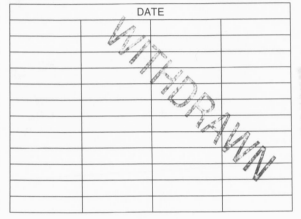

Also by Gabrielle Pina

B L I S S

CHASING SOPHEA

Gabrielle Pina

CHASING SOPHEA

a novel

One World · Ballantine Books · *New York*

Chasing Sophea is a work of fiction. Names, characters, places,
and incidents are the products of the author's imagination or are used
fictitiously. Any resemblance to actual events, locales, or persons,
living or dead, is entirely coincidental.

A One World Trade Paperback Original

Published in the United States by One World Books,
an imprint of The Random House Publishing Group, a division
of Random House, Inc., New York.

ONE WORLD is a registered trademark and the One World
colophon is a trademark of Random House, Inc.

READER'S CIRCLE and colophon are trademarks of Random House, Inc.

LIBRARY OF CONGRESS CATALOGING-IN-PUBLICATION DATA
Pina, Gabrielle.
Chasing Sophea : a novel / by Gabrielle Pina.
p.   cm.
Includes reading group guide.
ISBN 0-345-47619-0
1. Multiple personality—Fiction. 2. Psychological fiction. I. Title.
PS3616.I53C48 2006
813'.6—dc22   2006040005

Printed in the United States of America

www.readerscircle.com

2 4 6 8 9 7 5 3 1

Text design by Laurie Jewell

FOR RACHEL

In honor of your immeasurable courage
and unconditional love

FOR TAMARA

In honor of your grace, patience, and
unwavering loyalty

FOR TRACY ANN

In honor of your sheer determination, perseverance,
and passion for sisterhood

FOR GINA

In honor of your vibrancy, your voice of reason, and
for always infusing my life with laughter

I found God in myself & I loved her

I loved her fiercely.

—NTOZAKE SHANGE

ACKNOWLEDGMENTS

First and foremost, I want to thank the spirit that sustains me and allows me to keep writing, living, and loving. Thanks to my agent, Sasha Goodman, for always being there whenever I need you. Thank you to Melody Guy, my editor at Random House, for consistently being supportive of my work and for being patient as well. I sincerely appreciate your efforts on my behalf. Thanks also to Danielle Durkin and Porscha Burke at Random House for answering my calls and my questions.

My heartfelt thanks to the women in my life who constantly keep me on my toes: my mom, Diane Richardson, and my aunts Denise, Dolores, and Darlene and always my grandma, Marjorie Richardson, for your special kind of inspiration. Special thanks to my daughter, Maia Noelle, for not letting me pick my lip when I was stressed, bite my nails, or indulge in any other self-destructive behavior. Also, thank you to my son, Julian, for encouraging me every day and reminding me to breathe when I felt overwhelmed and for letting me make chicken pot pies every now and then.

Thank you Ron Kelly, for answering a multitude of rather sensitive questions over the past two years. You are unlike any mortician I have ever seen and that's a good thing. Thank you Dr. Richard Beyer, for all your help with the psychological aspects of this novel. Your insight was invaluable and the character was the better for it. And, of course, thank you to Dr. James Ragan, director of the Master of Professional Writing Program at the University of Southern California, for always being in my corner.

Many thanks to the Imani Book Club in Los Angeles for their nine years of sisterhood and loving support. Thank you to my spirited friend, Rebecca Huston, for being incredibly supportive and for introducing me to Tibetan food. Also, blessings to my very special friend Patricia Loar for your amazing guidance, love, and celestial inspiration. Finally, a million heartfelt thanks to my best friend, my soul mate, and my husband, Ron McCurdy, the absolute love of my life. Thank you for being so supportive and for loving me just the way I am. Thank you my love, for taking such good care of me, for kicking me out of bed at 4:00 A.M. to write when I was too tired, and for showing me every day, without hestitation or fanfare, what love truly is. With you I am safe. With you I am love. With you I am home.

CHASING SOPHEA

There was a tornado watch issued for the entire state of Texas the day my mama went crazy. Our block on Haven Street was buzzing about "the one" rotating its way through Tornado Alley stirring up all kinds of trouble. Showing out—that's what it was doing, twisting and twirling like it was mad at somebody. My Aunt Baby said that tornado looked mighty hungry and intended to suck up houses until it was full and satisfied.

"See," she said, "cars and trailer parks are only appetizers. This here tornado craves a five-course meal. The sky is talking up a storm today, Dahlia, and by the looks of it, we're all getting cursed out." She leaned down and whispered in my ear, "It's a bad one, though, baby doll. I can feel it in my bones."

The entire house always knew when a storm was brewing because some part of Aunt Baby's body would start aching, and on that day, she announced that all four of her corns were screaming bloody murder. I was scared after she said that, and she tried her best to reassure me, calm my nerves. She promised me our house wasn't anywhere near the suck zone. And besides, didn't I know by now that tornadoes skipped over funeral parlors? "Tornadoes only like foolin' with live people, and we have way too many stiffs up yonder to interest that old twister. So don't worry, baby doll," she cooed. "Don't worry."

People don't usually name tornadoes, but that year, Daddy insisted.

"Dahlia, darlin'," he said, "any twister that beautiful and that dangerous can only be female. Reminds me of a woman I used to know named Sophea." He laughed. "Sophea, Sophea." His eyes twinkled when that name rolled off his tongue, and his laughter that night was loud, full, and contagious.

Aunt Baby opened every window in the house and turned off the electricity after we caught a glimpse of Miss Sophea on the news. She was mesmerizing and terrifying at the same time and, as expected, terrorized trailer parks up and down the Lone Star State. But you know, despite Sophea's petulant disposition, I longed to just run up to her and thrust my hand somewhere deep in the middle. You know, introduce myself and make her acquaintance. To me, she resembled one of those peculiar van Gogh paintings, except it's flying at you at a hundred and fifty miles per hour. And all the while you think you comprehend what you're looking at until you're tempted to look a little closer.

Anyway, while most of Dallas County was worried about being swept clear to Oklahoma, I was wondering if my mother was going to make it through another day without creating a catastrophe. She didn't.

And now that I think about it, since you are forcing me to remember it, that morning began the same as any other. We had just decorated the house the night before for Christmas. Daddy had to stop twice to go set the features on two cases—you know, fix the eyes, cheekbones, basically make the nonviewable viewable. He possessed an extraordinary gift for such things, restructuring dead people, re-creating bone. He could transform just about anybody into someone acceptable to gawk at on a Sunday afternoon. People who weren't even related to the families would come to wakes sometimes just to marvel at the artistry of my father's work. He probably should have been a surgeon, although I don't think that would have made his life any easier. You see, the phone never stopped ringing for him as it was.

People seemed to be dying a lot that year, dropping like flies, ultimately ending up downstairs in my house cold and stiff, waiting to have their fluids flushed by my father. Oh, I'm sorry. You seem surprised. I can understand that. I mean, who would ever guess how bizarre my upbringing was just by looking at me? And you want to know one of the things I remember the most? The clothes. You wouldn't believe the getups some people dressed their relatives in after they died. Ridiculous ensembles that would kill the dead all over again if they woke up and saw themselves.

Anyway, Daddy was extremely busy that day. There was plenty of prep work to do because there were five bodies that had to be bathed, embalmed, and made up. Mercy Blue, the girl in charge of postlife makeovers, was wearing a tight red dress. Red was her favorite color. Go figure. And it was a Tuesday because John Coltrane resonated from every corner of the house. Daddy always listened to 'Trane on Tuesdays. Daddy was in a manageable mood, too, because Uncle Brother—that's what we've always called him—was back from New Orleans. Daddy didn't like to admit it, but he depended on Uncle Brother to lighten his mood on the days when Mama was having one of her brain tantrums. Aunt Baby was on the other side of town mixing up some concoction for somebody, I can't recall exactly. I just remember that she wasn't there. If only she had been there . . .

My mother was scurrying from one room to the next like a rat with a cat hot on its tail. She was a blur, a brown blur. You know, she always did that, zipped around from place to place as if her life was getting ready to end and she just had to complete one last task before her heart stopped beating. Haste was an ongoing obsession with her. Sometimes, I swear, she moved so quickly it looked like she was gliding on air. Mama swore the earth would swallow her whole if she stood still for any length of time. Really. I'm completely serious. It's confounding, I know.

Okay, let me clarify this madness for you. You see, if she was sitting on a chair with her feet up, that would be acceptable, but her legs could never ever touch the ground for more than a couple of minutes. Clearly my mother was, shall we say, not playing with a full deck or was four cans short of a six-pack. How about missing two digits in her phone number? Bread was half-baked? Elevator didn't rise all the way to the top? You get the picture? She even propped her feet on a stool when she went to the bathroom.

That being said, avoiding well-placed stools became something of a military exercise in my house. We used to pretend like they were land mines ready to blow us to kingdom come if we disturbed them an inch. Jesus, she was crazy. Mama had those stools placed just so because she needed to be able to leap up on one in case the floor started to buckle and suck her under. My brother and sister and I navigated around them with extreme caution. But I said that already, didn't I? You'll have to excuse my redundancy.

I was eleven. My brother was seven, and my sister was three, I think. Anyway, my brother, Jazz, loved trains. He had this LGB train set that Aunt Baby ordered from a Sears catalog. He adored it and, much to everyone's dismay, usually played with it early in the mornings. The sound of the train annoyed me, so I went downstairs to check on Mama. Keeping an eye on Mama was my responsibility since I was the oldest. She looked and sounded almost normal that day, you know, like she used to.

"Good morning, baby doll. Help me get everybody dressed. I feel like going for a drive this morning."

"What about the tornado, mama?"

"You think I'm afraid of a little old tornado?"

"Mama, they said on channel 8 that Miss Sophea had a big fat core! I'm gonna get to see a real live twister!"

"Hush that talk now, you hear. We've got things to do and places to go."

She was smiling and she had combed her hair, and I swear to God I thought maybe we were going to Swensons to get ice cream. She used to take me there and allowed me to get two scoops of lemon custard even though I always managed to drop the top one on the seat of her car.

"Jazz! Jazz! Stop fooling around with that train and get dressed. Mama said we're going somewhere."

I rushed to get the baby ready. I was so excited at the prospect of having a normal mother again. And outside, Miss Sophea seemed like a distant relative. You know if I close my eyes, I can still hear 'Trane playing in my head, smooth and melodious. It was "In a Sentimental Mood" da de da da da de da da. You know, the version he recorded with Duke Ellington.

"Baby doll, hurry up now," Mama whispered. "We have to get out of here. This hell of a house doesn't want to let us go, and it'll die trying to hold us in."

I was so giddy about wrapping my tongue around that damn sugar cone that I didn't remember to tell anyone that we were leaving. I didn't tell my father, and I was supposed to. You understand. It was my responsibility. Anyway, it was extremely windy outside, and I remember struggling a little to get in the car. It was a burgundy Mercedes with a beige leather interior, and it smelled of strawberries and Chanel Number 5. I remember consoling my baby sister, Livia, because she couldn't quite figure out how to tie her shoes. I remember Uncle Brother running, sprinting out of the front door, and the urgency in his tone yelling for my mother to come back.

"Reva! Reva! Come back here, Reva! Do you hear me? Come back."

Oh, and Jazz's sweet face. I remember Jazz's sweet face. I remember driving past Swensons on Parker Avenue and feeling my stomach starting to swirl. I remember thinking that something was terribly wrong, and I remember now how normal Mama looked when she turned around and smiled.

"Hey, baby doll," she said, "how about I take y'all to see a real, live choo-choo train?"

FALLING APART

CHAPTER 1

It was happening again: that feeling of being adrift in her own body, mystified by the simplest of things. Like a mourned lover, it had crept up on her out of nowhere, intoxicating her senses, and she struggled to remain focused on the task at hand. But what was the task? And how long would it be before she remembered—seconds like before or hours? Days perhaps. Unfortunately, time for her had become much too easy to lose.

Dahlia paused at the light on the corner of Colorado Boulevard and Orange Grove and wondered where she would end up this time. The signal changed, horns sounded, and still confusion in all its glory danced around in her head, spinning and twirling with reckless abandon. She was aware that she was somehow off balance, but she was at a loss for how to identify the cause of her difficulty. If anyone were to ask her, she wouldn't know how to adequately articulate how she felt without sounding like she was in desperate need of a padded room and wrist restraints. No, there was nothing to be revealed to anyone about these random spells that were beginning to occur more and more frequently. She would work through them—lean into the curve, so to speak—and in time, this one would pass just like the others and she would be no worse for wear. Wrinkled a little, yes, but not shredded into countless pieces—not right now, anyway. Dahlia pressed her foot on the accelerator and followed the gold Mercedes in front of her onto the 134 freeway. Today she'd go west toward Los Angeles, toward the ocean.

Oftentimes during moments like these, Dahlia reached for an emotional anchor to weigh her down and keep her grounded— a fond memory to calm her insides—but memories good or bad hid from her religiously. She guessed they lingered in her mind trapped in tight spaces unwilling to make an appearance. She longed to remember what it felt like not to be nearly hysterical twenty-four hours a day, but she didn't have the energy to go chasing after any phantom recollections. Lately it seemed she didn't have the energy to do much of anything—work, play, or love intensely the way she used to. Her life was escaping from her in minuscule increments day by day, and God help her, sometimes she wanted to simply turn herself off, give in to the pressure and be done with breathing already. But she was stronger than that. Or at least that's what she always told herself in the midnight hour when thoughts of suicide attempted to seduce her.

Last night had been more of the usual tossing and turning, screaming and sweating, and this morning her depression was compounded by the lone gray hair she discovered languishing in her punanni as if it belonged there, as if it were finally home. She'd gasped in horror and imagined herself at ninety years old napping in a wheelchair smelling of Bengay and peppermint patties. She'd grabbed tweezers and plucked wildly, trying desperately not to cry in front of her amused husband. He'd laughed, of course, and teased her until that heavy feeling in her chest subsided. "Welcome to my world," he'd said with a broad grin, and she did feel better for a while or at least until she walked out the door. He was good at that, though, making her forget herself at times. But now even he couldn't control what was happening to her, and neither, it appeared, could she. She blinked back tears and rummaged around in her purse for Excedrin, Advil, or anything that would make her head stop aching. "No," she whispered. "Go away." But the pain persisted, and she kept driving, oblivious to the sugarcoated life waiting for her on the other side of town.

CHAPTER 2

"Dahlia, baby, it's time to get up. I don't want you to be late again."

"Late for what? What are you talking about?"

"I've taken care of everything. All you have to do is shower, dress, and get in the car."

Dahlia pressed her face deeper into her goose-down pillow. It was so fluffy and obviously new, but she didn't remember buying it, and Michael—or Milky, as she liked to call him—would never purchase such a luxury. Normally she would be up, out the door, and on her way to the Coffee Bean for a nonfat pure vanilla ice blended. This morning it didn't seem to matter that she had thirty-odd students at Pasadena City College waiting impatiently for her to give a lecture on God knows what. Lying in bed all day daydreaming seemed preferable to actually opening her eyes or even moving. Maybe, just maybe, if she didn't move, kept still like the dead, he'd have mercy on her and leave her be for a moment longer. She wasn't ready. Why couldn't he tell that she wasn't ready? Couldn't a woman be depressed and suicidal in peace? Jesus.

Still somewhat oblivious to Michael's pleas for acknowledgment, Dahlia continued to think about the benefits of remaining buried under a mountain of hand-stitched quilts until the familiar intrusion of cool air jolted her back to the now, to the what is. Real life began to tickle the underside of her toes and disturb the cozy cocoon she'd managed to create for herself. Like yesterday and the day before, Michael had removed the covers and proceeded to swing her legs over the side of the bed as if she were a disobedient child. Despite her budding anger, she decided that she should be grateful for the distraction. If it weren't for him pushing her forward lately, she'd be a mess, an absolute zombie stumbling around Pasadena proper in Jimmy Choo shoes.

"Dahlia, I want you to talk to a doctor about this."

"Milky, I'm just tired, that's all."

"You're always tired, Dahlia. You go to sleep and wake up tired. And frankly, I'm tired of you being tired. I want you to make an appointment to see someone today. I mean it. I spoke to Stan and got the name of a good doctor."

"Are you attempting to tell me what to do, Milky?"

"Something is not right here, Dahlia, and we have to find out what it is. Maybe you have chronic fatigue syndrome or—" Dahlia interrupted before he prattled off an endless list of possibilities that could explain her exhaustion. He was a lists man. She'd learned early on in their relationship to ask questions that had only one answer if time was a consideration because Michael was always prepared with countless options. If only he wanted to be a game show contestant, they'd be millionaires by now.

"If this has anything do with last night, I just didn't feel like it, okay? The world is not going to end because you didn't get any from your wife."

"Don't give me that bullshit, Dahl. Are you intimating that I care more about having sex with you than I do about your health? Or perhaps you think I enjoy making love to a vegetable? Woman, you must be losing your mind."

"Fuck you, Michael."

"I'd love to oblige you, baby, but unfortunately at the moment there's no time and my desire has waned considerably. Make the appointment, Dahlia, or I'll make it for you." Michael turned her head to face him. "And, yes, in case you don't understand me, I am now officially telling you what to do."

Dahlia stared at herself in the mirror for quite some time after she dressed. Michael's voice seemed to be emanating from everywhere, echoing from her brain, bouncing off the hand-painted tiles in the bathroom . . . *You think I like making love to a vegetable? . . . You must be losing your mind.* What the hell did he know, anyway? Everything in his life had been perfect, no glitches or unexpected bumps in the road, just smooth sailing for him and his precious family. Well, no matter what Michael said. Today, she sensed, was not a good day, and she knew instinctively that once she stepped one foot out the door, it would immediately begin to rain on her head. She'd say the hell with it and stay home if Michael weren't hovering, waiting to see if she made it to the driveway. It was only a matter of time before he began to follow her to work or slapped one of those steel contraptions around her ankle like she was some runaway convict.

She fought her first impulse to drive through the alley, sneak back into her own house, and hide underneath the covers until the oddness passed. It wasn't anything she could put her finger on exactly. It was simply a feeling of bewilderment that she couldn't quite shake. What was happening to her? She used to be able to move from one day to the next with some semblance of comfort. Living, breathing, and loving had never been this difficult. She had a family to take care of, classes to teach, and a business to help run. Those were her priorities, and whatever was happening to her had to take a backseat. So what if she was fatigued? She'd been fatigued all her life and had managed just fine, thank you. She didn't need some quack to tell her to take a vacation and get more sleep. She'd always managed to expertly cover her tracks when these random spells hit and interrupted her structured life of details.

She'd have to pull it together so Michael could relax and stop worrying so much. She needed to make him believe that everything was all right. This time she managed to convince herself that he was simply perturbed because she hadn't returned his affections last night or the night before. Was there some law against a wife being too exhausted to make love with her husband? She assumed that after eight years of marriage, he'd understand that her lack of desire was merely temporary and had nothing whatsoever to do with him. Men were always so dramatic and impatient. They constantly believed the world revolved around them and their needs. Nevertheless, she intended to make it up to him. As soon as this latest spell passed, she planned to seduce him, intrigue him, and make him fall in love with her all over again.

Dahlia surveyed her restless class and began collecting assignments from the previous week. Many of her colleagues were baffled about her decision to teach; they considered it a waste of time. "It's not like you need the money," they'd say. "You can do anything you want."

"Exactly," she'd reply with a smile. She adored teaching and considered it to be something of an art form. Her enthusiasm was infectious, and even below-average students thrived under her tutelage. She had built a successful public relations firm, sold it, and discovered that she still required another venture of sorts to keep her focused, so she began teaching part-time at the city college. She felt calmer—for a while, anyway—and almost normal.

"All right, all right. Settle down, people. I'm here. My apologies for being late again. It was unavoidable." Dahlia didn't much remember what she lectured on after that initial greeting or how long she stood in front of the chalkboard before the unthinkable happened.

She convinced herself that if she just kept lecturing, no one would notice the warm fluid swirling around her leg, quickly fanning into a bright yellow puddle on the floor. She closed her eyes and willed the entire class to disappear, but when she opened them, they were still there, staring dumbfounded.

"That's enough for today," she whispered in a small voice, yet no one budged.

And in that moment, the lesson plan in her head vanished, and there was nothing left to recall, no witty anecdote to share, and no new innovative assignment to give. The class remained unmovable, almost appearing cemented to their desks, waiting for the next scene, the next act, or the inevitable conclusion to a play gone wrong. A tense moment passed, and in that space of time, she couldn't remember why she was there. After peering into startled eyes peering back at her, she decided that there was nothing left for her to do but leave, simply disappear as quickly and unobtrusively as she had arrived. And so, she reached for her purse, grabbed her briefcase, and made damn sure that her cocoa brown suede coat never grazed the miniature pond creeping hopelessly across the floor.

CHAPTER 3

There came a time in Michael Chang's life when he knew that he was most likely going to be alone for the long haul, recognized that there would be no wife, no heirs, and no Little League games to attend on Saturday afternoons. Reaching this crucial point was neither difficult nor painful; Michael accepted the inevitability of his aloneness like rain. He didn't know when complete solitude was coming to settle, but he knew it would show up eventually, armed and with a purpose. He was a forty-year-old accomplished chef with a successful restaurant and a quiet desire for an unfettered life. His life was the way he chose, and he took full responsibility for his decision not to marry a woman simply to plant his seed and produce an instant family to make other people happy—well, mainly his mother. So, somewhere around thirty-five, he had begun to surround himself with the three things that brought him the most pleasure and security: money, vintage Bob Marley recordings, and Baccarat crystal filled with Cabernet Sauvignon.

He was never a man to have a bevy of women or even a steady girlfriend. He was an only child and quite accustomed to entertaining himself, and much to the dismay of his mother, he considered being alone to be a blessing. It's not that he didn't like women—he did. He appreciated the many delicate gifts they offered the world. He was attracted to all that they were and often delighted in spending time in their company. But he had never found "the one" until Dahlia Culpepper crossed his path in a pair of tight black leather pants some eight years ago. She was beautiful and mysterious, and made him laugh. She teased him that night, took him home, and wore him out for hours—something that she now denied. She was a dichotomy, a whirlwind of conflicting emotions, but he fell for her anyway. She captivated him, and he couldn't explain his growing fascination. For the life of him, he didn't understand how a woman could be so aggressive one day and completely modest and shy the next. It unnerved him in the beginning and yet turned him on at the same time. And now, much to his chagrin, he could barely remember his previous existence before he took her into his arms, his heart, and his life.

She had been gone a mere five minutes before he began rummaging through her belongings, like a thief without enough time to steal. There had to be some tangible explanation for her behavior. He prayed that she didn't have some degenerative disease or a neurological disorder. *Christ, what if it's a brain tumor or early-onset Alzheimer's? Or dementia. Maybe it was dementia? Maybe she simply needed some Prozac and a trip to a day spa. Or a Xanax.* He'd heard that Xanax could be quite effective in situations like these. After riffling through countless desk drawers and a multitude of shoe boxes in the closet, he found nothing to substantiate his mounting suspicions. One minute his wife was the woman he married, sensual and spontaneous; the next she was diffident and aloof.

He knew he'd been questioning her incessantly, but he needed some answers. He had always taken her word for everything, since there had never been a reason to doubt her before. But their lives had changed, and he found himself frequently questioning her whereabouts, their marriage, and most often his sanity. He sat down on the edge of the bed, perplexed and frustrated. Maybe she was having an affair. Maybe she was a closeted lesbian and was leaving him for another woman named Mike. Maybe he should have followed her to work like before. Maybe he should consider hiring a private investigator. Maybe he should retain an attorney. Or maybe, just maybe, he was the one losing his fucking mind after all. Only time would tell, and either way, something had to give. She'd see a doctor and they would both finally have answers, understand precisely what they were dealing with, and then their lives could feasibly return to normal.

Michael retreated to the kitchen and listed in his head all the things he would do for her before she came home. Peel about eight cloves of garlic for one. Dahlia adored garlic. Draw her a hot bath and fill it with that lavender aromatherapy oil she was so fond of. Pick some pearl onions from the back garden and take frozen chicken stock out of the freezer to thaw. Stop by Pier 1 on Lake Avenue to get more candles. Make sure he had enough dry red wine for the sauce and buy more cognac—lots of it. Call work and tell them he wasn't coming in today. Tell Lydia to cancel the rest of his appointments. Stop by Bristol Farms and get fresh chicken breast, and let's see, . . . he was out of flat-leaf parsley and whole black peppercorns. And most important, love her—love her with everything he had until whatever this was left them the hell alone.

CHAPTER 4

The house breathed, and that's all she remembered. It seemed alive, and sometimes when she paused for too long, she could feel it in her chest pulsating—that thumpity thump thump, rhythmic and intrusive. As a child, she wanted to walk around screaming "What is wrong with you people! Can't you hear it? Can't anyone hear it?" The house, with all its hidden rooms and never-ending secrets, was a living, breathing entity that crawled inside your brain and took root there like some renegade cell. Slowly, methodically, it confiscated your sanity and doled it back to you piece by piece.

For years after she left home, Dahlia would tell herself that her memories were preposterous fabrications of a bizarre childhood, but pockets of truth always surfaced and battered her around a bit until she released the façade. Her life was her life, her family was hers and hers alone, and all the therapy in the world couldn't change who she was, or what happened or didn't happen in that house.

She reclined and inhaled deeply. All this nonsense about getting in touch with your inner child was overrated anyway. Her father always told her that she didn't suffer fools easily, so why was she sitting here across from some pinch-faced stranger in a pea green office attempting to regurgitate her life? She couldn't get over the fact that she was paying someone to tell her what to do when her husband could order her around for free. That alone should be enough to declare her insane. Most likely this man believed her to be demented, perhaps suffering from some sort of paranoid delusion? Admittedly, she was strange, but so what? She'd accepted that fact at least a couple of decades ago, which was why she kept her strangeness to herself.

Lately, though, strangeness had begun to escape her grasp in small increments, dripping from her fingertips and affecting the way other people perceived her. Attention was not something she craved on any level or felt she never had enough of. She was a background girl, always had been. She wasn't visiting a shrink because of her peculiar dreams, the reoccurring ones where she called out the names of people she didn't quite remember. Nor was she here to discuss her weird obsession with purchasing way more lavender panties than she would ever need. And she certainly wasn't here because her husband ordered her to come like some crusty three-year-old who couldn't follow directions. She wasn't even here because she sensed that she was one step closer to becoming hysterical twenty-four hours a day. Fear compelled her kicking and screaming in search of an elusive truth—fear of the one thing that taunted her when she inhaled too deeply and caused her to wonder just how much longer before it was her turn. Bottom line, she needed this therapist—who insisted on asking her twenty million questions—to clearly understand that she was finally here because, just a few hours ago, she damn near had to water-ski out of her own classroom.

Dr. Trevor Kelly was irritated at having to stay late. He didn't normally alter his plans to accommodate last-minute appointments. He lived a scheduled life, and unwanted interruptions soured his mood and affected his peaking libido. He was odd that way. He was supposed to be having dinner with his thirty-six-year-old wife, Cassandra. He was quite pleased with himself indeed. At sixty-one, he could still turn a few heads. He'd have been long gone by now, but he'd received an urgent call from a colleague to see a new patient as a favor, at four thirty in the afternoon, no less. His lovely wife had made reservations at the Parkway Grill for five fifteen. She knew that was his favorite restaurant in Pasadena. She was well versed in what pleased him, and he adored that about her. She was a wildcat, that one—spontaneous and sexually liberated. He eyed his watch. Shit, he was never going to make it.

Since he'd be forced to miss cocktails, he hoped that this was someone with a genuine problem. Lately he'd been ministering to people with the usual mundane textbook dilemmas. He treated patients who were navigating difficult divorces, pseudo-masculine men who were too petrified to come out of the closet, and of course, he dabbled in routine sexual abuse cases—if such a thing could ever be deemed routine. He'd been practicing for more than twenty-five years, and he had yet to run across anyone who bloody warranted a footnote in the *American Journal of Psychiatry*—which was smashing for society, of course, but crap for his career. Like any good health practitioner, he longed to make a difference, make a valuable contribution to his field, but more important, he longed for a byline. He heard faint knocking at the outer door and reluctantly prepared for another typical session. She was finally here. He checked the time.

"Dr. Kelly, I presume?"

"Yes. Dahlia, right? Dahlia Chang?"

"Yes."

"Please have a seat." Dr. Kelly observed her closely. He noticed right away that it was a challenge for her to maintain eye contact. He also suspected from her demeanor that she wasn't accustomed to sharing more than she needed to, and she definitely didn't want to be in his office. Right now, he didn't either. There, they already had something in common. His mind had since wandered to a chilled cosmopolitan and a coco crêpe. He quickly refocused on the woman fidgeting in front of him. "Dahlia, what seems to be the problem?" He waited. Note: The patient repeatedly avoids eye contact and has difficulty answering direct questions.

"I'm tired," she stated, and stared out the window.

"Please go on." Dr. Kelly settled into his chair. These initial sessions, he knew from previous experience, would be like watching paint dry. The patient wasn't prepared to communicate, and he wasn't about to force the issue. He closed his eyes and imagined Cassandra in a French maid's uniform. He decided right then that he would give Dahlia forty-five minutes and not a blasted second more. Time was money, and at the rate she was going, he'd be driving down Arroyo Parkway in no time.

"Dr. Kelly."

"Yes."

"I need to go home. I need to sleep."

"All right, then. Shall we schedule another appointment?"

Sadly, "Yes." Dr. Kelly glanced at his appointment book, relieved that she had elected to end so quickly.

"How about next Thursday at three o'clock?"

"Fine."

And then she was gone. Dr. Kelly glanced at the gold clock mounted on the wall next to his beloved picture of Margaret Thatcher and reached for his tape recorder. Patient was noncommunicative. Patient was extremely attractive and very well dressed. Patient refused eye contact. Patient seemed distracted and decidedly uncomfortable. Patient was borderline hostile.

Although Dr. Kelly was pleased that he would be able to join his wife, something in Dahlia's manner troubled him. He sighed and reached for his jacket. Deep down in his gut, he sensed that Dahlia Chang was going to be one tough nut to crack.

Later on that night, Dahlia woke up again, screaming names that she couldn't remember. From a corner long forgotten in her mind, she could hear Milky calling for her and she was torn. There were mangled voices in her dreams, and then there was the voice that would lead her home like now, like always. She concentrated on his voice and struggled to escape the tornado in her brain that was wreaking havoc on her very person. Still, the same old hauntings gripped her insides, squeezed, and threw her around like a rag doll. When she finally awoke, it was as if she had never slept at all.

"Honey, talk to me. Can you remember anything this time?" Milky prodded, caressing the side of her face.

The feelings of terror that she experienced in her sleep were so real, so visceral that they forced her into the unknown, a place that she didn't recall but that felt familiar, and a place that reminded her of home. And anything that reminded her of the funeral parlor sent her into an emotional tailspin. She was a little girl in the dream wearing a blue dress with red stripes. Her hair was in two ponytails pinned on top of her head like Aunt Baby's, and she was pointing at something. Any other time when she was lucid, she couldn't remember what she looked like as a child at all and barely had any recollection of the place she used to call home. But in her nightmares, the figure pointing was unmistakable, that much was apparent. This time, though, she heard multiple voices and screams that pierced right through her. She could never call to mind exactly what she was dreaming about, and perhaps that was for the best.

"Oh God, Milky, what is happening to me? And why is it happening now?"

"Try, honey. Can you remember something, anything?"

She fell into her husband's embrace and searched her mind for an answer to his question as well as her own. "No, I can't remember anything at all. When I wake up, it's all gone. I can't explain it to you any other way." Dahlia rose abruptly to take a shower. She was drenched with perspiration, and as usual, she had to remove any traces of the demon that delighted in stalking her. She stood under the powerful streams with her hands pressed against the tile. She didn't know why she lied back there to her husband. God knows he was only trying to help. But somehow lying seemed the appropriate thing to do. The truth was becoming more than she could handle, and if she couldn't make sense of what was going on in her dreams, how could she begin to explain it to him? She feared she was losing the battle, and she couldn't allow him to go down with her.

CHAPTER 5

Phoebe allowed the man, Stephan something or other, to massage her neck. He begged to massage other parts of her body as well, but she wasn't in the mood for a casual dalliance.

"Hey, Steven, hands above the shoulders."

"Stephan," he corrected, as he attempted to inch his hand up the back of her tank top. They met at the gym a few weeks ago, and he finally convinced her to accept his invitation for drinks. Naturally, after three heavenly mojitos at Xiomara, they ended up at his ornate town house on Marengo, where they experimented with banal conversation and plenty of Russian vodka. Most times this sort of thing didn't interest her. She liked men, yes, but she didn't usually have time to entertain such frivolity.

"Look, Soren, I said watch yourself. I agreed to drinks, nothing else."

"Aw, come on, baby. You know you want me. I can feel it. I've seen the way you stare at the gym. I have a hunch that every time you do a squat, you're thinking about me wiggling around underneath you."

"Servon, please, I'm not that drunk."

"Stephan. My name is Stephan." She sensed that he was becoming irritated with her.

Phoebe considered her options. It had certainly been a while, and her body was pleading with her to acquiesce. But even intoxicated, her mind had already wandered to another man, the only man. Quite expectedly, like last time and the time before that, the man in front of her hastily removing his clothes had become an annoyance, an unwelcome diversion from the target at hand. Who said she had to settle for some jack-off she didn't want? She had waited this long, a little while longer wouldn't kill her—frustrate her to no end perhaps, but certainly not kill her.

"Simon, I have to go. Get off me." She yanked her foot from his mouth and attempted to stand. He bit her big toe. She administered a roundhouse to the head courtesy of kickboxing class three times a week with Mauricio, the Brazilian. He fell backward. She ran out the door toward her car. She heard him cursing her in another language that she didn't recognize. She laughed at the hilarity of it all. *What a freak,* she thought.

It was nearly dawn, and as the alcohol began to wear off, the reality of her situation overwhelmed her. Once again, she was back at square one and had gained nothing. If she wanted to survive, she had to start making serious strides toward independence. Progress was a key to success here. With that in mind, she sped to the one place that inspired her to dream.

Thirty-two fifty-two San Rafael Drive. That was the address this time. All Phoebe had to do was knock on the door, and the world as she knew it would end. The anticipation of impending chaos was strangely intoxicating. She imagined walking up the long driveway, and she imagined the look on his face when she told him that his life was a cleverly crafted work of fiction. She had lingered outside their house often and fantasized about a multitude of possible outcomes and, of course, how she would handle herself if the unspeakable happened. She wondered what it would feel like to betray the woman she had spent a lifetime protecting. What if he didn't believe her? She'd probably have to convince him, dig into her bag of tricks. Maybe Dahlia would try to silence her, but Phoebe was the strong one. She was the survivor, and in her gut, Dahlia had to know that. One day soon, she intended to have answers to her questions, but not today. Today their world could keep revolving for a little while longer.

Phoebe maneuvered the house keys back and forth in the palm of her hand. She could feel the grooves pressing roughly against her fingers. The sensation was so appealing that she almost wept. She had stolen the keys from Dahlia months ago, slipped them in her pocket one day when her friend wasn't paying attention. Having carte blanche access to Dahlia's life had always been necessary. She figured this day was coming anyway. She wasn't stupid. From the beginning, there had always been some problem that only she could solve. Phoebe was a born fixer. She was the one who had calmed the storm when the storm descended out of nowhere hell bent on wiping out everything in its path. She was the one who had made a way out of no way. And now, without any warning, she had become the storm, and no one on this earth could make her change course. There was enough power in her truth to blow this family to pieces.

For a long time, she'd held back because she loved Dahlia and protected her fiercely, but she smelled change in the air, and change for her wasn't necessarily a good thing. Change meant that her relationship with Dahlia was in jeopardy, and she had been around too long to suddenly become a vague memory or a footnote in somebody's life. No. It could not be, and she would not—could not—sit idly by while Dahlia tried to erase her. Suddenly her life wasn't about Dahlia's survival anymore. It was high time she battled for her own.

It hadn't always been this way. In the past, she didn't mind being in the background. Now she realized after all these years that living in the background certainly had its disadvantages. No one had any idea how hard she'd worked or the sacrifices she'd made over the years. All she wanted was a little recognition for her contributions. Phoebe Graham was tired of being a nonentity, a ghost in the land of the living. And more important, she was tired of craving someone else's life.

CHAPTER 6

It was storming outside when Dahlia left Dr. Kelly's office. Fat droplets of Southern California rain decorated her camel-colored suede duster. It was November, two weeks before Thanksgiving, and she was cold, shivering on the way to her car. She was cold a lot these days, even when it wasn't raining outside. Despite the cold, she adored the rain. It soothed her soul and reminded her of home, and today, for some odd reason, she was comforted. She adjusted the hood and tied the duster tighter around her body. It was a long coat designed to accentuate her tall frame. She preferred long coats. They covered everything and left room for an active imagination. She didn't feel any better, though—not that she'd expected to. Perhaps it was because she couldn't bring herself to say barely two words to the man. Why again, she asked herself, was she suffering such humiliation? And what was the point of spending $150 an hour if she wasn't going to open her mouth? Aunt Baby would be disgusted with her wasting her money on such foolishness, and on a crazy people's doctor no less. She could hear her now: *"You might as well go on* Oprah, *telling all your business like that to a perfect stranger."*

Aunt Baby's voice was an invisible cord to her past, a rock that anchored her when her feet threatened to leave stable ground. Aunt Baby was her grandfather's baby sister on her father's side. She was diminutive in size but powerful nevertheless. She was obsessed with good posture and walked with the same determined strides she did when she was thirty. She was nearly a legend at home, the way a person could be in a small, close-knit community. She was a formidable woman quite well known for her quirky one-liners and recipes for life. She was famous for having a recipe for anything that plagued your mind, body, or soul. Whether your man left you or your hair was falling out at the roots, Aunt Baby had the solution. Although her recipes were somewhat unconventional, people back home still religiously wrote down every word. It was a wonder her picture wasn't hanging up in some folk's houses along with cheesy velvet paintings of Jesus, Martin, and JFK.

Once, when Dahlia was fifteen, this woman from Fort Worth stood in the kitchen scratching and rubbing off anything on her body that wasn't attached by bone. The whole house was convinced that she'd pluck herself to death right there on the linoleum, which incidentally would have been fine considering that the embalming room was right down the hall. Aunt Baby told her to repeat the Twenty-third Psalm each time she had an inclination to scrub her birthmark with steel wool. She also prescribed a pot of collard greens with twenty cloves of garlic for ten days. In two weeks' time, the itchy lady was raving about Aunt Baby just like everybody else.

Dahlia missed her terribly, and lately their phone conversations hadn't been enough to sustain her. They were a few days overdue for their weekly chat, but Dahlia needed to settle down first and calm her nerves. Concealing anything from that woman was impossible, so she attempted to relax and stop the hemorrhaging of her spirit with emotional Band-Aids. Pretending that everything was perfect had become a familiar routine, one that she depended on to float her from week to week.

She drove the long way home to San Rafael, a quiet neighborhood on the west side of Pasadena, and tried to figure out what on earth she was going to say to Milky. They'd met some years ago in an upscale restaurant when he offered to buy her a cocktail. He was such a unique-looking man, unlike any man she had ever seen. He was tall and brown like a cup of coffee with two teaspoons of cream. He had jet-black hair that curled at the ends, and his eyes slanted when he smiled. Normally, she didn't make it a habit of flirting with men more attractive than she, but she was drawn to him in a way that she couldn't quite explain. It was as if he really saw her and liked her anyway. Oddly enough, he behaved as if he had known her for years. Although she politely declined his offer, explaining that she didn't drink, he insisted that she sample her favorite, a specialty of the house. He returned shortly with cold chocolate milk in a martini glass dusted with the most decadent cocoa she'd ever tasted. She'd been calling him Milky ever since.

She knew he was worried about her. He'd been asking a lot of questions lately, attempting to pick her brain apart when she wasn't paying attention. She suspected he was trying to catch her off guard. It was difficult for her to hold his gaze anymore for any length of time. She was sure he was beginning to see it in her eyes, an unraveling that was happening from the inside out.

Finally, she stood in front of her house and took a deep breath and admired the colorful jacaranda tree that always welcomed her home. She counted backward from a hundred and hummed "Love and Happiness" by Al Green. And then, like magic, confused, unhappy Dahlia was gone and Mommy was home.

CHAPTER 7

Wednesday • November 15 • 7:00 p.m.

Whoever said you were supposed to be sane 100 percent of the time anyway? So what if a little craziness sneaks up on you? Most people can snap themselves out of it, you know, get back to the tuna casserole they were making or the blow job they were giving. For others, time passes and passes some more until one day they look up and twenty years have swept by, leaving them old, wrinkled, and tormented by cellulite.

What happens when you wake up and realize that you're no better than anyone else? You know what? You stand in front of the mirror lamenting how badly you screwed up your life. You blame your mama, your brother, and your crazy Uncle Scooter, too, for never believing in you and always telling you you'd never be someone anyone would want to know. Well, I say the hell with that bullshit. If you wake up one morning and the grass is blue or the sky is green, call a doctor and get a damn pill. Remedy your situation and move the fuck on. Next! I mean, seriously, there comes a time when you have to grow up and live your life. Blame and guilt are wasted emotions, and I seriously don't have time for either of them.

Dahlia doesn't understand this kindergarten concept, and I'm tired of trying to explain it to her. I swear that woman has turned *denial into a one-act play on Broadway. She just doesn't want to put the past behind her. She'd rather piss on herself in public and listen to old-ass music. Jesus, Mary, and Joseph save me from the drama. If I have to listen to one more Al Green CD, I'm going to bang my head against the dashboard and pray that I go deaf. She is plucking my last nerve with this piss-poor, melancholy attitude. Whine, whine, whine, moan, moan, moan, bitch, bitch, bitch.*

Whatever happened to being grateful for what you have? Whatever happened to counting your blessings and playing the cards you're dealt? Aunt Baby always did say she was prone to having brain tantrums like her mama. I mean, she has to know that most women would kill for her life: a bulging bank account, a scrumptious-looking husband, and a kid you can halfway stand to be around. Although as much as she's been pissing me off lately, I can't help worrying about her. That Milky is so sweet and attentive, too. In a way, I wish I could warn the poor bastard—tell him to build a bomb shelter because a nuke is coming straight for his ass.

Phoebe closed her journal and reached for a joint. She should try calling Dahlia again and leaving her a message—or she should mind her own damn business for a change. Who would have thought it would come to this? Phoebe wondered when and if Dahlia would tell Michael what happened. She needed to tell somebody something, because God only knew what was going to happen next, what with the cheese beginning to slide off her cracker. Either way, though, Phoebe decided that she would take over if need be, pick up the pieces when Dahlia crashed. Simply do whatever was necessary if her friend's mind spiraled in a thousand different directions.

CHAPTER 8

Milky paced the floor and tried to stop himself from think-ing the worst. She was late again, and he couldn't find her any-where. There was no answer at work, and she wasn't picking up her cell phone. What was he supposed to think at a time like this? What would any man think under such circumstances? *She's probably screwing somebody's brains out right now, or she's emptying the bank accounts and running off to an exotic getaway with our life savings—maybe Switzerland. She always wanted to go to Switzerland.*

"Daddy, Daddy."

"Yeah, princess," Milky answered, still plagued by the ongo-ing dialogue he was having with himself. *No. No, man, she's just late again.*

"Daddy, when is Mommy coming home? I'm getting hun-gry."

Milky felt his right hand ball up into a fist. *Calm down, Michael, don't jump to conclusions.* He didn't know what to tell his child anymore. He watched her bounce around the living room with limitless energy and wished he could predict when Dahlia was coming home. He reached for the phone again.

Dammit. He couldn't go on this way. If she didn't answer, he would go look for her himself. And this time, she was going to explain everything—account for each moment that she had been gone. This time, he would force her to tell him the truth even if it destroyed them both.

"Daddy!"

"Soon, baby girl. She's coming home real soon. Dinner will be ready in about five minutes. Can you hold on until then?"

"Daddy!"

"Isabel, I said—"

"Daddy, Mommy's car is in the driveway. Look!"

"What?"

Milky raced over to the window and saw his wife standing outside underneath the jacaranda tree holding herself, shivering as if she were cold. In that moment, she reminded him of Isabel, lost and alone in a place where he couldn't reach her. He almost ran to her then, but he didn't want to intrude on whatever was happening outside. His heart was no longer racing or contemplating the unknown, and for that he was grateful. His wife was home again safe and sound, and he could breathe a little easier for now.

CHAPTER 9

"Mommy, you're home!" Isabel squealed, jumping up and down. "Daddy's making cocopan. Can you smell it?"

Dahlia opened her arms to her six-year-old daughter and held on for dear life. Much to Dahlia's dismay, Isabel became a life preserver from the moment she was born. Dahlia had never intended to put so much pressure on the child, but who was she to break the cycle? Mothers eventually devoured their daughters. Wasn't that in the manual? No matter, in spite of earlier challenges, right now she was Mama. Tonight she would be a wife, and tomorrow . . . Well, tomorrow was a whole new day altogether. She was home sans some wet clothes and a bad attitude, and that was progress. She was accounted for and prepared to play the role to which she had been assigned. Twenty-seven cleansing breaths and her willingness for normalcy had to count for something.

"Yes, Izzy girl, I can smell your daddy's cooking. I'm sure the entire block can smell what's cooking in here."

"I went to ballet today, Mama. Chandler Guzman pulled my hair."

"Really? That wasn't very nice."

Milky watched their interaction from the kitchen. He couldn't quite gauge Dahlia's mood yet. Still, before he uttered one word, he needed to ascertain exactly how the evening was going to progress. His wife and their daughter looked so beautiful together, laughing and touching like it was the most normal thing in the world. If only this moment could stretch into tomorrow and the day after that. If only . . . He continued to eavesdrop, waiting for a tone, a facial expression, any sign that would indicate whether he needed to break open another bottle of Extra Strength Excedrin.

"What did you do in school today, pumpkin?" he heard Dahlia ask.

He'd considered calling Aunt Baby or even the father-in-law whom he'd never met for help but knew Dahlia would strangle him for sure.

"I went outside. I took a nap. I played with toys," Isabel continued in a singsong voice.

"That sounds like fun, honey." Dahlia laughed. "So, overall, you had a good day, then?"

All neck wringing aside, Milky decided right then in the archway of his ultramodern kitchen to do whatever was necessary to save their marriage even if it meant further alienating his wife. Maybe he should travel to Dallas first, feel her family out. It was time, he thought, after eight years of marriage, that they all got to know one another.

"Yeppy," Isabel responded, nodding her head. "What about you, Mama? Did you have a good day, too?"

Time immediately seemed to slow down while Milky waited for an answer. He could smell the simmering chicken and hear Jill Scott singing powerfully in the background: *"You woo me, you court me, you tease me, you please me."* He watched Dahlia intently then. *"Invite me, you ignite me, you co-write me, you love me."* Jill crooned on, and their eyes met, and he knew that she knew what he was waiting for.

"Yes, pumpkin," she said, looking straight at him. "I had a very good day."

Milky rested on the edge of the bathtub and decided to draw a bath for his wife while she read Isabel "The Stinky Cheese Man" for the fourth time. He hadn't realized how much he missed such simple pleasures. Perhaps the worst was over. Perhaps his coq au vin did possess some medicinal qualities after all. His mother, Miko, always swore that his cooking could make a blind man see, a deaf man hear, and a bowlegged woman straighten up and walk like she had some sense. He chuckled absentmindedly and tested the temperature of the water. He wondered and hoped that Dahlia missed him as much as he longed for her. And then she was there, kissing his neck and massaging his shoulders. He ached to confess just how much he adored her. He needed her to know that he'd do anything to make her life easier, anything to make her happy. He wanted her to trust him enough to share what was happening to them but didn't want to push her any further away than he already had.

"I thought maybe you'd like to relax in the Jacuzzi and have a long, hot soak," he said softly, without turning around.

"I would, but only if you'd join me."

"Are you sure? I don't want to—"

"Shhhhh," she interrupted. "I'm sure."

Milky stood and turned to face his wife. When he looked in her eyes, he saw their lives together, and that was all he needed to take another step closer. They undressed each other silently and lowered themselves into the water. It was almost as if he were being transported into another world, a world where nothing could touch them—no headaches, no arguments, no blackouts. The oval-shaped tub was somehow reminiscent of a womb, and he imagined that every man longed to feel this good, this safe, this complete. Soon long legs wrapped around his waist and mercifully intruded on his complicated daydreams. She pulled him closer.

"Do you still love me?" she asked matter-of-factly, reaching for him under the water.

"Every moment of my life," he answered.

"Then show me, Milky. Show me."

He guided her on top of him and made love to her as if his life depended on it, slowing just enough to leave her thirsting and impatient, wanting and out of breath. And when she was at her zenith, ready to explode around him, he maneuvered her hips in front of one of the swirling jets and smiled as she screamed his name for the first time in a long while.

CHAPTER 10

Lucius Jeremiah Culpepper walked around in circles and tried to ignore the nagging pain in his chest. He was certain it wasn't the kind that was supposed to warn him of an impending heart attack. It was the kind threatening to put him down, though, just the same, flat on his back, or curled up in a fetal position in a corner somewhere. He'd been carrying such a load on his heart for so long, the weight of additional emotional pounds was becoming more than he could bear. Sadly, it appeared that nothing he did could lighten the massiveness that now caused him to feel unsteady on his feet.

So what in God's name was he supposed to do now? He was, or had been, a champion at expertly navigating every crisis or catastrophe that crossed his path. He was a rock, plain and simple. Hell, the whole town knew it. Everyone counted on him to make their world a better place, smooth things over, fix the unfixable, and he had—except for this. Somehow he'd thought, hoped, believed that time would heal his wounds, her wounds, make every unpleasant emotion disappear. Well, time hadn't healed a damn thing, and he'd wasted so much of it waiting for a resolution that obviously didn't exist. Inexplicably, he felt like he'd aged twenty years overnight. December 15 came around every year, and every year he had been able to work right through it, pretend like it was just another ordinary day. God only knew why he was unable to do that now.

He leaned against the wall in Reva's old sitting room and closed his eyes. It must have been a Saturday because he heard "Now's the Time" in his head—a spirited blues tune by the troubled Yardbird. Bird knew trouble was coming. Why didn't he? He could envision them all now laughing in the living room. He could even see Dahlia. She must have been about nine then and was begging him to lift her up so she could put a star on top of the Christmas tree. She was so beautiful and smart, kept him on his toes, that one. He'd started saving for Harvard the day she was born. He knew fathers weren't supposed to have a favorite child, but he couldn't help utterly spoiling her. Dahlia looked and acted so much like him that denying her anything was tantamount to denying himself. All he could do was adore her. He loved all his children, but he loved her the most, and he'd failed the one he loved the most. And in failing her, he'd failed himself. He began to weep silently and became disgusted at himself, crying in the middle of the day like a damn baby. He comforted other people when they cried. He didn't cry. He was really losing it. He'd be walking into walls next if he weren't careful.

He heard footsteps and quickly regained his composure. No one could ever see him like this. Weak. Lucius wiped his face with the back of his hand and prepared to go back to work on Buster Perkins. Poor old crusty bastard caught a stroke wiggling and carrying on underneath his nineteen-year-old girlfriend, Portia. The family, including Buster's wife, Sister Pearl, ordered him to remove the peculiar grin that seemed to be plastered all over Buster's face. So, nervous breakdown aside, it was back to business as usual because rocks didn't weep.

"Lucius, what are you doing up here? I thought you didn't come in here anymore," Aunt Baby inquired gently.

"I don't know. I just felt compelled to visit this old room. There's a lot of history in this room."

"Lucius Culpepper, have you been crying?"

"No, of course not. Don't be ridiculous. Got a little chemical in my eyes. Today is the day, you know. Anyway, when was the last time you spoke to my daughter?"

"I know, I know. I talked to her a couple of weeks ago, I think."

"And?"

"We didn't really talk about anything important."

"Do you ever?"

"Sometimes. Sometimes, Lucius, but I don't push. I never push. She's not ready."

"It's been nearly twenty-five years, Aunt Baby. If she isn't ready by now, I don't think she'll ever be. She won't talk to me, you know. It's like she's erased me from her memory. I suffered, too, Baby. God knows we all suffered behind what happened."

"Yes, Lucius, but you were a grown man, and she was a child. Children suffer differently from grown folk."

"Hell, suffering is suffering. Why couldn't we suffer together? Families are supposed to suffer together."

"Your wife, her mama. Different relationship, different pain."

"Maybe she thinks I didn't experience enough pain. How could she think that? How could anyone think that?"

"Nephew, everyone expresses their pain differently. And, well, frankly you can't blame the girl for not understanding how you chose to express yours. Hell, none of us understood that."

Lucius raised an eyebrow and inhaled deeply. How did this conversation turn into an analysis of his personal life? Why couldn't she just stick to the subject at hand and leave Mercy out of this? He attempted to refocus Aunt Baby on the issue at hand.

"Okay, what about that husband of hers, the half-black China-man, and my grandchild that I've only seen pictures of? If it weren't for you, I wouldn't know anything about my own daughter. I've lost her, Aunt Baby. I've lost her for good."

"Well, then, nephew, there's only one thing left to do. Find her; fight for her before it's too late."

"What if it's already too late?"

"Boy, it ain't never too late to save your soul. Hers or yours."

"She'll hate me. She'll hate me for bringing all of this up again."

"She'll hate you if you don't. It's time now, Lucius. You should have done this thing long ago. I always told you that the way you handled it wasn't natural. But, see, you were hardheaded just like any other man. It's not your fault, though; you come by it honestly. I told you then that this would come back to haunt you."

"I just couldn't handle it."

"Well, Dahlia couldn't either, but she was a child—a child that you—"

Lucius interrupted before she could finish. "Don't say it, Aunt Baby. I . . . I just couldn't do it. Why can't you understand that?"

"Boy, who do you think you're talking to? You could have done what needed to be done, Lucius. You just chose not to, and now you have to. You can do this, my love. And anyway, I have a bad feeling right about now. The joints in my left knee have been throbbing for damn near a week. Now you and I both know that's a bad sign."

Lucius left Aunt Baby feeling just a little bit worse and wandered around the grounds until he found his way to his office on the north side of the funeral home. He pressed a button on a shiny silver remote control and reclined as Miles Davis's *Kind of Blue* filled the space where he came to hide. He only played Miles when he was feeling out of sorts, lost inside himself. All this time, he had been managing his life, his wife, his home, and his business with a kind of determined calmness. He had somehow accepted that not having a relationship with his firstborn was completely normal. He moved from day to day, year to year, surviving, pretending that it wasn't killing him, a malignancy consuming his soul. Aunt Baby was right. If he didn't do something now, they would both be lost in a tragedy that never seemed to end. How did he get here? When did it all start to fall apart? And how, in God's name, could he have let it go this far? What kind of man was he? He leaned back when the answers were not forthcoming, closed his eyes, and allowed the sounds of a forlorn trumpet to steal him away until the urgency of the moment left him—if only for a little while.

CHAPTER 11

Phoebe slammed the phone down for no reason in particular. She was irritated more than usual today and couldn't quite figure out why. She hastily surveyed her split-level condominium and plopped down on the couch like a thickster who'd lost her balance. Truth be told, she knew exactly what or who was bothering her, getting her panties all twisted, making her butt hurt. She hadn't heard one word from that pain in the ass Dahlia, not one word. Phoebe narrowed her eyes. She did not appreciate being ignored. She'd been to hell and back with Dahlia, and this was how she was repaid? Ungrateful self-absorbed bitch. It seemed to Phoebe that Dahlia was trying to come down with amnesia, straight out pretend like she didn't exist at all. And really, why shouldn't she? Feigning like a problem or a person wasn't real was nothing new to Dahlia. She'd managed to make her own daddy disappear somewhere in no-man's-land, and now it was obviously Phoebe's turn. After all these years, Dahlia was still merely surviving, struggling desperately to go it alone when she didn't have to.

Bottom line, maybe it was time for Phoebe to just leave her

alone, focus on her own uneventful life. She was a grown woman, easy on the eyes, and completely bored out of her damned mind. She didn't have to work, but she was considering opening some kind of business, a gallery maybe, in Pasadena. Although Dahlia would probably think she was stalking her if she moved to her neck of the woods. She had to face that her preoccupation with Dahlia was turning into some kind of freak obsession. But God help her, she couldn't all of a sudden stop caring, stop loving, and stop protecting the best friend she'd ever had. If it weren't for Phoebe, who knew where Miss High and Mighty would be? Most likely tripping up and down Hollywood Boulevard with a venereal disease and some lopsided silicone tits. Certainly not thriving with two careers, a family, and enough shoes to rival Imelda Marcos. In spite of Dahlia's pissy attitude, abandoning her just didn't seem like the right thing to do. Wasn't that the same as kicking someone when they were down? Couldn't a person go straight to hell for something like that?

Still, she yearned to be free to live her own life without being consumed with Dahlia's. It was time for her to relax, prop her feet up, and throw back a couple of apple martinis. Shit, it was time for her to get a life. She had to face the fact that maybe she'd finally done enough, worried enough, and yelled enough for the both of them.

She simply needed to unwind and find a man to help occupy her time. Yeah, baby, some suave Mandingo with perfect pectorals to titillate her and numb her mind when her life began slipping into an abyss of monotony. Come to think of it, she couldn't remember the last time she had an orgasm without Roscoe, her fourteen-hundred-dollar blow-up doll. It was a pity she wasn't allergic to latex. That would at least force her to find a real flesh-and-blood man.

She should be a good friend and go spend some quality time with Milky. He, like she, was most assuredly in need. All men were in need, and she was such a giving and compassionate woman. Really, just because Dahlia had stopped contributing to their relationship didn't mean she had to be equally distant, did it?

Phoebe smiled and sipped on a glass of Sangiovese. Well, then, it was settled. She was just going to have to drive on over there and graciously offer her support. She flipped open her journal and began writing furiously. Timing was everything.

CHAPTER 12

Mercy smoothed the folds of her crimson dress and re-freshed her matching lipstick, Lancôme 452. She was diminutive in size, but that never affected her vivacious disposition. She admired her flawless deep brown skin in a full-length mirror and wondered aloud how in the world her husband could keep his hands off her. She was ebony perfection, a work of art constantly in progress. Mercy Culpepper was forty-one, svelte, and tired as hell of being cooped up in a creepy old mortuary with people who refused to appreciate her God-given talents. Folks around here would rather pay more attention to formaldehyde than ac-knowledge the work of art gracing their presence every day. There was only so much shopping a woman could do.

Of course, she never thought she'd ever ponder such a notion, but the truth of the matter was, she needed some serious maneu-verability in her life. Suddenly, prowling the aisles of Neiman Marcus wasn't as fascinating as it used to be—and neither was her husband. Lucius used to be such a mystery to her, someone to dismantle, decipher, and then reassemble again like a jigsaw puzzle. Ah, Lucius—handsome, moody, eccentric Lucius. She had been young then and somewhat idealistic when she believed that she could make him happy, keep his mind from venturing too far into the past. But no matter what she did, how beautiful she became, or how many times she shimmied buck-naked in his office, he looked right through her. Soon she realized, not long after they married, that she'd become an annoyance, an unwanted distraction. And maybe, just maybe, she always had been.

She'd thought about leaving him, starting over somewhere else, Miami maybe, but she'd been with Lucius Culpepper for too long now. Packing her life up in five Louis Vuitton bags seemed so implausible. Although she believed that she would walk away with a little nest egg if they divorced, she also believed that Aunt Baby would cast some kind of backwoods New Orleans voodoo on her. That old witch was hell on wheels, and the best that Mercy could hope for was a quick, unexpected death sometime soon. She'd heard stories about Aunt Baby for a long time, and truth be told, she did not intend to become a chapter in her book of "get rid of the trifling wife" spells. So she would bide her time and wait for the inevitable. Everybody had to die sometime. In the meantime, she'd make nice like she always did and continue to pretend that the mere sight of Lucius's aunt didn't make her face twitch.

She couldn't find her moody husband anywhere, so she took a deep breath, made the sign of the cross, and went to look for Aunt Baby instead. She found her ten minutes later bent over the dining room table writing furiously.

"What are you doing, Aunt Baby?"

"Minding my own damn business."

Mercy rolled her eyes and tried to will her face to be still. "Have you seen Lucius? I've been looking for him all day."

"Maybe he doesn't want to be found. Have you considered that? And stand up straight, for the love of God."

"Look, I don't wanna start a ruckus, Baby. I just need to talk to my husband, ifn that's okay by you."

"My, my, my that fancy talk of yours sure seems to disappear when you get all riled up."

Mercy felt her face twitching so hard she thought she'd blow up right then and there. She itched to slap an apology clean out of the old woman's mouth. Lord knows she had never hated another woman as much as she hated Aunt Baby. No wonder Lucius's first wife went crazy. Who wouldn't lose all their marbles living in the same house with the wife of Satan cleverly disguised as an evil-ass old woman? "Are you going to answer me or not?" she asked in her sweetest voice, with her hands on her hips.

"Lucius had a meeting to attend in North Dallas. Why don't you take a drive over that way and see if you can find him on the freeway? And while you're at it, stop by NorthPark and buy yourself another red dress."

"Now was that so difficult? Goodness, you'd think I was asking you for a kidney or something."

Mercy sauntered off feeling as if she'd won some kind of door prize. Perhaps before all was said and done she'd win Aunt Baby over, convince the old bat to retire to a nice old folks home someplace a million miles away. Mercy slid into her red CLK 55 Mercedes-Benz. *Dream on, sucker,* she thought. *Fat chance. That old biddy is going to stay alive out of spite just to antagonize me. She won't be happy until I'm twitching like an epileptic.*

Not five minutes later, Aunt Baby watched Mercy peel out of the driveway in search of a husband who was on the other side of the house. She shook her head in amusement. Dumb bunny, that's what she was, a dumb bunny in a red dress. It never occurred to Mercy to walk through the house and listen for any Miles, 'Trane, or Bird. Even the dead knew how to find Lucius when he was on the premises. She'd slept in the same bed with the man every night for over twenty-four years and still hadn't figured out how to follow the music. Her brain had obviously traveled down to her ass. She didn't even ask where the meeting was. The demented heffa was probably going to drive up and down the expressway looking for a black Jaguar that was parked out front. She was a real mental giant, that one. And Lucius thought his first wife was touched in the head. Crazy bastard. He sure could pick them, her nephew—out of the frying pan and straight into the fire.

Aunt Baby stared out the window and massaged her throbbing knee. She had no intention of allowing anyone to disturb Lucius during this crucial time—least of all his dim-witted, tic-faced wife. This family was finally changing course, and even though she knew the journey was destined to be painful, it was necessary if everything was ever going to be all right again. Yes, Lord, change was coming, and she had to be certain that they were all ready. She'd made a decision long ago on that awful day that before she left this earth, she would do all that she could to glue the fragments of her family's life back together—even if it meant shattering it to pieces all over again. Aunt Baby continued to write her letter. She was going to California for a while. Someone had to plow the road for Lucius.

CHAPTER 13

"Relax, Dahlia. I'm not your enemy."

"How many people have you said that to?"

"Why is that important?"

"I don't know. I guess I feel like I'm being forced to be here. This is our fourth session, and I don't feel any different. I mean, I know obviously something is going on with me, but I don't appreciate being ordered to see you."

"Understandable, but now that you are here, why don't we make the best of our time together, hmmmm?"

"Whatever you say."

"Dahlia, give me a chance to help you. Help me help you."

"What is it that you want from me? I'm here, aren't I? That should count for something."

"Why are you here, Dahlia? I know you've said your husband ordered you to come. What was it exactly that prompted this visit?"

"You get right to the point, don't you, Doc?"

Dahlia reclined and found it difficult to respond. But at last the words found a place in her throat and regrettably slid out of her mouth. "I . . . I soiled myself in front of my students."

"What do you mean, exactly, soiled yourself?"

"And they tell me you have a Ph.D."

"All right. For clarification purposes, liquid or solid?"

"Liquid."

"Oh. I see. Try and remember precisely what you were doing and feeling before this happened."

"I don't know. I've been trying to block the entire incident out of my mind. Milky doesn't even know about it. I am—I was too humiliated to tell him."

"Try to remember how the day began, and we'll work from there."

"I didn't want to get out of bed that morning. God, I was so exhausted. I'm always so wiped out. I remember arriving to class late, and then I remember feeling wet. That's it. I don't even remember leaving."

"Do you remember where you went after you left the school?"

"Yes, I think I went home because I had a headache."

"What did you do then?"

"I changed my clothes." Dr. Kelly noticed that she looked puzzled.

"Did anything else unusual happen that day?"

"You mean other than the puddle around my leg thing?"

"Yes, anything in addition to that."

"Nothing that I want to mention right now."

"All right."

"Can we move on?" Dahlia asked, somewhat irritated.

"You've been having a lot of headaches lately, yes?"

"Unfortunately, yes."

"Are these headaches affecting your relationship with your husband and your daughter, Isabel?"

Dahlia looked away. She was still tired—tired of feeling tired and tired of this conversation.

"Dahlia, have you ever considered that maybe this isn't as urgent as you imagined? Stress could be a factor, and you might just have a bladder-control problem."

"I don't think so, Dr. Kelly. I'm thirty-five years old. I usually know when I have to pee."

"All right, then. We'll move on." Dr. Kelly referred to his notes. "Let's try and start from the very beginning again. Relax, take a deep breath, and picture yourself back in the home that you grew up in. Tell me what you see. Are your parents there?"

Dahlia sat up abruptly and glanced at her watch. "Sorry, Doc. Time's up."

CHAPTER 14

There are people in this world who always seem to inspire a bit of fascination. No one quite knows what to make of them, but they know enough to leave them be and watch in wonder as they find their place in the world. And then there are those people who are simply strange. Not strange in a "We need to keep that one in a room behind the shed before he hurts somebody" kind of way but strange in a "Best to just leave that child alone before you find something wrong with you" kind of way.

Percival Tweed fell into this category. From the moment he slipped out of his mother's womb, his beingness perplexed everyone around him. He was an anomaly, a walking mystery of the universe, a peculiar contradiction of sorts—both black and white at the same time. It was said that his mama, Caldonia Tweed, was visiting with Aunt Baby's Indian mother, Oceola Moon, the day she went into labor prematurely. Supposedly, as the story goes, she saw a haint in the stairwell of the funeral home winking at her, and as a result, the baby she carried in her womb didn't have a chance in hell of being born normal. Her sheer terror on that day, people swore, plum scared the black straight off of Percival. After Percival was born, Caldonia Tweed was never quite the same again. But Percival, despite his statements to the contrary, became something of a legend.

Back when Percival Tweed was a boy, some fifty-sixty-odd years ago, the white folk didn't even fool around with him. Rumor had it that anyone who had ever tried to hurt Percival Tweed mysteriously ended up with a curious affliction of sorts. Once when Percival Tweed was fourteen, the O'Shannon boys tried to teach him a lesson for not jumping off the sidewalk quickly enough to let decent folk pass. Billy O'Shannon had pushed him then and threatened to string him up from the nearest magnolia tree. The next day, as sure as the sun rose, Billy O'Shannon lost all ten of his fingers in a meat press over at the sausage plant downtown. Each O'Shannon in that group on the sidewalk that day was struck with a painful calamity. Coincidence perhaps, some pondered, but nobody in five counties was willing to take any chances with the blond-haired black boy who lived behind the Negro funeral home.

And that was a blessing because Percival Tweed never meant to hurt anyone. For a long time, he, too, believed he was some kind of freak, a boy put on the earth just so other people could exercise their eyeballs and flap their lips when they looked upon him. He was of average height, five feet eleven or so, and lean of build. His body was chiseled from years of manual labor, and his skin was so white that it was nearly translucent. His mother used to proclaim that the sun came up every morning just to try and brown him up some. The hue of his skin alone would have been enough to get tongues wagging, but God had blessed Percival Tweed with an eerie sixth sense and the most extraordinary canary yellow eyes anyone had ever seen. He had always been alone, and for the most part, he liked it that way. The only woman he'd ever wanted was the one he couldn't have, so being alone suited him just fine.

Percival Tweed arose and said his prayers on his knees like he'd done every morning of his life. His mother had been a stickler for such things. Life was calmer, and he'd had no reason to complain for a while. He lived in a modest house on the outskirts of the Culpepper property and had been there for as long as he could remember. Old man Culpepper had invited him many times to move closer to the main house with the family, but he'd always declined. Percival Tweed knew he was peculiar, but he had no intention of seeing anything or anyone else peculiar up in that house. Looking in the mirror every morning was enough for him.

He'd ventured into the Culpepper house once back in the spring of 1949, and that was the last time he'd ever stepped foot in that place. His mama always claimed that there were haints in that house, and Percival Tweed didn't fool around with no haints. They'd already caused him enough trouble. He savored a slice of honey wheat bread baked with bourbon and molasses, grabbed his trademark wide-brimmed gray hat, and loaded up the truck. His work list would be posted on the back door of the funeral home. Oddly enough, he'd never had to check it. He'd always known exactly how many graves to dig on any given day. It was a gift. Percival Tweed was a man of many gifts.

CHAPTER 15

Aunt Baby watched him from the window upstairs in the corner room—the one no one went in anymore on account of the unexplained frigid temperature. It was cold, but then again it was always cold in a funeral parlor—cold from refrigeration or cold from all the spirits hovering around begging for attention. No matter what you told people, sometimes they just couldn't get used to the obvious. Truth for the feebleminded was too exhausting. She pinned her long salt-and-pepper braids on top of her head, sat for a spell, and enjoyed the view.

He was an unusual man, that Percival Tweed, but he intrigued her just the same—always had. They never spoke much, just managed to exchange pleasantries every now and then. She knew that he knew that she watched him, and she also knew that he liked it, counted on it to jump-start his day. Although he tried, he couldn't fool her. Hell, nobody could. It didn't matter much, though, because neither of them would ever attempt to initiate any contact. For some odd reason, they only seemed to like each other from a distance. Folks always said that Percival Tweed was too strange a fellow to be fooling around with, but Aunt Baby also knew folks had whispered the same nonsense about her since she was knee-high to a bullfrog. She pondered, What were the odds of having two bizarre people in one town who weren't related?

Decades had passed and they'd never had so much as a real conversation except for that one awful day. And after that, it didn't seem like there was any more left to say. They had never really been in each other's lives, but she found that she missed him like she'd miss a husband if she'd ever had one. Her life had always consisted of her family, her family's business, and her back-porch remedies. Before she knew it, in the blink of an eye, she was a grown woman with no husband or children of her own. It didn't bother her too much. She never thought she'd have children anyway. She had accepted the vacancy sign that had become permanently attached to her womb. And there was always somebody else or somebody else's child who needed tending. When Dante came along out of the blue, thoughts of a husband that had been lingering in her imagination and casually invading her dreams vanished almost overnight. But still, even now, after all this time, when she looked at Percival, she was reminded of a life she could have had, a husband she would have loved, and a time that was long gone.

CHAPTER 16

Mercy had driven to NorthPark and back twice before she realized that she'd seen the black Jaguar parked out front next to Uncle Brother's Lexus. She berated herself for being so gullible, so naïve, so utterly stupid. She had unwittingly been entertainment for Aunt Baby again. Right now, at this moment, she should be staring into the eyes of a man who loved her instead of driving around town like a maniac searching for a car that had been in front of her the whole time. She was disgusted with herself, and the three new red dresses she had charged from Nordstrom didn't make her feel any less dim-witted.

Being around Aunt Baby made her so jittery that she couldn't complete the simplest of tasks without appearing like she suffered from Tourette's syndrome. One minute she was perusing catalogs in her lavishly furnished bedroom, and the next she was twitching through the funeral parlor, most likely putting on a show for the dead along with the staff. Her face had become a sitcom, and much to her chagrin, TicTock had become her middle name. For the life of her, she couldn't comprehend how one cantankerous old woman could have such an effect on her. Somehow, since entering this house, she had been reduced to an incomparable twit, someone who couldn't walk and chew gum at the same time, someone who didn't know her ass from her elbow, someone who couldn't control her own facial muscles without downing a shot of Cognac. This was not supposed to be her life. She had always been a reasonably intelligent girl. She could have made something of herself. She should have done something with her life instead of settling for a man who couldn't love her and a house that would never be her home.

The truth of her life was overwhelming. Who she was and what she had done settled into her bones and unfurled like cancer. She realized that she had no one to blame but herself. Her life was the way it was because of the choices she'd made. She had always been able to write her own ticket, and in doing so, she had invariably sent herself to hell. Her existence was less than desirable because, when she was sixteen years old, she had told her mama that she wanted to marry Lucius Culpepper. And like always, her parents had obliged her. She wished now that they hadn't constantly given her everything she ever wanted. She wished that her parents had expected more of her. What teenager is allowed to decide her entire life? What the hell had she known at sixteen? Frankly, what the hell did she know now? All of her life, she had been told she was special, and she'd believed it until she married Lucius Culpepper. Now she felt trapped in a spiral of wrong decisions, and there was nothing she could do about it. She was being punished. She knew it.

If only she could go back and make adult choices. If only she could undo the damage she had done so carelessly. If only . . . she could press rewind and relive that one day, all would be forgiven and she would have the life she deserved. But no, as usual, she had gotten precisely what she asked for, and the realization of that was almost more than she could bear. Defeated in her scarlet red Mercedes with her hands clenched tightly around the steering wheel, Mercy Lucille Blue flirted with a nervous breakdown. What if, after all this time, her parents had lied to her? Maybe she wasn't so extraordinary after all. Maybe her life had been one big mistake from the very beginning.

CHAPTER 17

"Quit fussin' over me now. I can figure out how to get on a damn train. I'm old; I'm not stupid." Aunt Baby slapped Uncle Brother's arm away as he tried to help her onboard.

"Don't you run back and tell that boy I'm leaving, hear. Let him find my note in his own time."

"Are you sure you know what you're doing, Mama?" Brother asked, shaking his head. "You know, some things need to be left unsaid. I think—"

Aunt Baby sternly interrupted him. "Boy, I don't recall asking you what you think. Hell, did I even ask you to drive me down here? Furthermore, did I ask you to cut your hair like that? You look like a damn chicken."

"No, Mama." Brother sighed.

"Well, then, don't just stand there. Help me with my bags."

"Yes, ma'am."

"Brother."

"Yes, ma'am?"

"You take care of Lucius while I'm gone."

"Hmmm."

"Brother."

"You come with Lucius when it's time to bring me home."

"All right," Brother agreed, with a raised eyebrow.

"And, Brother."

"Hmmmm."

"When you come to California, don't let him bring TicTock. She'll only make matters worse. You and I both know she likes to stir up a fresh batch of hell every chance she gets. I mean, what kind of woman buys over forty red dresses? One that's not quite right in the head, that's what kind. Just a plain nutcase, if you ask me."

"Well, there's a lot of that going around."

"Hush your mouth. You know that girl has a head chock-full of peanuts," Aunt Baby whispered, stifling a giggle.

"Aw, Mama, that is his wife. Maybe she's just color-blind and can't see any other color but red," Brother added, trying desperately not to join in his mother's laughter at the expense of his cousin's wife.

"Just hear what I say. Make sure somebody watches Mercy while y'all are gone or else the entire house will be looted, picked clean like a drumstick on New Year's Day. Watch her now, son. Keep one eye on her at all times."

"Okay, Mama, okay. You're about to miss the train now. Hurry up."

"Brother."

"Yes."

"I love you, son, you hear."

"I love you, too," Brother responded gently, and embraced the only mother he had ever known.

"And, Brother."

"Yes, Mama."

"Did any bread come today?"

"It's Wednesday, Mama, and fresh loaves always come on Wednesdays. They have for as long as I can remember."

"All right, then. Oh, Brother."

"Yes, Mama."

"Well, did you pack some in my bags?"

"Of course."

"What kind is it this time?"

"Does it really matter?"

Aunt Baby raised her eyebrow, and Dante sighed before replying.

"Some kind of sweet potato bread, I guess."

"I better get going, but listen to me. I know what I'm doing. Tell your cousin that I know what I'm doing. And, Brother."

"What! For Christ's sake."

"Watch your mouth, boy. You know I didn't raise you to take the Lord's name in vain."

"Yes, yes. What is it now?"

"Tell that red-dress-wearing heffa that I'm coming back, so don't go repainting any rooms or rearranging any furniture. She don't own nothing up in there."

Aunt Baby watched Brother get smaller and smaller as the train pulled away from the station. If she didn't know any better, she'd have sworn she had given birth to that boy herself, squeezed him right on out of her womb. It was impossible, she knew, but he was beginning to look more and more like her every day—a paler version, anyway. Frankly, she had no idea what the boy was. Everyone in the family always suspected there was a drop of black blood coursing through his veins because of the light brown hue that mysteriously crept up on him sometime during the middle of July. Hell, for all she knew, that could be just a tan, a tan on a white man. He was damn near white, with green eyes, a long nose, and a sweet disposition—which was amazing considering how his life began.

Some forty years ago, his mama or somebody left him on the front porch of the house, which wasn't connected to the funeral parlor at the time. There was a pounding on the door, and of course, at that time of night, they all naturally assumed that there was a dead body somewhere for her father, Marcel, to pick up. Lucius was about twelve or thirteen then, and he was the one who answered the door. He busted in her room looking wild and crazy and screamed that somebody had left a burned-up baby on their doorstep. She remembered it like it was yesterday. Everyone flew downstairs and gawked at the miniature horror writhing before them. Brother was only a few weeks old then, and he was in so much pain—poor little thing, he could barely scream. He was wrapped loosely in a cotton blanket that stuck to his skin, and he was burned so badly that no one was able to figure out if he was black, white, or any color in between.

That night, Brother looked straight through her and asked her to be his mother. She picked him up then and declared it her mission to make him well and whole from that moment on. She nurtured the scars right off his body and poured liquid love all over his soul. She mixed, boiled, concocted every herbal salve she could think of and kept that boy slathered in it for nearly three straight years. And then one day, she unwrapped him, and like magic he looked as normal as the rest of them, except for being a few shades lighter. She couldn't have loved that boy any more if she had given birth to him herself. He was in her blood and always would be.

They never discovered who abandoned him on that doorstep or why. It was just as well, though, because Lord knows she would have killed somebody dead if they'd ever tried to take that boy away from her. For all intents and purposes, he was her son and that was that. Brother was good for Lucius, too, a godsend for the Culpepper family. Almost overnight, he became the little brother Lucius never had. Aunt Baby named him Dante because he had already been through several levels of hell, but everyone called him Brother. And when Lucius's children were born, he became Uncle Brother.

Aunt Baby reclined in her deluxe room and fingered the loaf of bread that Dante had packed for her. It was still warm and smelled of sweet potatoes and nutmeg. Fresh bread had been a part of their lives for such a long time. Baskets of it began arriving at the funeral parlor more than thirty-five years ago. No one knew where it came from, but it was always there—every kind of bread imaginable. Loaves of sourdough rye, rosemary garlic-infused baguettes, and herb parmesan something or other had graced the Culpepper doorstep as if they were permanent fixtures, attachments to the architecture. Aunt Baby knew that Percival received Wednesday baskets as well, and that brought her a certain level of comfort. Someone loved them dearly, and at one time, she considered trying to figure out who it was, but in the end, her son was right—some things were best left unsaid. Aunt Baby closed her eyes and allowed her mind to finally rest. It would take forty-three hours before she arrived in Los Angeles, and she needed every hour of sleep she could get. She had to be on her toes when she stepped off that train, and she knew instinctively that she had to be ready for anything.

CHAPTER 18

"We need to talk." Milky paced the floor. It seemed he was constantly pacing the floor.

"What is it, honey?"

"What is going on, Dahlia? What is happening to you?"

"What are you complaining about now, Milky? I'm here. I'm home." Dahlia refused to look up from the *O* magazine she was pretending to read. She finally had a moment to breathe, and here he was interrogating her, treating her like a suspect. Hadn't she been questioned enough? Wasn't she doing enough?

"Look at me, dammit. I am your husband." Milky snatched the magazine from her hand. Dahlia stood and faced him. It was difficult, but she had to let him know that she was trying. God, she was trying.

"What do you want from me, Milky?"

"I want you to talk to me. I want you to be an active participant in our marriage. I want you to be a mother to our daughter. I want you to come home when you say you're coming home. I want to know where you are when you're supposed to be here with me, with Isabel. Shall I go on?"

"Jesus, what else do you want me to do? I've done everything that you've asked of me. I don't know what's happening to me. I just know that—"

Milky interrupted, somewhat exasperated. "Look, I know you've been going to see Dr. Kelly. Have your sessions with him been helpful at all? Tell me—"

"No!" Dahlia screamed. "I'm seeing Dr. Kelly because you said I had to. Talking to you about it wasn't part of the agreement. Why can't you just leave me alone and let me sort this out for myself? I meet with the shrink once a week. Why isn't that enough for you?"

"I think we need to consider some other options here."

"No. That won't be necessary. I think I just need more time."

"More time, Dahlia? It's been over a month, and nothing in your behavior has changed. As a matter of fact, things between us have gotten worse. You've gotten worse."

"I think you're exaggerating, Milky. You and I both know you have a penchant for making a mountain out of a molehill."

"Really?"

"Yes, really." Dahlia reached for the discarded magazine. Milky pushed it away from her grasp.

"Where is Isabel, Dahlia?"

"What?"

"You heard me. Where is your daughter?" Silence. "What kind of mother doesn't ask about her daughter when she comes home?"

"What are you implying here, Milky?"

"You have a master's degree. I think you know exactly what I'm saying."

"Are you accusing me of being a bad mother?"

"I'm accusing you of being a bad everything. Look at you. Look at us. Something is missing here, Dahlia, and we can't continue, I can't continue, until we figure out what it is."

"What are you saying?"

"I don't trust you anymore, and neither does Isabel. How do you think that makes us feel, Dahlia?" Dahlia looked away.

"I know you take good care of Isabel," Dahlia whispered. "I know I don't have to worry about her."

"Yes, that's convenient, Dahlia, but I shouldn't be the only one taking care of our daughter. And she's at my mom's, by the way, just in case some unaffected part of you was wondering."

"Go to hell."

"Are you having an affair?"

"Don't be ridiculous."

"Answer me, dammit. Are you having an affair? Who is it?"

Dahlia stormed past him toward the winding staircase. He grabbed her by the arm and spun her around to face him.

"And all this time, I thought you were the brilliant one in this relationship," Dahlia retorted.

"And what the hell is that supposed to mean?"

"Think about it, Einstein. I'm too exhausted to fuck you most of the time. What makes you think I have the energy to open my legs for anyone else?"

Milky felt her jerk away and watched her disappear into another part of the house. Now he was more confused than ever. This was a side of his wife that he had never seen, and he didn't like it. He didn't like anything about his marriage anymore. The love of his life was only a few feet away, and yet he was more alone than he had ever been. He sat and stared at a painting of a Tuareg woman that hung above the fireplace. They'd bought it together a few years ago at a gallery in Ojai, California. He smiled at the memory and became wistful. They were happy then, or maybe they weren't. This kind of unraveling couldn't have happened overnight. He couldn't have missed a character flaw this monumental, or could he? He hungered for the woman he'd fallen in love with, and he had to find a way to get her back, for his sake and for Isabel's. He wished he could share his dilemma with his wife, his lover, his confidante. But he couldn't because he didn't know the woman upstairs anymore, and it amazed him just how long it had taken her to become a stranger.

He gritted his teeth and picked up the phone. It was up to him now to do what was best for their family. "Mom," he said, "I need you to keep your granddaughter for a while longer."

CHAPTER 19

Mercy, that's what her parents named her, because she was a miracle baby, and Mercy was the first word uttered from her daddy's mouth on the day she was born. She came at a time when her mother, Lucille, believed that her period was gone forever, lost in that faraway place with her rock-hard thighs and twenty-eight-inch hips. Her head had swirled along with her stomach back then as she wondered how in the world she could possibly have been pregnant. For years, the Lord had never seen fit to bless her with a child, and then suddenly, at age forty-eight, she had an unfathomable craving for liverwurst and deviled eggs. It took her at least a month of throwing up her breakfast before she was able to accept the inexplicable.

And Mercy's father, Leander, was just as dumbfounded. As he had been cursed with a limp tool for most of his adult life, he couldn't imagine that any of his spermatozoa had the energy or wherewithal to swim anywhere. Attaining an erection for him was the same as trying to find a pearl in an oyster. It was possible but highly unlikely. He had been married to Lucille for nearly twenty-five years, and her presence still baffled him every time he woke up and saw her pretty brown face. Still, when he opened his eyes every morning, he just knew she would be long gone—stolen by a younger man with a working johnson and an agile tongue.

On the day that Lucille announced she was with child, Leander was incredulous. He couldn't figure out how it happened and swore it was akin to the Immaculate Conception. Mercy, he kept repeating over and over again, this pregnancy was a blessing from the Almighty because the child was conceived in the oddest of ways. That night, Lucille was in desperate need of the kind of intimacy that she'd always dreamed about but never experienced with Leander. It had been years, and she yearned for a feeling, an emotion, anything to remind her of who she once was before she settled for Leander. Of course, Leander attempted to satisfy her urges. He performed the best that he could, but his best never became firm enough to reach that warm place inside her that ached for attention. Exhausted by the effort, Lucille turned away and wept just in time to feel him release himself on her left leg right above the knee. Shortly thereafter, her cravings began, and their blessing came through her womb straight from the heavens above.

It didn't take long for Lucille and Leander to realize that Mercy was an exceptional child marked for greatness. They both knew she had maneuvered quite a distance up her mama's leg to come into the world. And from the moment she was born, they showered her with anything that she ever wanted. She was supposed to be on this earth, and no one could convince them otherwise. She was a walking miracle, a gift from Jehovah, and they told her so almost every day of her charmed life. They would have signed their souls over to the devil and sold everything they owned to make her happy, but in the end, all Mercy ever wanted was Lucius Culpepper. And despite Lucille's misgivings about her only child's peculiar request, she sent Leander to the Culpepper place to inquire about a job for Mercy when she was seventeen years old. Lucille wanted her daughter to have her heart's desire. After all, Mercy had worked so hard and crawled so far to be a part of creation.

CHAPTER 20

Friday · December 1 · 9:06 a.m.

Am I a horrible person for even contemplating this insanity? Well, under the circumstances, I guess I am. Attempting to justify my feelings is a sure sign that I'm just no damn good. Clearly, there's no way around it. I am a horrible person, a wretched, conniving ho, tramp, slut. I deserve happiness, don't I? Doesn't everyone? I deserve to live my life free of Dahlia. She's had her chance to be blissful all these years. Is it my fault that she can't hold her life together? No. Hell no. Why should she continue to have everything while I continue to have nothing? No one has ever helped me do a damn thing. No one has ever supported me. Why, why, why do I have to live like this? Locked up like a genie in a bottle.

Who is going to pick me up when I fall? Who do I have to turn to in a crisis? Shit, no one but Roscoe, and he's half the man he used to be ever since he sprang that leak. All I have ever done is protect her, keep her from harm's way, and remind her that she was not alone. For years, I've been there. Me, propping her up, propelling her forward, reinforcing that she could survive what happened. And now she abandons me! Well, I'm abandoning her first. I've been there for every major event in her life, and now it's my turn in the spotlight. I'm taking the microphone, baby doll, so you get your ass *in the background where you belong. From now on, I'm looking out for me, paying attention to what I want and what I need. That doesn't make me psycho, does it? Right now, I figure it makes me sane, focused. Hey, I'm not the one peeing on my damn self in front of a room full of people. I know I'm not perfect, but I have talents. I do. I have gifts. I can pretty much do whatever I set my mind to. I'm smart. I'm attractive. I'm financially independent. I take care of myself, dammit. I'm a warrior, and Dahlia better not fucking forget it. I'm owed here, and if she won't give me what I'm due, well, then, I'll just have to go and take what's rightfully mine.*

Phoebe closed her journal, licked the rim of her wineglass, and danced around her apartment naked. She casually admired her taut backside in a full-length mirror and scanned her closet for possibilities. Every aspect of this plan had to be executed perfectly. She was determined to make a good impression. She wanted Milky to realize that he had chosen incorrectly. After all, she'd seen him first, and she wanted him to rectify his mistake no matter what the cost. She knew that Dahlia would find out eventually and that their relationship would never be the same again. She accepted that this was an act of betrayal on her part, and she knew deep down that she was wrong for planning to seduce her best friend's husband; she simply didn't care. There was no turning back now. She craved Dahlia's life. Every sacred part of her that she cherished—love, friendship, honor—had all suddenly become figments of her imagination, concepts that no longer resided in her soul. In the scheme of things, they were no longer relevant to her survival. Nor were Dahlia and Isabel. They, too, were expendable. Nothing or no one mattered anymore. Phoebe slid her hand down her lavender lace panties and smiled. She was alone, but she wouldn't be for long.

CHAPTER 21

"Okay, where did we leave off?"

"I don't know, Dr. Kelly. Don't I pay you enough to answer these kinds of questions yourself?"

Dr. Kelly glanced at his notes. He knew exactly where they left off the last time, but he sensed that he needed to be especially cautious. The patient became increasingly edgy and aloof when he inquired about her family. She always steered the conversation to another topic or quickly ended the sessions. He couldn't force her to stay, of course, so he had to find a way to convince her that his questions were nonthreatening. He had already posed a series of reality-based questions, and her answers were textbook. On the surface, she appeared to be normal and somewhat well-adjusted, but his twenty-five years of experience assured him otherwise. Perhaps it was time he attempted another approach. Instead of moving from childhood to the present, he decided to work backward—in a way, psychologically tricking her into believing he was no longer interested in a certain area of her life. He scribbled new notes on his pad and prepared himself for a heated exchange. "Do you like your husband?"

"What kind of question is that?"

"A very direct one, I would say. Well?"

"Yes, I like my husband. I even love my husband—most of the time, anyway."

"What do you love about him, exactly? In fact, tell me how you met."

"The thing I love about him the most is that he loves me. And he's stable and so secure about himself. He is the most openly defined person that I have ever known."

"What do you mean 'openly defined'?"

"You know, no surprises. I always know what to expect from him. He is who he says he is, and unlike some people, he's incapable of any unexpected diversions."

"I'm sorry, I don't follow."

"He's predictable. No bombshells. No shocks in the middle of the night."

"So I gather you don't like surprises."

"No, I don't."

"Why not?"

"I just don't, okay? Do you want to hear the rest of this or not?"

"Yes, please continue." Dr. Kelly watched her closely. "Now tell me how you met Michael."

"Geez, that seems like a lifetime ago. I walked into his restaurant one day after shopping in Old Town. He took one look at me and brought me a martini glass filled with milk. I liked him and he liked me. The rest is history."

"That's it. No fireworks. No passion."

"Why the surprise, Dr. Kelly? Were you expecting a Lifetime story?"

"Let's switch tracks for a moment. How do you think your daughter perceives you?"

"What do you mean?"

"If I were to ask Isabel what kind of mother you were, what would she say?"

"God, I don't know. That sounds pathetic, I realize. I'd hope that she would say that I love her. I try to love her."

"How do you connect with her? You are obviously a busy woman. How do you stay connected to Isabel?"

"I guess I do regular motherly stuff. I read to her. I try to spend quality time with her when I can. Right now, Dr. Kelly, I am doing the very best that I can. I thank God for Milky, though, because he picks up the slack. Isabel is much more attached to her father than she is to me."

"And how does this make you feel?"

"Sometimes I'm jealous when I see the two of them together, and sadly, other times I'm relieved because Isabel's preoccupation with her father takes the pressure off of me. Most times, I feel inadequate with Isabel. I don't feel like I give her what she needs. No, that's an untruth. I know I don't give her what she needs. I fail her in some way every day."

"And what about you, Dahlia? Have you always gotten what you needed? When you were Isabel's age, do you believe your mother felt the same way about you as you now feel about Isabel? Did your mother fail you?"

Dahlia heard the question. It was unexpected, but somehow she'd suspected that he would try to go there, pry into the locked room in her head. It had been eons since she'd thought about her mother, and she wasn't about to start now. There were times when a part of her tried to remember something from her childhood, but remembering soon became a futile effort. Still, her inability to recall certain moments from her past haunted her and spawned intense bouts of confusion that inevitably morphed into an internal tantrum. Inside herself, she was jumping up and down, kicking, screaming, and ramming her head against an emotional wall. And then a voice deep inside her hissed that she was damaged goods. She'd heard that voice before, a persistent nagging behind her ear, but it was louder now and becoming more difficult to silence.

"I've noticed that every time I begin to talk about your family, you avoid the subject at all costs. I'm starting to suspect that you experienced a traumatic event in your childhood."

Dahlia began to cry silently. Traumatic event. She'd heard those words before once. Minutes later, she stood, glared at the doctor, and gathered her purse to leave.

"Clever, clever therapist," she quipped. "Did you figure that out all by yourself, or do you have a team of monkeys feeding you through an earpiece?"

"Are you all right, Dahlia?" he inquired, writing furiously on his notepad.

"What a fucking idiot," she said, and walked hurriedly toward the door.

CHAPTER 22

"Morning, Mr. Culpepper."

Lucius nodded and surveyed the grounds of the Culpepper estate. Over the years, it had grown considerably. It used to be one rather large house where the Culpepper family lived, worked, and died. Everything was done in one structure. The family would eat upstairs while the neighborhood was being embalmed two levels down. His line of work seemed to bother some, but it was the only life he had ever known. Almost.

"Who's on limo today?" Lucius inquired. He didn't really give a damn, but his staff needed to feel his presence.

"Remo."

"Remo? What happened to Boogie?"

"Dante—I mean Mr. Culpepper—said Boogie couldn't drive no more on account of what happened at the Harper service."

Lucius stared at his assistant, a skinny boy named Freddy with a lazy eye. He sighed and continued toward his office. He was feeling somewhat melancholy this morning, but then wasn't he always? He couldn't remember the last time when his mind or his body was relaxed. Today was a moderately busy day, and that was just as well because he needed to keep occupied. Three services were being performed, which meant he had to check behind people, ensure that they were not embarrassing him and the Culpepper name. He didn't embalm so much anymore unless someone specifically requested that he do the work. That happened from time to time, and he always acquiesced. Uncle Brother usually handled all the daily administrative duties, but Lucius consistently approved every single body that was prepped in his funeral home. He was still a hands-on kind of guy.

He reclined in his office, put on some Bird, and scanned the obits. He always listened to Bird when he read the obituaries. It was becoming more and more difficult to focus on the everyday minutiae of his life. His mind always seemed to creep to the inevitable. He thought about Mercy, Uncle Brother, his mama, his grandfather, Aunt Baby, and even his father, and Lord knows he hadn't thought about him in a month of Sundays. He tried desperately to fill his head with every thought, every memory that wasn't reminiscent of Dahlia and his family, his life before that day. Thankfully, right as his chest was beginning to tighten, Freddy began pounding on the door.

"Mr. Culpepper, Mr. Culpepper, there's been an accident."

He'd heard those words before, and although Freddy kept blabbering on, Lucius was already lost in the moment, reliving that day, that space when every cell in his body changed forever. He froze and it was 1981 all over again. He inhaled deeply and fought the battle waging in his head as his mind threatened to explode with memories buried under a volcano. It was windy outside, and there was a tornado. Sophea, he'd named her Sophea. He remembered he was busy that day, up to his neck in stubborn corpses. Two elderly people had expired at the local nursing home, and one was curled up in a fetal position. He'd needed to concentrate on his work, and he remembered Uncle Brother screaming something, something he couldn't quite make out. And then Mercy rushed in with the phone. "Lucius, there's been an accident," someone had said.

"Mr. Culpepper, Mr. Culpepper, did you hear what I said? Three people died today. Families are calling. I need some help out here, sir. How should I schedule the viewings? Who should I send to pick up these bodies? Mr. Culpepper!"

Sweet Jesus, help me, Lucius prayed. Why was this happening to him now after all these years? What had he ever done to deserve this hell? *Breathe,* he thought, *or die.* He peered out the window as he quietly answered his assistant. "Go find my brother, Freddy. He'll tell you exactly what to do."

"Yes, sir, Mr. Culpepper. Should I send for Percival Tweed, too? We're going to need . . ."

Lucius held his fingers to his lips and continued to stare toward the cemetery. Percival Tweed tipped his hat, and Lucius knew instinctively that the old albino had already dug six graves.

CHAPTER 23

Milky hurriedly packed suitcases for him and Isabel. He had spoken to his mother, Miko, and she had agreed to keep Izzy while he went away for a few days. He told his mom that Dahlia was ill with the flu and needed a while to recuperate, but he knew that she suspected he was lying. He would have to tell her some part of the truth when he dropped Izzy's luggage off or she would never let him leave. He'd bought an e-ticket to Dallas and was due to land at DFW at around 8:00 p.m.

He'd told no one of his plans and was beginning to question his impending interference. He felt the truth of this trip, though, inside himself. And his insides never lied. Reality was buried in the way he felt, and he had been feeling odd about the Culpepper family for quite some time. Christ, he'd never even spoken to her father. Still, questions plagued him, and he couldn't help imagining the worst conceivable outcomes. Like what if Dahlia found out and divorced him? What if her father loathed him or harbored some freak hatred of Chinese people? What if his wife came from a family of psychopaths and his daughter had inherited some mutated mortician gene? Really, what kind of people operated a funeral parlor for eight generations anyway? He'd al-

ways thought anyone in that particular business had to be a little bit off somehow, different, unique. What if? What if? The
possibilities were endless, and he nearly gave himself an aneurysm
contemplating every aspect of his trip. This all seemed so insane,
but something was gnawing at him, and he was compelled to
find out what it was.

The relationship between Dahlia and her family was always
puzzling, but she had been adamant about her decision to stay
away, deal with them in her own way. "You wouldn't understand," she'd say. "Your family is so normal." Well, that was
nearly a decade ago, and he had been remiss for not insisting on
introductions or traveling to Dallas sooner. So he would go and
intrude in the lives of his wife's bizarre family, his daughter's
family, but a family nevertheless. He'd made reservations at the
Adolphus downtown. He didn't want to inconvenience anyone,
and he had no intention of closing his eyes in a damn funeral
parlor. He grabbed his luggage to leave, and then the doorbell
rang.

CHAPTER 24

Dante Culpepper hung up the phone and shook his head in disgust. After all this time, people still surprised him. Sandra-Ann Patterson, the local pastor's wife, wanted the jewelry from her dead brother's body before the man's wife came to claim him. Oftentimes death brought out the worst in people. He'd witnessed it time and time again—ordinary folk turning into demons when they thought they were entitled to the life a dead person left behind. Hell, he'd seen an entire family ripped apart over a deuce and a quarter that none of them could drive.

These days, he found that he was revolted with people most of the time. He needed a change in his life, a distraction of sorts to break up the monotony of bodies, economy packages, and casket receipts. Maybe it was time to take another trip, one of his special excursions where no one knew him or knew what he did for a living. Not that he was ashamed of his line of work, but he didn't get as much action when he told women that his nickname was the Bone Collector. Man, they ran from him like convicts in a prison raid. He was forced to invent a more ambiguous description of his profession. However, he was and had always been unable to lie, and so if he couldn't avoid the "Hey, what do you do?" question, he answered with his trademark response: "I'm a thanatologist, and my word, your eyes are absolutely mesmerizing." Go figure, women just naturally assumed that he was some type of surgeon. In a way, he was, so it wasn't a complete fabrication. And anyway, he couldn't find a decent date in Dallas, not even with a full head of "good hair" and a platinum American Express card. Everyone seemed to know his business—what he did, where he lived, how his real mother had abandoned him like a burned-up marshmallow on the Culpepper doorstep. It was an old story, and he had become increasingly annoyed at constantly being reminded of his painful beginnings.

Dante "Uncle Brother" Culpepper was forty-one years old, and he was finally ready to settle down. He had to find the right woman, though, a woman who could love him in spite of his profession—a woman who could live at the Culpepper estate and meld with his family, a woman who wouldn't antagonize his mother. Ironically, at that moment, Mercy switched by wearing a crimson dress that had obviously been made to cling to the curves that blessed her body. She spoke softly, and he readied himself for innocent conversation, conversation that he wouldn't be ashamed of.

"Dante, may I speak to you for a minute? I heard it's been a dreadful day." Mercy never called him Uncle Brother. She always thought his first name was much more sophisticated.

"Well, yes—dreadful for the people who aren't breathing anymore but not dreadful for us. On the contrary, we've had a very lucrative day."

"That's horrible. I'm sure God doesn't think that's so amusing."

"Yeah, well, the Almighty had more to do with them being dead than we did," Dante said, smiling just a little. "How are you, Mercy girl? Is everything all right?"

"As all right as it can be, I guess. Dante?"

"Hmmmm."

"Where do you go when you leave here?"

"Away." Dante turned to face her, and for a split second, he felt as if he was doing something wrong. And as usual, he pushed the thought out of his head. "Can I help you with anything, Mercy? I'm kind of busy here."

"Um-hmm. My husband. Have you seen him, by chance?"

"Yeah, he walked toward the chapel a while ago." Dante pointed down a long hall.

"Thanks. I'll see you around."

"I'm always here," he replied, as he watched her walk away from him. His brother had been trying desperately to avoid Mercy for days, and here he was sending the woman in his direction. If only he were able to lie just a little. He returned to his paperwork relieved that she'd gone and was immediately startled by a voice he'd heard his entire life.

"One of these days, boy, the devil's going to win you over," Lucius quipped from an adjoining door.

"How long have you been standing there?"

"Long enough to know that you liked the way my wife looked in that dress."

"Lucius, please."

Lucius waved his hand and eyed his brother suspiciously. "What the hell is going on here, Dante?"

"What are you talking about? Nothing—"

"I'm talking about this." Lucius pushed Aunt Baby's letter across the mahogany table. "Where in God's name is Aunt Baby? Where is your mother?"

Dante walked around and stood facing the only sibling he would ever have. "You know where she is, Lucius."

"When did she leave? Why didn't she tell me?" Lucius yelled. His eyes began to fill with tears that he wouldn't allow to fall. "Jesus, Mary, and Joseph, Brother. What if I'm not ready for this? What if I fail her? I can't go through that again. I can't lose her again."

"You have to be ready." Dante glanced at his watch. "Because my mother is already there by now fussing at your daughter, trying to convince her to come home, and most likely telling her to stand up straight. It's time, big brother. You have to slay this dragon, put it out of its misery once and for all."

"I know," Lucius said, as he sat and buried his face in his hands. "I know."

CHAPTER 25

Phoebe knew he was in there; she could hear determined footsteps on the other side of the door. She inhaled deeply. There was still time to reconsider, walk away, but she'd never walked away from anything, so why should now be the first time? The door opened and her new life began.

"What are you doing here, and why are you ringing the doorbell?"

"I thought I'd surprise you," Phoebe said seductively, and walked past him into the house. "It's been a while, sexy. Haven't you missed me?"

"Of course."

"Good. Now that's what a girl likes to hear. You know, the truth will set you free." Phoebe scanned the room and noticed the garment bag draped across the couch. "Going somewhere, Michael?"

"Umm, no. Just donating some old suits to charity." Milky glanced at his watch.

"What's the rush? Surely you can spare a moment to chat, catch up on life."

"Are you serious?"

Phoebe sat on the couch, parted her legs just so, and beckoned for him to join her. "I can only imagine how difficult it's been for you lately, and I just thought I'd come over and offer you a welcome distraction. You know, an afternoon pick-me-up, a little bump and grind, if you will."

"Is that right? What brought this on?" Milky asked suspiciously. "What's gotten into you?"

"What? Don't look at me like that. You know you want it."

Phoebe caressed the side of his face and whispered in his ear. "I know I can make you happy, Michael. Come on, baby, let me give you what you need."

Aunt Baby rolled into Union Station with a strong spirit and a throbbing bunion. All hell was about to break loose. "Lord Jesus, give me strength," she sighed. The ride had been a troubled one filled with painful memories and unrealistic expectations. She found a half-dressed girl with a plethora of tattoos to hail her a cab. *Lord, these children today,* she thought. "Pasadena" she called to the driver. "Carry me to Pasadena, 3252 San Rafael Avenue. And hurry. My grandniece is waiting."

Sitting in the back of the cab, she prayed fervently that she'd misread the entire situation. Dahlia was fine, Milky was wonderful, and her family was whole and intact. But Baby Marseli Culpepper had never misjudged anything or anyone in her sixty-four years on this planet. She was blessed that way, and sometimes she hated the realness of it, like now. For as long as she could remember, she was the way she was. Gifted, knowing, but this—this here was a problem even she didn't know how to solve. All the herbal remedies in the world couldn't fix what was ailing Dahlia. Only God knew what could. But Heaven help her, she would try. Aunt Baby would try until she couldn't try anymore. And she intended to keep trying until Dahlia remembered everything. Dahlia had to return home, face the pain in that house, and let it float up to Jesus, where it belonged.

So much had happened over the years. Time passed and memories became trapped in the rooms of the funeral parlor, invading the very air they breathed, reminding them of what they'd lost. The house coveted every moment that passed in the Culpepper family, nurturing them, keeping them alive. To this day, there were some rooms in the Culpepper place folks couldn't step foot in without becoming severely affected. Of course, nothing like that ever happened to Aunt Baby. She was seasoned in distress and had seen far too much, although when she walked into certain rooms, she was filled with recollections of her life there—some good, some bad, and some she could definitely do without. She wasn't ready to think about those now. They would be upon her soon enough. She smiled, though, and recalled the night her nephew Lucius was born. He took a long time to come into this world. His poor mama was in labor for sixty-two straight hours, God rest her soul. It was almost as if Lucius knew what awaited him and decided to lounge in the comfort of the womb until he was evicted. The midwife tried everything, but he was stubborn even then, refusing to glimpse the light of day. His father, Lucius Senior, put on some Duke, and—wouldn't you know it?—that boy slid right out of there like he was coated with Crisco. Turned out, all he needed was the right kind of coaxing. Some things never changed.

"We're here, ma'am. Would you like help with your bags?"

"Well, hell, you didn't think I was going to carry them, did you?"

Aunt Baby marveled at the enormity of her niece's home. It was kind of pinkish in color and resembled a Spanish-style house she'd just seen in one of those fancy architectural magazines. It was spectacular, and for a moment, Aunt Baby beamed with pride until she remembered why she was there. Fortunately the gates were open, so the driver was able to drop her off at the front door. She hadn't once worried about how she was going to get in or if anybody was going to be home. Things like this always managed to work out for her. She tipped the driver and set about finding something to calm her nerves. No one appeared to be home, and that was just as well. She needed to prepare alone.

Phoebe walked around Dahlia's house slowly, methodically inspecting everything that would be hers. She envied the king-sized mahogany bed and matching etched armoire, which probably came from some piss-poor country on the other side of the world. Dahlia had always been into that whole ethnic thing. Personally she preferred clean lines and tended to shy away from any object that was made in Mexico or imported from Taiwan. Some of the clothes she recognized from her closet, and that further infuriated her. The woman had nerve—she had to give her that. Phoebe remained inside wandering around until she had inhaled Dahlia's life room by room. Once she made sure Dahlia was a memory, she would definitely have to redecorate—every piece of furniture, every painting, and everything else in between. Dahlia's house lacked imagination. The woman lived like a Carmelite nun. Brown and tan hues dominated the main rooms, and to make matters worse, there were too many damn plants. How many plants did one woman need, anyway? What was she trying to do, simulate the Amazon? Freak. Even Isabel's room was a pale, sallow pink unfit for an energetic six-year-old girl. Michael's daughter deserved better.

Phoebe was preparing to search the medicine cabinet in the master suite when she heard a noise downstairs. She smiled. He'd decided to come back to her after all. She refreshed her lipstick and began to remove her clothes. This time he couldn't possibly deny her. This time the world belonged to her.

CHAPTER 26

Lucius paced upstairs in his bedroom, a place where he hadn't been spending much time lately. Everything real—bodies, paperwork, caskets—masqueraded as distractions. Concentration on the tasks at hand eluded him, and no amount of Miles Davis would soothe his insides or ease the tension creeping through his veins. He longed to know what was happening two thousand miles away. He wanted to know if he was any closer to holding his daughter, any closer to meeting his grandchild. He'd picked up the phone to call eight times, and eight times he had hung up defeated and ashamed. He had always known Dahlia's number. He'd just been too much of a coward to use it. God, what could he possibly say?

Ever since he discovered Aunt Baby's letter, he'd been disturbed in the worst way. One part of him was furious at her for meddling in his affairs and sneaking off like a child. And the other was grateful that she loved him enough to intervene at all. She had always been there for him, always tried to clean up his messes. So whatever irritation he was experiencing due to Aunt Baby's unexpected departure was insignificant. He could never be angry with her. He had no right and he knew it. There were others who could benefit from his indignation if he allowed himself to feel anything. But there was only one who deserved his rage, only one who still tormented him when no one was watching.

Lucius felt a name swirling around in his mouth that he had forbidden to pass his lips or anyone else's in twenty-five years. "Reva, help me, goddamn you. Jesus H. Christ, it's the least you can do." He threw up his hands in desperation and was greeted by the woman he'd spent the last few years trying desperately to avoid, his wife.

"Lucius, here you are. I've been looking for you all day. Where have you been?"

"Here. Working. That's what I do. That's what I've always done."

"You didn't hear me calling you? Didn't Dante tell you that I was trying to find you?"

"It's a big place, Mercy," Lucius responded, eyeing the French doors that separated him from temporary freedom. What if Dahlia never wanted to come home again? What if he died without ever seeing her face?

"It's not that big. But you know what, the space between us is a lot bigger than this damn house."

"Don't start with the melodrama, Mercy. Today is not a good day to have this conversation."

"Then when, Lucius? When is it ever going to be a good day to talk to your wife? How long do I have to chase you?"

It pained Lucius to look at her, so he didn't. He couldn't necessarily articulate his disdain. It's not like the withdrawal happened overnight, but somehow, in spite of her willingness to love him, he became more and more emotionally distant until there was a chasm between them. It permeated the house, the business, and inevitably his heart. Mercy had come into his life at a time when he was unable to think or function like a normal man, a man in control. Then he would have done anything to make the pain go away, including wedding a girl young enough to be his daughter. One day little Mercy, Lucille and Leander's baby girl, was making up the expired, and the next she was his wife. He had no concept of time then or decorum or anything else that was supposed to matter. The day he married her, he remembered feeling appreciative for the interruption in the hell that had become his life. She was young and vibrant, and all she ever wanted to do was please him. She was determined to keep his mind from ever drifting to the event that had altered the course of both their lives.

In the beginning, she wanted what all young women wanted—shopping sprees, pedicures, an occasional trip to a vacation spot featured in *Jet* magazine—and he obliged her. She was coveted medicine for a soulache that never subsided. He knew, though, that she yearned for the one thing he was emotionally incapable of giving her. But how in God's name could he love her? How could he love anyone when he could barely stand the sight of himself?

"Lucius! Are you going to answer me, or do I have to stand here and talk to myself? I'm tired of talking to myself. I'm tired of talking to everyone in this place but you."

"Hey, I have an idea. Why don't you go shopping?" Lucius reached in his pocket, and Mercy began to scream. She tore at her dress as if she were on fire. He ran to her, but nothing he said stopped her screaming. It was emanating from inside her, somewhere that he was unable to reach. "Mercy, please, you're going to wake the dead." And still she screamed. "Dammit, Mercy, stop it! Stop it! Do you hear me?" He shook her repeatedly and was about to slap the hysteria out of her throat when Dante burst through the door and grabbed his hand. Lucius saw the disappointment in his brother's eyes and backed away.

"What have you done, Lucius?" he asked.

"Nothing," Lucius mumbled. "I don't understand what's wrong with her. I just told her to go shopping. What woman wouldn't want to go shopping?"

"What?"

"Mercy, for God's sake," Lucius pleaded, annoyed that his brother, his staff, and the rest of Haven Street were now privy to another one of his failures. "I have to go. I have to get out of here. Mercy—"

"Go, Lucius."

"Dante, . . . I—"

"Just go. I'll take care of her."

Mercy continued to cry for the lie that was trapped in her soul threatening to strangle her alive. She sobbed because her husband, the only man she had ever loved, would ultimately hate her more than he did right now, and she sank to the floor because she knew that the worst was yet to come.

In the corner of a room that never really belonged to her, she lay whimpering in the arms of a man who dried her tears, covered her nakedness, and whispered words that soothed her pain.

"Mercy girl," he said, "don't worry. Everything's going to be all right."

He saw her in all her misery, and for the moment, she didn't feel so invisible.

CHAPTER 27

There was a tempest brewing. Percival Tweed could smell it as soon as the sun kissed his face. Much like his beloved, he could sense turbulence on the horizon—not meteorological disturbances, though, but pure emotional upheavals. For a while now, there had been a cloud hovering over the Culpepper place, and now there would be a deluge. Sweet rain had a distinctive smell, and so did tribulation. Percival Tweed didn't make it a habit, wafting around in other folks' business, but this was a different kind of situation. He figured he was drawn to this house and this family from the moment he was born. When he was younger, he assumed his attraction had everything to do with the strangeness of it all. Here in the place that most people prayed to stay away from, he felt right at home. Now that he was getting up in age and could go anywhere he wanted to go, he still chose to remain in the comfort of the familiar. She was here, and he would always protect her, even if it were from a distance.

Percival stood out front and scanned the grounds. He didn't know why, but he was supposed to linger out front this morning even though he was finished for the day. It was an easy day. He'd had only two graves to dig. There was some kind of commotion going on up at the house, and he was glad Baby Marseli wasn't here to referee such nonsense. He was sure she already had enough to deal with where she was. Baby needed his help, and help her was what he intended to do. So when he saw the curiously brown fellow approach the road, he knew what had to be done. He watched him get out of the car and look around. He watched him tentatively make his way toward the entrance. Percival Tweed adjusted his wide-brimmed hat to block his face from the sun and started toward the stranger. There was no time to waste.

Dante held her close until her screams abated to a soft whimper. She was drowning and he felt her clinging to him, and much to his shame, he liked it. The voice inside his head whispered for him to leave quietly and unobtrusively, break away while he was still able, but his heart wanted to love her, and his heart was what he decided to listen to. He didn't know what happened in this room before he arrived, and maybe that was the way it should remain.

He loved his brother, God knows he did, but he'd never approved of the way he ran the family after the accident. In all the years that they'd lived together and worked side by side, there had never been a harsh word uttered between them. When Dante began to feel overwhelmed, he disappeared, plain and simple—took one of his trips until his spirit calmed. Even though he fully accepted that he was a Culpepper, sometimes he expected Lucius to remind him that no one really knew who he was. But that day hadn't come yet, and he didn't know if it ever would. When old man Culpepper died, no one knew for sure what was in his will. Everyone expected—rightfully so—that Lucius and Aunt Baby would inherit the bulk of the estate. After all, Dante was considered Aunt Baby's boy, but the old man had shocked them all. He divided his assets equally between his two boys, and that had made all the difference in the world to Dante. And here he sat on the verge of jeopardizing it all. He exhaled and tried to talk himself out of the inevitable.

"Dante," Mercy murmured, "don't leave me."

Dante lifted her and gently placed her on the bed, the bed that she shared with his brother. He averted his eyes so as not to gaze on the cranberry red bra and panties that were cleverly exposed through the tears in her dress, but she caressed his face and found his eyes. She wanted him to see her.

"Mercy, no," he said, sure of his decision.

"No?" she choked in what was left of her voice.

"Not here," he continued, as he lifted her again.

CHAPTER 28

It was an ancient observation. No one knows why bad things happen to good people. Normally Aunt Baby didn't question the reasons for unfortunate events or tragic occurrences. Life happened, and every second of every day, you had to move through it—that was the secret—a body, a soul had to keep moving, lean into the curves, so to speak. When Dante appeared all those years ago, she didn't dare question how a mother could abandon her child charred on a stranger's doorstep. She automatically believed that she had been given an opportunity to be somebody's mother. And wasn't that what she wanted? Of course, she'd convinced herself that she was content with her life, but the truth be told, she'd yearned to love someone of her very own, and like magic, one day she had a son. So she accepted that the Almighty always had a plan, but God help her, even she couldn't fathom the purpose for this.

She sipped on a glass of red wine she'd poured from a crystal decanter, and before she knew it, she was on her second glass. Baby Marseli had never been much of a drinker—alcohol interfered with her God-given talents—but an occasional indulgence was necessary when life ebbed instead of flowed. Her tense muscles began to relax, and against her better judgment, she reflected on her sixty-odd years and began to reminisce about what could have been, what should have been, and what was about to be. She closed her eyes and it was 1949. Harry Truman was president, and the country had just jumped off the World War II war train. Thelonious Monk, Billie Holiday, and Ella Fitzgerald flowed through the funeral parlor. Putting dinner on the table was a challenge for many, but the climate of the time—tense with racial strife and anticommunist propaganda—seemingly had no effect on the Culpeppers. People were dying, and their doors were constantly open. Five years before she was born, her parents had moved from New Orleans to Dallas. Her father's brother stayed behind to run the business in Louisiana, and her father braved uncharted territory to build a new one. She and Lucius were born in the same house she would probably die in.

Prettybaby—that's what they called her back then—was fifteen and full of dreams. It wasn't fashionable for a black girl in those days to dream of traveling the world and becoming someone everyone wanted to know, but she was thought to be kind of peculiar, so most folk left her to her sugar-coated fantasies. Born to a very shrewd black father, Marcel Lucius Culpepper, and a full-blooded Choctaw Indian mother, Oceola Moon, Lucius Senior and Baby Marseli were the talk of the town at their respective births. However, when Marseli was born some ten years after Lucius, her father took one look at her and immediately planned her entire life. Marcel Culpepper was notoriously protective of his family, and the arrival of Marseli hardened his resolve even more. Marseli was unlike any infant he had ever seen, and by God, she was his. From the moment she was born, her presence filled the room, so filling his heart was easy. She was so breathtakingly beautiful that although her mama named her Marseli after him, he immediately started to call her Prettybaby, and everyone else followed suit.

Marcel Culpepper decided that Prettybaby was to remain

where he could always keep a watchful eye on her. It wasn't his Prettybaby he didn't trust; it was the boys and men who couldn't seem to stay away from her. Being in her presence was addictive. Everywhere they went, people stopped and commented on what a striking daughter he had. He trusted no one, barred all of his male acquaintances from the house, and attempted to hide his daughter from the outside world. Marcel wasn't taking any chances. As God was his witness, he would die first and take half the world with him before he allowed any harm to befall his wife and children. That was his way, and his way was the only way.

The Culpeppers had been in the funeral business for eight generations before Prettybaby was born. Bodies—or here-no-mores, as her mother called them—never frightened her. Death, she sensed even then, was part of a never-ending circle and was nothing to be afraid of. Grown folk, people in the neighborhood, gossiped behind her parents' back that it was unnatural to keep a growing girl locked up in a funeral parlor, but Prettybaby didn't seem to mind, which, of course, added fuel to the fire about her being somewhat touched in the head. The life she lived every day was normal to her. The life her big brother described outside sounded foreign and strange. He was allowed an existence beyond the funeral home: school, friends, Saturday afternoons at the ballpark. Her father didn't permit her to attend school outside of the home. A female tutor taught her upstairs as soon as she was of school age while her mother looked on. Occasionally her father would ask her if she wanted to play with other girls. She did, but other girls didn't want to play with her, so she learned to appreciate being alone.

When she wasn't immersed in reading about the pyramids of Egypt and computing advanced mathematics, she studied the properties and medicinal qualities of the unusual growings in her mother's greenhouse. She also found that she had an uncanny effect on the bereaved when they arrived to visit their loved ones. Word of mouth spread through Dallas, and the same people who had scoffed at her upbringing began to seek her assistance for a multitude of problems. By the time she was seventeen, she could cure almost anything, and by thirty, she had become a legend. Here, at sixty-four, she could not, would not be defeated. She called on her mama for guidance and centered her breathing. Nothing had ever scared her until now.

CHAPTER 29

It was two o'clock in the morning, and Trevor Kelly was still poring over his notes at home, something he hadn't done in a long time. He'd made love to his wife for hours until she nearly collapsed from exhaustion. Now she was sleeping like a baby two rooms over, and he was berating himself for not having taken yoga earlier in his life. It affected him in ways he and Cassandra had never expected. He was performing better at sixty-one than he ever had at thirty-five. Go figure.

He refocused his attention on Dahlia Chang's case and poured his third cup of coffee, something his wife would not approve of. He'd been toying with a diagnosis and subsequent treatment for Dahlia, but a certain aspect of her case still perplexed him. She wasn't a manic-depressive or an incest survivor, but something was indeed triggering her bizarre behavior. The answer was hidden in his notes, in the dialogue they'd shared, in the manner she answered gentle inquiries about her childhood and her family life.

People were like complicated jigsaw puzzles with a thousand scattered pieces. You just had to take the time, examine each piece one by one, and ultimately marvel at the finished product.

He leaned back in his chair, pushed Play on his tape recorder, and carefully listened to every conversation he and Dahlia had ever had over the past six weeks. Dahlia was counting on him, and he didn't want to be on the long list of people who'd obviously failed her. He glanced at the *Diagnostic and Statistical Manual of Mental Disorders* open on his desk and began flipping through the pages. He listened to her soft voice fill the room while simultaneously listing her symptoms in his head: depression, mood swings, panic disorders, sleep disorders, and he believed that she had suicidal tendencies. Several of these symptoms were common to many mental disorders, and that thought alone confounded him. And of course, they'd had sessions when she appeared to be fine and in complete control of her behavior, which he found odd.

Trevor suspected that a lot of time had passed in her life between dissociative episodes, and for the most part, Dahlia had been living a normal, albeit unusual, existence; however, he still couldn't believe that she'd never sought help until now. It was amazing that she'd made it this far without having a more serious breakdown. His patient clearly had a severe mental disorder; he just didn't know which one.

He leaned back in his chair and closed his eyes. He feared he was getting a tension headache, and the caffeine wasn't helping. Perhaps if he stepped away for a moment and cleared his head, the answer would miraculously come to him. "Shit! Shit! Shit!" he yelled, and pounded his fist onto his desk in frustration when his mind remained blank. "What the fucking hell is going on here?" Trevor contemplated all the disorders, conditions, and illnesses he had diagnosed in his professional career. Over the past twenty-five years, nothing compared to this. He kept a little red notebook in his desk with notable disorders and subsequent treatments to remind himself every now and then, when his practice became tedious and irritating, that he was a real psychologist. There was Darlina Carsey, a balding second-rate actress, who suffered from a severe form of narcissistic disorder, not to mention the worst case of body odor he had ever experienced. Jesus, she could have caused a natural disaster. She'd been delusional most of her adult life, and he'd finally had to commit her to an institution in Victorville. And then there was Tabitha Luckner, who struggled with schizophrenia in addition to a mood disorder with psychotic features. And Erick Hayes, the poor bastard, suffered from Tourette's syndrome and Asperger's syndrome. The bloody wanker would be on medication for the rest of his natural life.

Trevor scanned down the list and still nothing caught his attention, but then words leaped off page 339 of the manual and began swimming rapidly through his mind. They came so quickly that it was difficult for him to form a coherent thought. Dissociation. Trauma. Emergency defense system. Trancelike behavior. The signs had been in front of him the whole time, and he had missed them entirely. How could he have missed them? Why had he taken so long to figure it out? He knew, albeit subconsciously, that this would be a controversial diagnosis, one that would make or break his solid reputation. He would either be hailed as a bloody genius or ridiculed as a completely incompetent asshole. He jumped up in excitement and was immediately certain of his conclusion. Normally DID individuals are not diagnosed until they approach adulthood because DID most often masquerades as something else. But out of all severe mental disorders, DID has one of the best prognoses. Dahlia would have a chance if he could gain her trust and convince her to accept the diagnosis and subsequent treatment. He wanted to shout from the rooftops that he'd made the diagnosis of his career, but more important, he wanted to locate Dahlia before she deteriorated any further. She needed his help, and she needed it as soon as possible.

He had never diagnosed a patient with DID, let alone prescribed a course of treatment. A part of him wanted to refer

Dahlia to a more-qualified doctor, but he quickly recognized his own contaminated thought process, a benefit of being a psychologist. He was a qualified therapist with two degrees from Harvard, a thriving practice, and more than two decades of experience. He was the right psychologist for the job, and he was determined to be the one who cured her. It would take dedication, determination, and a long-term commitment of four to seven years. If Dahlia was willing, Trevor intended to be ready.

He reviewed related texts from his extensive home library in South Pasadena and settled in for the rest of the night. He scoured papers, reread articles, and left an urgent message for a colleague he respected. He continued to research every available document on DID or MPD and prepared himself for the long road ahead.

CHAPTER 30

Phoebe waited nearly nude upstairs in Dahlia's bed for Michael to come ravish her. She'd put on one of his silk shirts and fantasized about how he would feel inside her. Was he fast and rough or slow and gentle? She assumed from listening to Dahlia that he preferred to take his time, and her body spasmed in anticipation. She had been imagining this moment for years, and she wanted this reality to replace the one still lingering inside the house. What was taking him so long? What if he was having second thoughts? What if he didn't want her? She smirked. That would be impossible. Everyone wanted her. She would tell him that Dahlia had left him and who knew if she'd ever come back. She would tell him that she was all the woman he would ever need. Phoebe was determined to make him forget that Dahlia ever existed.

After several minutes, she tired of the world of make-believe and decided to take matters into her own hands. Choosing to have an affair couldn't be an easy decision for a man like Michael, but Phoebe was committed to helping him make the right choice, guiding him to the promised land. She headed downstairs determined and confident. She could hear him clinking around in the kitchen. He was probably pouring glasses of Cabernet or soaking plump strawberries in Grand Marnier. He was imaginative that way. Aroused, she rounded the corner at the end of the stairwell and came face-to-face with Aunt Baby. They stared at each other briefly, and Phoebe composed herself. The enemy was here, and she hadn't spoken to the enemy in quite some time.

"Well, well, well, the world must be coming to an end if you're standing here. That is what you do, right? Show up out of nowhere after the show is over." Silence followed. Phoebe continued while Baby watched her every move. "Well, Baby Marseli Culpepper—you're two for two. You were too late then, and you're damn sure too late now."

Aunt Baby heard the familiar hostility in her voice. After all these years, it hadn't changed, nothing had. She shook her head in disbelief and eyeballed the woman who stood half-dressed in her niece's house. Sweet Jesus, what a mess. The woman, this Phoebe, had hated her when she was a girl, and it was obvious from the tone of her voice and the look on her face that she hated her still. It was of no consequence. Aunt Baby pinned her braids back on top of her head and steeled herself for a confrontation.

"Where is Dahlia?"

"Far, far away, I imagine."

"How long have you been here, child?"

"Here in general or here in her house?"

"Don't you sass me, girl. Just answer my question plain and simple."

"Well, you know exactly to the day how long I've been around. Why would you ask a question that you already know the answer to? I thought you were gifted. I thought you had talent."

"Where is Michael? And where is Isabel?"

"Unfortunately, Michael had to go run some ridiculous errand, and I don't know where the girl is. It's not like she's my daughter." Phoebe adjusted her thong and sat down. "What are you doing here anyway, Baby? I know Dahlia didn't call you. She doesn't call anybody anymore."

"I'm here to help my niece."

"Help your niece? You aren't serious?"

"I don't know what devilment you've done, but if I have to go through you to get her back, I will."

Phoebe laughed and reached for Baby's glass of wine.

"You always have tried to bite off more than you can chew. And, yes, what you're probably thinking right now is true. Before it's all said and done, one of us will be gone for good. And just so you know—this time, I'm here to stay. No more coming and going whenever poor little Dahlia works herself into a tizzy."

"You don't mean that, child. Let me help you. I know there's—"

"No!" Phoebe interrupted. "Get it through your head, Baby, this is one problem that you just can't fix. Go home, old woman; you're way out of your league here."

Aunt Baby chanted a prayer under her breath, the same prayer she said every time she'd had to deal with Phoebe in the past. God help her, it had to work. "The hell you say," the older woman spoke, swiftly reaching for Phoebe from across the table and holding on to her wrists as tightly as she could.

"Baby doll," she said softly, "it's me, Aunt Baby. I know you're in there. Come on out, my love, and talk to me. Come on, now. This time I'm here, and I'm not going anywhere."

Phoebe glared at Aunt Baby and tried in vain to twist away from the warm hands that restrained her. She fought to stay focused but her head began to throb, and then in spite of her struggle, blackness consumed her.

THE SPACE BETWEEN

CHAPTER 31

Incredulous, Michael absorbed the sight before him. He had never seen such an opulent funeral home owned and operated by people of color. The house, or the main structure, resembled an old plantation of sorts, and sat on acres and acres of land. In fact, the property was captivating in a way he couldn't quite define. He felt at peace and yet conflicted at the same time. The experience intrigued him, and he wished to know why. The journey itself from the moment he left home was beyond bizarre, and he didn't know how to respond or what to say. Dahlia was behaving more and more erratically—ringing the doorbell like she was crazy and trying to seduce him in the middle of the afternoon. Under normal circumstances, he would have been thrilled to participate in an impromptu freak fantasy. What man wouldn't? But for some reason, the nature of the action contrasted with who she was. It felt counterfeit and forced. It was almost as if she were someone else. He pushed the thought from his mind and focused on the sole purpose of his visit. His goal was to unravel a mystery, not manufacture new problems to solve.

He drove through the enormous iron gates up the extended

driveway toward the entrance. It was hard to imagine that his wife ever grew up in a place like this. It was not at all what he expected. He briefly considered turning around and flying home, but the house pulled him closer, and in the end, his feet would only move forward. He decided that he should locate his father-in-law first. That was the right thing to do under the circumstances. He would introduce himself, present the man with photos of Isabel, apologize for not coming sooner, and ask him why he and Dahlia hadn't spoken in more than a decade. He reached for the doorbell filled with a mélange of emotions when he felt a firm hand on his shoulder.

"No, son. Now is not a good time."

Michael stared into the eyes of the whitest black man he had ever seen. He was a tall ghost with yellow eyes, but he had tight blond curls and full lips, a wide nose, and a deep voice. Michael attempted casual conversation and prayed that the man could not sense his discomfort. "Maybe you can . . . can help me. I . . . I'm looking for Lucius Culpepper."

The strange man turned him away from the door. "I know who you're looking for," he said. "He's around, but best if you talk to him later on. I imagine you have a lot of questions."

"I'm Michael Chang, Dahlia's husband." Michael extended his hand.

"I know who you are."

"How can that be, sir? I've never been here before, and we've never met."

"Son, I know everybody around these parts and everything about this family. Who else could you possibly be?"

"Who are you?" Michael asked, perplexed. "Are you related to this family, Dahlia's family?"

"I tell you what. You come sit with me for a spell, and I'll answer some of your questions. The others? Well, you'll have to see Lucius for those."

Michael paused and contemplated his options. Solving the

mystery of his wife's life had begun. He turned to the man with the yellow eyes and opened to the possibilities. "What did you say your name was again?"

"I didn't say, but it's Percival. Percival Tweed."

"What do you do here, Mr. Tweed? What's your connection to this family?"

"Well, you could say I secure and maintain the final resting place."

"You mean like the casket?"

"No. The ground."

"Oh." Michael paused and digested the information. "Do you know my wife?"

"Since the day she was born. C'mon, let's take a walk."

"All right, then, I'll go along for now."

Percival Tweed nodded and motioned for Michael to follow.

"Where are we going, anyway?"

"Back to the beginning, son, the very beginning."

CHAPTER 32

Lucius felt as if he'd been lingering in a daze emotionally drunk for more than a millennium while the world passed him by. He was approaching a moment of sobriety and was humbled by its intensity. It pervaded every corner of his body, tightened his chest, and caused his eyes to water profusely. He imagined that his imperfections were boring holes in his body from the inside out for everyone to see. When he looked at himself and saw all that he had become, he realized that he was being held together by a string that was slowly beginning to disintegrate. Lucius had been a bystander in his own life or, worse yet, a nonentity, a voyeur of sorts.

It hadn't really hit him until now—the magnitude of his own desertion. For years since that wretched day, he'd blocked out every emotion that made him the least bit uncomfortable lest he be tricked into becoming an active participant in his existence. At the time, he believed his decision to be a brilliant strategy for survival—his and Dahlia's. After years of denial and ignoring the obvious, Lucius Culpepper became trapped in a spiral of regret. Only now, at fifty-five, could he begin to admit to himself that he had possibly erred in judgment. He clenched his fists and knew that if he allowed himself to stop and feel the history of the moment, it would be the end of him, and maybe that wasn't a bad thing. He had taken the cowardly way, done what his grandfather would never have done. Marcel would have died before he allowed any harm to come to his family, period. His grandfather had been a warrior that way, and yet he'd protected himself, concentrated on his own survival as if saving himself was the right course of action. *I'm going straight to hell,* he thought, and wondered how much worse hell could be than the life he was already living. No wonder Dahlia had banished him from her life. When she needed him the most, he had abandoned her for solitude, work, and a seventeen-year-old makeup girl he didn't love.

Back then, he couldn't fathom how his course of action had destroyed those around him, torn away at them piece by piece. Perched on a hill overlooking all that he had been the beneficiary of—like his father and his father before him—Lucius Culpepper slowly began to hold himself accountable. Despite his best efforts for almost half of his life to remain separate from all that resided inside him, truth gradually began to crawl back into his bones. Reacquainting himself with reality was a painful experience that caused his heart to spasm with surprise at the welcome intrusion. His heart was startled by the sudden activity, and it somersaulted in anticipation of more distress because there was so much more, and it remembered. Denial left him as quickly as it had come, and God help him, he was relieved; but atonement, however much he desired it, was still a world away.

Revelations aside, his heart began to splinter all over again, and this time, he absorbed the blow and allowed twenty-five years' worth of pain to writhe out of his chest and invade every pore of his body. He gasped from the impact, fell to his knees, and opened a dialogue with the one he'd believed had abandoned him. "Father God, help me," he prayed. "Tell me what to do now." Amazingly, the answer was swift and decisive. "Brace yourself, my son," the voice whispered in his head. "A reckoning is coming."

CHAPTER 33

Back when she was a girl, Prettybaby used to watch her mama grind herbs with a pestle and mortar and turn concoctions into miracles. Ailments and maladies seemed so simple back then. Cures, medicines, conversations were effortless, and afflictions were familiar. She should have smelled this creeping up on her long ago. Failure. Nothing good lasts forever, and she wasn't as pure as her mother. Her life had been much too easy. Now her time had come to be tested. Most likely because she had taken her gift for granted—a sin—and somewhere down the line, she'd become too comfortable and missed an opportunity to heal.

It was true. She could admit that to herself now. She had seen Dahlia's wound then, held it in her hands, and given it right back to her. For once, she didn't know what else to do or where to begin, and there was no one to ask. She'd prayed for years that the wound would mend on its own, but despite her prayers, it had grown and eventually swallowed the sweet little girl she used to know. Aunt Baby was not acquainted with defeat, and failure was an unfamiliar concept associated with other people. After all, she was a restorer, a giver of that which made you well. Healing was what she had been born to do. Her mama had always reminded her that she'd agreed to this work before she was born, and her soul would rebel if she ever denied what the creator planted firmly inside her, wrapped around her veins.

People thought her mother to be one of those moonstruck Indians. Her mother, Oceola Moon, wasn't considered good or bad, just different, and Prettybaby was moonstruck by association. "The apple"—they used to say whenever she and her mother took long strolls at sunset—"the apple don't fall far from the tree. Yes, Lawd." For a while, the characterization used to annoy Baby because her mother behaved as if they lived on another planet. They were the normal ones, with their caskets and herbs and rituals. It was everyone else in their community who was drowning in abject confusion.

No matter what people said or how they stared when she and her mama stepped into the light of day, Aunt Baby never saw her mother withhold healing from anyone. There had never been an ailment, a condition, or a situation that Oceola couldn't conquer. There were times, though, that she chose not to intervene because she explained that a person's destiny was not to be tampered with. Somehow she always knew who was supposed to be returned to health and who was supposed to return to the oneness and begin again.

Aunt Baby lightly stroked the sleeping figure next to her. She couldn't recall an herb, a plant, or a chant to heal what ailed Dahlia. She would have to travel inward, down deep toward her sacred space, and call on her ancestors for guidance. If she faltered, she was prepared to do something that she'd never had to do in all her years. She'd take Dahlia bound and gagged to one of those fancy head doctors herself if it came down to it. This sickness ravishing Dahlia's spirit would not be the end of her or

Dahlia. She breathed deeply and centered herself in the moment. Losing this child, after everything she had gone through, was not an option. In the end, Baby Marseli Culpepper was Oceola Moon's daughter, a healer of the Choctaw nation, and that had to count for something.

CHAPTER 34

There were no words spoken, explanations offered, or glances of silent regret. Dante and Mercy became lost in their betrayal without hesitation. The house could have burned to the ground and its nonbreathing occupants could have screamed out loud, and it still wouldn't have stopped Dante Culpepper from finally making love to his brother's wife. He found that he couldn't remove her clothes fast enough to quench his thirst for her. He could not imagine what she was thinking now as her hands began to roam his body. He only hoped that she wanted this moment as badly as he wanted her. He accepted, as did everyone, that she had always been in love with Lucius. But now was his time, and he intended to make every moment worth remembering. He planned never to be forgotten and never to be regarded as a mistake in a vulnerable moment.

For him, this coming together was the realization of a forbidden fantasy, one that he'd kept locked away in his dreams, hidden between family dinners and casual conversation. She was the reason he remained at the funeral home, and she was the reason he often had to leave it. No matter how hard he struggled to erase her from his mind, she haunted him and he ached for her still. As he lay close to her unclothed, he so desperately wanted to reveal himself, confess that he'd loved her from the moment she graced the back porch and offered herself on a silver platter to his brother.

He silenced the persistent voice in his head that tempted him with the righteous course and concentrated on the woman quivering naked beneath him. Finally he reached for her, and she opened for him all that she had previously been unable to give. He explored every inch of her brownness and paid special attention to areas that he felt had been particularly neglected. There were sighs and moans and an intense urgency to feel her throbbing around him. He pressed her hands down with his palms and entered her with more than two decades' worth of repressed passion.

Mercy felt him inside of her moving rhythmically to the melody in her head. She couldn't really identify the song, but Dante heard it just the same, seeping out of her pores, imploring him for more. More of what he was offering and more of that when he was done. She could not believe herself. Who was this woman making love to her husband's brother? She was a stranger, but at the same time, Mercy was more herself, more alive than she had ever been. She could have walked away, saved them both, but this space in time was intoxicating, and she soon became drunk with pleasure and possibilities. She rocked with him as if she had a thousand times before and, in so doing, realized precisely what her body was for. She welcomed the intense heat that was spreading rapidly throughout her body and wrapped her legs around the only man who'd ever made her scream out loud.

They stayed folded into each other until reality started to creep upstairs and steal down the hall into the room where everyone else was afraid to go. They heard footsteps and assumed the outside world was coming for them with Lucius in tow. Strangely unafraid of discovery, they embraced and remained undisturbed. Mercy swallowed and prepared to speak; there were things that needed to be said. The window of bliss was closed, and her husband was only a few feet away.

"Shhh," Dante whispered. "Me first. I know that we probably should have exercised better judgment. I know that when we leave this room, you'll still be my sister-in-law. I know that I am in love with you, and watching you with him in this house destroys a piece of me every day. And before you ask, I can't pretend like I don't know what the inside of you feels like—"

"Dante," Mercy interrupted.

"Mercy," he continued, "this was a mistake for obvious reasons, but mainly because now I can't . . . I won't let you go."

"Dante, I never guessed that you felt this way."

"I know," Dante responded, and rose to look out the window. "I'm here, Mercy, and I've always been here waiting, devoting too much time to a pipe dream. And anyway, you've always seen what you wanted to see."

"That's not fair. I was young and naïve when I married him. I didn't know what I wanted. I didn't know what I was doing. I realize that now." Mercy partially covered her nakedness. "God, Dante, I've made so many mistakes—some of which I don't expect to be forgiven by Lucius, by you, or by God."

"Why do you say that? What could you possibly have done to make you believe such a thing?"

Mercy looked away and staved off another breakdown. She wished she could tell him what she had done, but the truth of it had never passed her lips. And in the end, he would hate her like everyone else. The lie that had been coiled around her bones attached itself to her soul long ago. The thought of prying it loose took her breath away and caused her face to commit an act of betrayal. Twitching uncontrollably, she waited for Dante to question her further, but he wasn't looking at her anymore. Something else had his attention, something outside.

"Dante," she said. "Dante, what's the matter?" Mercy stood and joined him.

"Someone's here."

"Someone's always here."

"No," Dante replied, pointing out the window at the stranger walking with Percival Tweed.

"Who is that?" Mercy asked, somewhat disinterested, unaware that the unraveling had begun. Her deception at that moment was being pushed out of her stomach and up toward her esophagus. Soon it would ferment in the back of her throat and sneak its way along her tongue. Twitching was just the beginning. Dante hurriedly reached for his clothes.

"Probably just somebody nosing around the property. I'm sure it's nothing to worry about."

"Get your clothes on," Dante said firmly. "We have to leave here."

Dante continued to stare curiously out the window. He didn't recognize the man with Percival Tweed, and that concerned him. The grave digger wasn't known for wasting words on strangers. And yet there they were strolling in the direction of Percival's house like it was the most normal thing in the world. But Dante knew better. Normal was a town in Illinois. It certainly didn't exist here, and never had for as long as he could remember. His heart began to beat faster while everything else around him stood still.

The room they were in rested on the third level of the house. It boasted a round window and crème-colored walls. The view of the grounds was exceptional, but no one ever braved the spiral staircase to appreciate the sight. People always said that they saw ghosts in the little round window staring longingly out at the outside world. It had been his experience that most folks averted their eyes from the window when they passed, but that wasn't the case here. Dante wasn't afraid of any ghosts, and apparently neither was the albino. For a few crucial seconds, Percival stopped walking and faced the circular window while Dante watched. Mercy reached for his face, and he stiffened.

"Don't tell me you see a ghost," she quipped lightly.

Dante narrowed his eyes. Words escaped him, and he was unable to express his growing trepidation to Mercy. She saw an old man standing in the middle of the grass gazing at the heavens. He saw chaos standing still and knew in that instant that nothing would ever be the same again.

Percival Tweed tipped his hat at the figure in the little round window and shook his head. Aunt Baby wasn't going to take too kindly to this turn of events, not too kindly at all.

CHAPTER 35

Trevor Kelly had been up for hours vacillating between attending to the intricacies of the Dahlia Chang case himself or consulting a colleague. He decided on the latter, as he had to be sure of his conclusion. He needed to be certain that he hadn't missed the mark altogether. By God, he recognized the symptoms and respected his intuition, but he had no tangible evidence that the patient had ever experienced any severe trauma at all. Through his own knowledge and subsequent research, he knew that the vast majority of DID patients have documented histories of repetitive, overwhelming, and often life-threatening trauma at a developmental stage of childhood and that the main types of abuse that are precipitants of DID are sexual, involving incest, rape, or some kind of molestation, and/or physical, involving beatings, burnings, and wretched incidents of that sort. Shit, if only he had more information. If only he could get through to Dahlia. She had suffered from something that had damaged her during her childhood. Of that he was certain.

Trevor Kelly had always followed his hunches, and at sixty-one years old, he wasn't about to make an about-face now. For Dahlia's sake, he had to dismiss his fear of being mocked by his peers and remember that he had a sizable set of balls after all. He reached for his jacket and grabbed his tape recorder. There was only one person he could talk to, one place he could go with this discovery. He flipped open his cell phone and dialed. "Let me speak to Dr. Lionel Durbin," he said with a steady voice. "This is an emergency."

CHAPTER 36

"Are you certain, Trevor? You know, I've never put much credence in these kinds of cases."

"I'm sure, Lionel. I've been practicing for many many years, my friend. I know what I'm saying, and more important, I know what I feel. The patient shows all the signs of DID. She's unable to remember entire portions of her childhood. She has excruciating headaches and often suffers from blackouts. Plus the alter that I encountered called me an idiot, and my patient would normally never speak in that manner."

"Very observant lady, I would say."

"Be serious. This is no time for jokes."

"All right, keep your knickers on. What about manic depression or neurosis? Surely there are other options to consider here."

"Something traumatic occurred in her childhood, Lionel, which caused her to dissociate, if you will, detach herself from reality and take on an alter. And what's most bizarre about this case is that the subject herself isn't aware of her condition. I'm still trying to determine just how long she's had DID or MPD. I assume the creation of the alter correlates with the traumatic experience. You and I both know that all thoughts and memories of the abuse in cases like these are psychologically separated from the child. I'm consulting with you, Lionel, because I have to be careful here. I know you'll tell me if I'm barking up the wrong tree."

"Do you have your notes? Tapes of your sessions?"

"Yes, of course."

"And you stand by this diagnosis with no reluctance?"

"Yes, yes, of course. Jesus, Lionel, the girl will split again if you don't have a look already."

"You know, old friend, if your patient in fact has this illness, she has a long, painful road to recovery ahead of her."

"Yes, I'm aware of how difficult it will be for her and her family."

"All right. I'll review your findings, and then we'll discuss how to proceed."

Dr. Trevor Kelly paced his mentor's office and wondered what Dahlia was doing right now. Was she in fact Dahlia or the other, the one who had snapped at him in his office and flipped him the bird as she stalked out the door? What was her name? How often did she make an appearance? When exactly was she born? And were there others? Bloody hell, he hoped there weren't others. He wondered if Dahlia's husband had any idea that his wife had someone else walking around inside her brain. The alter was clearly becoming more and more aggressive, and that meant that Dahlia was in jeopardy. In the medical journals, he'd read about cases of the alter's taking over the original personality completely. The mind was so powerful that it was capable of convincing a woman that she had to be someone else in order to survive. What, he wondered, in God's name could have happened to cause the brain to be in such turmoil? Dr. Durbin interrupted his thoughts.

"Trevor, I'd like to help you any way I can here. Perhaps I can observe a session with the two of you. Do you think your patient would agree to that?"

"I don't know. I'd have to ask her first, you know that. Although at this point, I don't know whom I'll be talking to. I'll gently suggest that the patient speak with her husband about her condition as well. Hopefully she'll agree. She needs all the support she can get."

"I concur. Call her and schedule an emergency appointment as soon as possible. So do you think the husband has any idea? Poor clueless bastard. I see here that they have a child as well. I'm sure he didn't count on marrying more than one woman when he said 'I do.' Jesus, how could he have bloody missed that?"

"Bollocks, Lionel, if the patient does agree to discuss her condition with her husband and allows him to come to a session, how am I going to tell him that his wife has dissociative identity disorder?"

"Very carefully, my friend. Very carefully."

Trevor glanced at his watch; he'd already canceled his dinner plans and promised his wife a hot-oil massage when he got home. She was waiting for him as usual, this time with a tangerine teddy and a shot of tequila.

"Trevor, I must say that if this is a genuine case of DID, you have to begin treatment immediately."

"Lionel?"

"Yeah."

"May I use your phone?"

"No time like the present, eh?"

CHAPTER 37

Dahlia awoke and reached blindly for the Extra Strength Excedrin she kept glued to her nightstand. She grasped nothing, so she opened her eyes and scanned her surroundings. She didn't know where she was, but the space felt vaguely familiar. Her sleep had been troubled and restless, but this time, she'd dreamed of Aunt Baby, and she was immediately grateful. For now, there were no mashed faces screaming at her and no sweating, just an overwhelming feeling of relief. She unclenched her fists and realized that she had been here before. She saw photos of Isabel and began to relax. She was home on her couch in her family room, although she couldn't remember how she got there. The pain in her head taunted her mercilessly, and her left foot throbbed. What was wrong with her foot? Milky must have put her here, or maybe she'd passed out again. She was tired. God, she was always so tired. She called out softly and winced at the sound of her own voice.

"Milky. Milky. Isabel. Anybody home?"

She attempted to stand, but her legs refused her. It was entirely expected, as she was already in pieces, left to somehow put herself back together. In the end, she was what she always thought she'd be. Alone. Her husband had probably abandoned her for good and taken Isabel with him. Her fate had been sealed. She would rot away on a green chenille couch and would eventually smell of pee and Oreo cookies.

Dahlia massaged her temple and managed to pull her legs toward her chest. Now what was she going to do? And how was she going to get her family back? So many questions were dancing around in her head when the intruder interrupted her thoughts. She closed her eyes and struggled to silence the voice now booming in her head. "Go away," it said calmly. "They don't love you anymore." She screamed. She was terrified and held herself as tightly as she could lest the rest of her fall apart. "Somebody help me," she cried. "Aunt Baby, where are you when I need you?"

"Here," a voice behind her answered softly. "I'm right here, baby doll."

Dahlia turned around and sobbed uncontrollably when she saw Aunt Baby standing over her. She stared in disbelief and clutched wildly at the woman in her dreams. She clung to her just like before, and for a moment, she was a child again lost in the storm while the tornado devoured everything around her.

"I know, baby. That's all right. Get it out, get it all out." Aunt Baby stroked her hair and offered words of solace until calmness replaced hysteria. Dahlia took a deep breath and briefly considered that she might be dreaming again. She touched one of Baby's long braids just to be sure that she wasn't slipping any further than she already had.

"What? How did you get here? When?" Dahlia asked hoarsely.

"It doesn't matter. I'm here now, and I'm not leaving anytime soon. I'm sorry, Dahlia. I'm sorry I haven't done enough to help you, and I'm sorry for not coming sooner."

"Aunt Baby, what's wrong with me? What is happening to me?"

Aunt Baby rose and handed her grandniece a cup of her special tea laced with kava kava and chamomile to calm her nerves.

"Drink up, now. We might not have much time."

"What are you talking about? You said you wouldn't leave me."

"Do you trust me, Dahlia?"

"Yes."

"You know I would never lie to you. That's not my way."

"I know you wouldn't." Dahlia sipped her tea. "Where are Milky and Isabel?"

"Honey, I don't know where your family is, but let's hope that wherever they are, they stay there until we tell them it's safe to come home."

"What do you mean safe to come home? I wouldn't hurt my family. I could never harm them."

"I know you wouldn't. Sit up straight now, and listen to me, child." Aunt Baby gently took the tea from Dahlia's unsteady hands and searched her eyes for any signs of the other one. This kind of truth-telling was serious business, and that other one seemed to thrive on keeping the truth from Dahlia. "Tell me, baby doll," she said, as she leaned closer, "just how much do you remember about your childhood?"

Dahlia stiffened and pulled her hands away. "What does my childhood have to do with anything that's happening here and now?"

"Everything. Everything that is happening to you now is a direct result of what happened to you then, and it's high time that we dealt with it once and for all."

"Well, that can't be, Aunt Baby, because I don't remember much. I remember you and Daddy. I kind of remember the house. Nothing happened in my childhood out of the ordinary that's worth discussing here."

Aunt Baby placed the tea back in Dahlia's hands and continued to study her grandniece's face. "Finish up now, before your tea gets cold." Sweet Jesus, this was far worse than she had anticipated. The child didn't remember a thing, not the tornado, the funeral home, the children, or Reva. The girl didn't even remember her own mama, and Lucius had always believed that was a good thing. Aunt Baby sighed. She didn't know where to begin. This was by far the strangest sickness she had ever come across. Something had snuck up into the girl's brain and commenced to raising pure hell.

She thought of Percival and wished she could see him now. She'd feel better, oddly enough, if she could just see his face. She couldn't explain their bizarre attraction to anyone, but he had always been a source of comfort and strength. And when she returned home, she would finally tell him so, practice a little truth-telling for her own soul. "Your father misses you, you know—asks about you and Isabel every day. He's getting older now, baby doll. We're all getting up in age—gonna be dead and stinking in a minute. You remember your father, don't you, child?" Silence.

"How is he?"

"Not well. He needs you, and by the looks of things here, you need him. I promise that the world will keep spinning on its axis if the two of you finally sit down and talk about what happened."

"I don't know what you're talking about," Dahlia insisted, becoming more and more frustrated. "Daddy and I just don't get along too well. You know that."

"It wasn't always that way, though," Baby added, hoping to jump-start her memory. "You and your father were inseparable before the tornado, before Reva—"

"Look, I see the man every time I look in the mirror. Isn't that enough?"

"No, it's not, and actually you look more like Reva, your

mother. Somebody had to give birth to you. Do you remember anything about that woman at all?"

Dahlia closed her eyes and squeezed her head between her palms in a viselike grip; the pain was almost unbearable. Aunt Baby knelt in front of her. "Stay with me, now. Hold on to my voice, baby doll. We can do this together, Dahlia. Dahlia, look at me." Aunt Baby waited for an answer, some sign of recognition, but it was too late. She had said too much too soon, and just like that, her Dahlia was gone.

"My God, old woman," the other one said, without missing a beat. "You're still here."

"I told you before that I'm not going anywhere, and I'm telling you again to watch your mouth. I'm not too old to slap some respect down the back of your throat." Aunt Baby stood to face her. "Remember that like you claim to remember everything else."

"I know you've never liked me, Baby, and that's cool because I've never been too fond of you either. And whether you believe it or not, the only person who can handle what you're itching to tell is me."

"Is that so?"

"I remember everything about Dahlia's childhood, her father, those kids, and that crazy-assed mama of hers. Hell, you should be grateful Dahlia doesn't remember anything. Who would want to?"

"Why don't you ever allow her to hear the truth for herself? How is she ever going to get past this thing, with you sneaking around in her head starting a ruckus?"

"Who says that she'll *ever* get past this thing? Most people couldn't get past what happened. Have you? Besides, I've always let her hear what she needed to hear."

"See, what you need to do is mind your business."

Phoebe smirked. "Don't you get it? Her business *is* my business and has been for quite some time."

"You are an abomination, girl, a freak of nature. Can't you feel that? You don't belong here, not in her life and not in this house. Go back to where you came from, do you hear me?"

Phoebe threw her head back and laughed. "Me. I'm the freak of nature. You and your dysfunctional family are the abominations, the ones who left Dahlia by the wayside all alone to fend for herself. Why didn't you drop her off in the middle of a freeway and watch her get run over? Now, that would have been more humane. The nerve of you people actually claiming that you're surprised she disappeared. Give me a break. Hey, I'm the normal one, the sane one, the courageous one. Your precious Dahlia, on the other hand, has blossomed into a walking wreck, a total whack job just like her demented mama. She's standing at the edge of a cliff here, Baby, barely holding on, and I'm just the person to give her the encouragement she needs to jump." Phoebe walked around and searched for her shoes.

"She's a lot stronger than you think, you know." Baby followed behind her.

"No, Aunt Baby, she's not. Strength has always been my area. I control what comes in and out of Dahlia's life, and I have since that day twenty-five years ago. I have protected her from your neglect and her father's pain. I have kept her safe from the rest of you and your backwards look-the-other-way bullshit. If it weren't for me, Dahlia would have slit her wrists years ago. Trust me. She actually thought about it, you know, ending her life, but I wouldn't let her. And do I get a thank-you? Hell, no! And why? Because no one has ever appreciated me, so kiss my ass and move out of my way."

"Where do you think you're going?"

"Wherever I feel like going. Where the hell is my purse, anyway?"

"You're not leaving this house until I get Dahlia back."

"And who's going to stop me? You? Please. I'm going home to take a nap, and when I come back, I want you gone—back to whatever tepee you crawled out of. This is my house now, my family, and we don't need you."

Aunt Baby silently asked her mother for guidance. She had prepared for this kind of setback. The main ingredient in her tea would take effect momentarily. The child would get to the door, but she'd never make it to the car. She was moving slower now. It was only a matter of time before she succumbed to the herbs.

"Phoebe," Aunt Baby called, and guided her back toward the couch, "why don't you take your nap here?"

"What did you do to me, Pocahontas?" Phoebe asked angrily, unable to control the lethargy that was spreading through her body. "You haven't stopped anything, you know," she added smugly, as Aunt Baby placed the blanket over her. "Dahlia still won't be here when I wake up, and there's nothing you can do about it."

"I know, Phoebe. Go on now and get some rest."

"Prettybaby," Phoebe whispered, before drifting off.

"Yes," Baby answered.

"You remembered my name."

Aunt Baby sat cross-legged and sang a prayer of gratefulness to her ancestors like Oceola had taught her. She'd won the battle this time, but the war would take much more effort. Phoebe would sleep for hours, and when she awoke, there would be hell to pay. Baby twisted her fingers, a habit she kept from childhood, and allowed herself to momentarily slip away. Her soul was exhausted, and begged to be free of the cumbersome body that held it in. She was almost there in that meditative space that replenished her, but a sudden distraction in the background hindered her from going any further. She disconnected and hurried toward the ringing intrusion. On the line was just the person she needed to speak to. Wouldn't you know it? Oceola Moon had heard her after all.

CHAPTER 38

It seemed as though they sat for hours before speaking, the anxious husband who required information and the albino poised with a story to tell. Much like an elephant, Percival Tweed remembered every happening—tragedy and triumph—that had befallen the Culpepper family, and his memories were filed, numbered, and categorized by name. He could, if he so chose, share with anyone what had happened to whom on any given day for the past five decades. He was a keen observer of human nature—a voyeur, if you will—and analyzing the people around him had been his true life's work. As all knew, he was indeed a man of few words and had never contemplated sharing his observations until now. He was simply a recorder of circumstances, and his reflections and opinions remained close to his heart, where they belonged. After all this time guarding the Culpepper history, he found it difficult to remove the first file—his: Percival Tweed, May 8, 1939. Finally, he opened his heart, and the words tumbled out eagerly in search of a new home.

"She was out back there picking tulips with her mother the first time I saw her. They did things like that every afternoon around the same time. Her mother was a full-blooded Choctaw, you know. Prettiest Indian gal you ever did see. My mama—Caldonia Tweed, God rest her soul—had recently gone to glory, and I was feeling mighty poorly. It's not like I ever had a porch full of kin to talk to like most folk. I went to see the elder Culpepper because I needed work, solitary work. As you may have guessed, I mostly keep to myself, and people tend to leave me alone around these here parts. I don't mess with nobody, and I don't want nobody messing with me. Anyways, seeing as how I was born in the house out yonder on the stairs in the main hall, I asked old man Marcel for a job. He liked my resolve, he said, and started me right away that same day digging graves and such. That was over forty years ago, and I've been here ever since.

"Later that same day, Prettybaby—that's what we called her back then—came to see me, which was a surprise because her father didn't allow her to keep company with anybody, and I can't say I rightly blamed him either. She didn't say much and neither did I, but somehow we understood each other. She held my hand for a long time, gave me a bowl full of funny-smelling cream, and told me that she'd be watching. We connected that day as sure as the sun rises, and I been here ever since watching her watch over me. She needed me; I could see it in her eyes even then."

"Why didn't you ever talk to her, let her know how you felt?" Milky inquired.

" 'Cause a man like me don't deserve a woman like her. We have what you young folk call an understanding, and I accept my place. I'm used to being by myself, and unlike a lot of y'all, I don't believe in forcing nothing. She has her role in this life, and I have mine. Well, I did try once to muster up the courage to approach her after the old man died, but I couldn't. She was busy with Dante, and, well, our time had passed."

Percival Tweed paused for a while and appeared to collect his thoughts. Milky respected his silence and waited. Rushing the old fellow would be futile, and he couldn't leave until he knew everything there was to know about his wife and her family. He thought of his daughter and became even more determined to stay the course. Isabel deserved a complete family, whole and intact, not the counterfeit version she had been relegated to. He wondered what Dahlia was doing now and whether she missed him. She would surely divorce him and inflict bodily harm if she discovered where he was and what he was doing. But he didn't care because his fear of not being able to help her outweighed the consequences. God, he loved her, and a part of him would wither away and die if he couldn't help her and their marriage didn't survive. He stared out the window just like Percival and fantasized about the Dahlia he used to know. It would take more than an hour before the albino began again.

"Marcel Culpepper was a proud man, you know. Some said he was a strange one, too, but that don't really mean nothing to somebody like me. He come up from New Orleans with his family to open up this here funeral home. My mama told me that the folk here took to him like gravy to corn pone. He was a hard man to get next to. Although he took care of folk during their time of need, he didn't trust nobody and never let no one get close to his family, especially after what happened to his boy. His wife and daughter were not allowed to go anywhere off this property without him. Now his son, Lucius Senior, Dahlia's grandfather, was given free rein to do whatever he wanted to do, provided he ended up home every night at a decent hour ready to work. And he did—most nights, anyway—from what I heard.

"When he was sixteen, you see, he put this girl across town in a family way, and old man Marcel was fit to be tied. He confined the boy to the house and made him marry the girl. No kin of his was coming up without his protection, he said. The girl's name was Livia, I believe, and she was younger than Lucius Senior by a hair. They had one son, Lucius Junior, Dahlia's daddy. Well, after a while, Lucius Senior and Livia couldn't stomach living and working in the family business, and they told Mr. Culpepper that they wanted to leave Dallas, travel, see the world. It hurt him, I think, his only son wanting to leave the business like that, but he was a very proud man. He offered them money and told them they could go, but they had to leave the boy, and they did. Lucius Junior was about five years old when his parents chose Paris over him.

"They'd been gone about six months when Livia sent word that Lucius Senior had caught some kind of crazy infection over there—scarlet fever something or other—and up and died on her. I was a young man then myself—about twelve or thirteen, same age as Prettybaby. The Culpepper women took it hard when they found out, and the old man locked himself in his office for days trying to get his son's body shipped back here. He never did, and when he finally came out of that room, he didn't allow anyone to mention his son, Livia, or what happened. As far as he was concerned, there was only one Lucius, and he raised that boy as if he were his son, not his grandson."

"Man, so what happened to Livia? Did she ever come back from Paris for Lucius Junior?"

"Well, the man is still here, ain't he, minus the junior? I think she knew Mr. Culpepper would never have let her take that child away. It didn't take long for Lucius to finally stop asking about his parents, and nobody heard from his mama again. Lucius was all right, though. He had his grandparents and his aunt, and his brother Dante kept him busy enough."

"I thought you said Livia and Lucius Senior had one child. Where did this brother come from?"

"Slow down, son. There were a lot of folk that asked that

same question. Why don't we make sure you have all the names right, 'cause this'll get mighty confusing if you ain't paying proper attention."

"I think I've kept up all right so far. We're talking about two people named Lucius here, parents, grandparents, aunts, and a mystery uncle, but by all means, feel free to go over it again in case I missed something."

"Okay, listen to me now. Marcel Lucius Culpepper was married to the Indian woman Oceola Moon. Remember I told you about that?"

"Right. Got that. Go on."

"Marcel and Oceola had two children, Lucius Senior and Baby Marseli Culpepper. Lucius Senior married a girl called Livia, and they had one child, Lucius Junior—your father-in-law. Baby Marseli had one child, a boy by the name of Dante. Junior married Reva, and Dahlia, your wife, is the child of that union."

"Okay, I think I've got it now. So Aunt Baby is Dahlia's grandfather's sister, right?"

"Good, good. It's about time you started keeping up."

"I'm trying to follow you here. Where are Dahlia's parents? And why doesn't she talk to them?"

"Well, that there is a mouthful, the question of all questions. Be patient, son. I'm coming to that part in due time. You young folk are so busy rushing to get somewhere that you don't pay attention to the signs, the little things that move you through life along the way. You've got to study every piece of a puzzle before you can put it together right. You've got to know about Dahlia's family, Dahlia's life, before you can begin to understand her, the woman that she turned out to be. Now I'm going to give you the pieces you need, and nobody has all of the pieces but me."

"Now old man Culpepper was extra hard on Lucius. He'd realized, I guess, the mistakes he'd made with his own son, and Lucius suffered. He listened to his grandfather and always did what he was told until he started smelling his own manhood, and then all hell broke loose. He was about seventeen, and the old man was on the warpath."

"Wait. You didn't tell me about Dante. You said he was Lucius's brother, and then you said he was Aunt Baby's son. Which one is it? How could he be both?"

Percival Tweed rose from his chair and walked into his small bedroom. No wonder he didn't go around running his mouth. All this questioning and interrupting was plucking his nerves but good. Maybe this wasn't the best notion after all, but then again, his mama, Caldonia Tweed, always told him that you couldn't meet your maker with a lie caught between your throat and your soul. Not that he was planning on dying anytime soon, but he had already lived longer than an albino was supposed to live, or so he'd been told by folk his entire life. All of this fat-lipping was new to him, and he needed to catch his breath to continue. He couldn't remember ever talking this much to anybody. It was downright exhausting. He was prepared to tell the boy everything about Dahlia, but he wasn't ready to discuss Dante Culpepper. As a matter of fact, he had planned on taking everything he knew about Dante Culpepper to his grave.

Percival Tweed had tried to maneuver the conversation toward other events, other pieces of the puzzle, but Michael wouldn't let him; the boy didn't miss a thing. How could he tell the story without admitting his truth and owning the part he had played in altering the lives of the only real family he had ever known? He walked back toward the living room, his mind racing, remembering, reclaiming yesterday's reality. And as fate would have it, there was now more than one person in his house waiting with bated breath for a mystery that had been buried for more than forty years.

"Don't keep us waiting any longer, Mr. Tweed," the man said calmly. "I've been waiting my entire life to hear what you have to say about me."

CHAPTER 39

Energy is a tangible force that ebbs and flows through people, places, and inanimate objects fluidly and without hesitation. This life force, often referred to as the exhalations of God, can't be seen by the naked eye, but casual intuitives can feel it swirling around them pushing, pulling, constant like rain. It shifts and reconfigures itself every moment of every day, affecting those in its path whether they realize it or not. It constantly seeks balance and expands naturally toward the greater good. It can easily be manipulated, and thus, it always pursues truth—the native tongue of the universe.

The energy pulsating through the Culpepper estate had transformed yet again into something Lucius did not recognize. It was alive and carried with it a certain foreboding, and to him, it smelled like trouble. The vibrations around him were unfamiliar, and he inhaled deeply, unafraid and with a heavy heart. Lucius wasn't anywhere near as gifted as his grandmother, Oceola Moon, or his daddy's baby sister, but some force that he couldn't identify inside the house caught his attention. He could feel it seeping from the walls attempting to bore into his pores, and it was strong and determined. He walked around inspecting nothing in particular and tried to isolate the cause of the shift, because he knew there had been one. He had always known when something didn't feel right; however, this was the first time he had actively sought the source of his discomfort. He had made a vow to the Almighty earlier. "I'm through running, Lord," he'd promised, prostrate in the corner of his office like a child, and this time, he swore he would live up to his word.

It was after six, and there were no services scheduled for the evening or for the next two days. He had sent everybody home at half past five, and now he found himself wandering through the halls as if he were a toddler searching for something to do, some complicated task to occupy his time. There was one body left in the cold room, but it didn't need to be fully prepped until Thursday of next week. He had thought that odd when cock-eyed Freddy had told him about the instructions but not odd enough to find out who was spending their "done-gone" days lounging in his funeral home. He preferred to move the dearly departed in and out, and that was all—no extra-lengthy services and no lingering visits from the dead who still longed to be attached to their physical bodies. There were enough of them hovering around the house already, causing a commotion from time to time, turning the lights on and off, and messing around with the thermostat. He'd thought he heard somebody walking around upstairs a while ago in the attic room with the round window, but nobody ever went up there anymore, so he assumed the haints were rabble-rousing and having some type of spook party. All the more reason he didn't want to tease any poor soul by hanging on to their body for too long. He wasn't superstitious per se; he just didn't believe in taking any unnecessary chances.

He chided himself for not knowing who lay there on cold steel waiting for a once-over from the boss. He'd been so busy wrestling with his own thoughts that he'd neglected his duties. There was a family somewhere in Dallas who needed his kind words to carry on or maybe a widow in distress who would appreciate consolation during her time of bereavement. He needed to be preoccupied, and work would keep his mind sharp and focused. Now had not been a good time for Mercy to fall apart. Jesus, Mary, and Joseph, didn't she know that he had enough to worry about without ripping her clothes to pieces and carrying on like a natural-born fool? Hell, she had been hysterical—damn near woke the dead with all that commotion. What else was he supposed to have done? Slapping the shit out of her seemed like the right thing to do at the time. Wasn't that what you did when someone became crazy in the head, hollering and acting like they didn't have the sense God gave them? He sighed and massaged his temple; he would have to deal with his wife at some point, and he wasn't looking forward to it. Staying busy sounded like a viable option.

He reached into his pocket for the familiar brown folded slip of paper, the one Aunt Baby had left, the same one with Dahlia's address and phone number scrawled on it. He picked up the phone to call and placed it on the receiver again for the eighth time in one day. He couldn't call her, not quite yet. Everything there had to be all right. He hadn't heard otherwise from Baby, so he figured an interruption—his kind of interruption—wasn't warranted.

He glanced at the paperwork hanging on the back of the door and prepared to give a Mrs. Leezel Diezman some special attention. Clearly, she'd been waiting long enough. Diezman—he'd never heard that name before. It turned out that she was being embalmed here and laid to rest out back with the colored folk. This was a special request from the late Mrs. Diezman herself, and Lucius was immediately puzzled. He'd accommodated special requests before—that in itself wasn't unusual—but he normally knew the family or they had known his father. Freddy reported that the uppity white family had been none too happy about dropping their mama off at the black funeral home, but Leezel Diezman had left strict instructions in her will. From what he could tell, Mrs. Diezman had amassed quite a fortune, and her children didn't want to run the risk of losing one dime by not honoring her bizarre request. Maybe she was someone he'd met at a conference, or perhaps she'd heard of his work. Lucius opened the refrigerated compartment that held the mystery woman and pulled down the sheet. She was a pale woman indeed, appeared to be in her seventies, and didn't have a defining mark on her face that he could see. Strange, though, she looked vaguely familiar, but he knew that was impossible because he had never seen her before and he never forgot a face. He scanned the paperwork again, unable to ascertain why she was here instead of at a funeral home in North Dallas, where she belonged.

It's not that he didn't embalm white people; he just didn't normally embalm them in the family establishment. When he was younger, he and his father often traveled to white funeral homes all over Dallas County and Fort Worth when there were special cases, disfigurements, reattachments, and so on. The Culpeppers were the best in the business, and were often sent for by white morticians who were not as endowed in the field of dead bone reconstruction. His father charged triple the fee for services rendered, and the two of them always had to enter through the back door so white family members wouldn't see them and know that brown hands were stitching up their loved ones. Sometimes they even took Percival Tweed along for the ride. His grandfather, Marcel, always said that Percival scared the bejesus out of white folk, which allowed him and his grandfather to do their job in peace—what with nobody wanting to be in the same room as a disfigured dead person and a black albino. Of course, Percival waited outside soon after they arrived, usually right after the white flight. He never did get used to being around dead folk, though, disfigured or otherwise, and Lucius never got used to him being there.

Lucius pushed number two on his compact disc changer, and

"A Love Supreme" filled the room and immediately began to calm his nerves. 'Trane had that effect on him, always had. Jazz acted as a powerful drug without the nasty hangover. The tension in his neck subsided, and he grabbed the requisite white latex gloves and removed the sheet covering the rest of her body. He had never seen burned tissue quite like hers. Scarred flesh completely enveloped the bottoms of her feet and crept up the sides of her ankles, much like ivy would on the face of an abandoned building. There were also burns on her hands, but none anywhere else on her body. Leezel Diezman was an enigma, and Lucius became more and more curious about who she was and why she was laid out in front of him. Maybe she was trying to tell him something. He racked his brain and scanned his files most of the night searching for any clue that might jump-start his memory. He recalled several years of families and funerals, and still her identity eluded him. Perhaps she was a stranger after all who had become familiar with his work through word of mouth. Or perhaps he was making something out of nothing— simply stalling, so he wouldn't have to go upstairs and have a conversation with his errant wife. True, there were other things, other people he could be attending to, but Leezel Diezman held him where he was. Something about her nagged at him, and he was loath to let it go. There was a puzzle here, and as God was his sacred judge, he was determined to solve it.

CHAPTER 40

After hours of staring into a face that he now realized he must have seen somewhere, Lucius was more determined than ever to figure out why Mrs. Diezman had chosen him to groom her for glory. He reexamined her file for the eleventh time and called one of her daughters, but the girl seemed just as perplexed by her mother's unusual request. "Did she ever mention me or my grandfather, Marcel Culpepper?" he'd asked, and "Did she attend a service here perhaps?" "No," the daughter had replied emphatically, "not to my knowledge," to every question he'd asked.

Finally he stood over the body and interrogated Mrs. Diezman as if he expected her to rise up and answer him. "Who are you?" he pressed. "And what are you doing here?" Lucius stroked the burned skin on her hands, admired the soft lines of her face, and the way her top lip protruded to the left just so. He'd seen a mouth like that before, and he'd seen this particular injury on someone else, but it was much worse then. It had been a long time ago, when he was a boy, but he remembered it like it was yesterday. And then a thought came to him, a thought so unbelievable that his mind could barely contain the possibility. The sheer force of it blew through his body and knocked him clean off his feet. He had to think, but focusing was difficult, as so many memories, conversations, and feelings were converging at once surrounding his one clear thought. It was insane, but then insanity had always been a part of his family, so why should now be any different? It had to be so because he felt the truth, her truth, twisting and prancing in the pit of his stomach, flirting with his demons. He sat down for a spell and closed his eyes, and when he opened them, he knew with certainty where he had seen her face before. It was a few hours ago when he looked into the eyes of his little brother. Lucius smiled a bit, relieved that, for once in his life, he had figured something out before it was too late. Have mercy, Leezel Diezman wasn't here for him at all.

Mystery solved, he was prepared to spend time with her remains, for the rest of the night if he had to, alone and in deep thought, until she was perfect. But he immediately realized that any form of introspection wasn't going to happen just yet. He recognized his brother's footsteps coming down the corridor and hurried to cover the body. He turned up the music and wished that he were riffing in a jazz club in New Orleans. But he wasn't; instead, he was planning on stopping his brother from getting any closer to the mother he would never know. In that moment, Lucius made a decision for Dante. If he had never seen his biological mother alive, it sure as hell didn't make any sense for him to see her dead. What purpose would that serve? They had both had enough pain in their lives, he and Dante, and Lucius wasn't going to invite any more agony to the party.

He began rereading old paperwork and waited somewhat annoyed for Dante to enter the room. He had to send him away from this room and away from her. Maybe if 'Trane were blowing loud enough, Dante would walk the other way and leave him to work alone. No such luck, though. The double doors swung open, and this time, he was ready to protect his family.

"Hey, you've been down here for hours. Need any help?" Dante asked.

"No, Brother. I think you've done enough helping for the day."

"Lucius, I—"

Lucius stopped him in midsentence. "It's okay, Brother. I'm glad you were there for Mercy. I don't know what got into her. It was bad, you know, but it could have been a lot worse. You're always there when I need you, and I appreciate you. I want you to know that."

Dante paused before answering. "Lucius, you know I love you, and I would never do anything intentionally to hurt you."

"Yeah, yeah—how many women have you told that line to?"

"Not many, man. Only one," Dante responded, and lifted the sheet, admiring his brother's meticulous preparation of the body on the table.

"Well, I hope she fell for it. Move outta the way, Brother," Lucius said, and stood in front of the body. "You're blocking my light."

"Who is this lady, anyway?" Dante inquired. "And how did she end up here?"

"What? Are you inferring that our fine establishment isn't good enough for her?" Lucius quickly re-covered Mrs. Diezman's feet and glanced at his paperwork. "Her name is Leezel Diezman, and she requested that we handle her remains, okay? That's all."

"Really? Do we know her family? Does she have some kin around here?"

"Look, I don't have an FBI file on the woman, Dante. I'm just trying to work here, not write a biography," Lucius snapped.

"All right, all right," Dante responded, and put his hands up. "Well, is there anything I can do to help you finish? Clean her up, grab another trocar? It looks like you've got your hands full."

"Yeah, now that you mention it, there *is* something you can do."

"What?" Dante questioned. "Whatever you need."

"Get the hell outta here, man. I'm okay . . . I just need some time to myself."

"Understood. I'm gone." Dante turned to leave. "Come find me if you change your mind."

"Brother."

"Yeah?"

"One more thing."

"Yeah, what is it?"

"One of these days, boy, the devil's gonna win you over."

Dante froze, unable to respond.

"No, seriously, man—could you check on Mercy for me before you go to bed? I'm going to be a while down here. Leezel here needs me."

"Sure," Dante managed to reply without turning around. "I think I can do that."

CHAPTER 41

Dr. Kelly clutched the receiver and repeated himself for the third time in five minutes. "I'm asking you if you'll consider coming in with your aunt."

"She's not my aunt. What are you, deaf? I've told you that already."

"All right, I'm sorry. Who is she to you, then? Tell me again, . . . Phoebe, is it?"

"Jesus, I can't believe you actually make money doing what you do. Aunt Baby isn't anything to me. She's Dahlia's aunt, that's all. We're not related in any way."

"I see. It sounds to me like she only has your best interest at heart."

"Really, and you were able to ascertain that in the five-minute conversation you had with her? You're a lot smarter than you look."

"Phoebe, you can come to my office alone or with her. The important thing here is that you come in to see me now."

"I'll think about it, but don't hold your breath, Doc."

Phoebe slammed the phone down and glared at Aunt Baby. "I know you. Don't think you're going to hold me here like some hostage. Don't get any crazy ideas, old woman, because I'm on to you, and by the way, I'm not drinking any more of your damn tea or anything else that you put in front of me. You're always trying to fix somebody. I ought to have you put away."

"Listen here, girl, if anybody's going to be put away, it's not going to be me. I'm not the one who has lost my damn mind . . . yet. One of us here has a screw loose. You either go with me to that fancy doctor or I'm going to make a phone call, and by the night's end, you'll be in a nuthouse somewhere in the desert with metal straps around your ankles calling for a mama that you never had."

"You can't be serious. You can't keep me here, Baby."

"You're right, I can't, but I sure can make it hard for you to go anywhere else. I went through all of your personals while you were sleeping. I took your money, your keys, and anything else of value you had wedged in that there shiny, overpriced bag. I know where you live, and I know what I'm willing to do to make sure you can't get there. I don't know how you've managed to get by this long without being discovered—renting apartments and doing God knows what. You think you're slick, girl, but you're just a common thief, trying to steal a life that doesn't belong to you. Oh, I've got your number, Phoebe. I might be old miss thing, but I'm wiser and stronger than you'll ever be."

Phoebe reached for her bag, examined the contents, and threw it against the wall in disgust. Baby had indeed taken everything except her journal, which she had probably read thoroughly. Nosy witch. She knew it would be futile to search for her belongings in this big house, and she also sensed that Baby would brain her with a stick if she tried. She sat heavily on the couch and kicked her Prada bag laying on the floor.

"Tell me something, Baby—if you're so damn smart, what took you so long?"

Baby sat on the couch and thought a while before she answered. "Well, I figured that question would come up sooner or later."

"And?" Phoebe pushed.

"Fear—simple as that. I can admit that now, before you—before God. I know you've been around for a long time, Phoebe. I know exactly the moment when you were born. I just didn't know how to fix you, fix Dahlia, and make all the pain go away. I didn't want you to be my first real failure. So I did nothing but watch from the sidelines, and you have survived because of my fear, my inability to take a chance. You see, Phoebe, I couldn't attack an illness that I didn't understand."

"Well, what makes you think you understand now? I told you before that you're not going to be able to just patch me up and expect a miracle to happen. And I'm not sick either, got it? Dahlia was sick, and you had your chance to help her. All of you did. Why can't you accept that she's gone? If Dahlia didn't want to disappear, do you really think I'd be here? Accept your failure and get a life."

"No. This is not the natural order of things. This is not the way it's supposed to be."

"Blah, blah, blah. Look, lady, I'm here to stay, and there's nothing you or any doctor can do about it."

"I'm not afraid anymore, Phoebe. Did I mention that? I'm not meeting my maker with fear etched on my heart for you or anybody else, you hear me? I've got to always be able to say that I did my best in every situation, and honey, my best is yet to come. So grab your empty bag and do whatever it is that you have to do in the next twenty minutes. We've got an appointment to keep."

Defiant, Phoebe snatched her purse from the floor and headed toward a room with heavy doors. She needed a moment to compose herself and rewire her brain. Being dragged to a shrink was not part of the plan. She had to think quickly and change course, set a new agenda and get back on track. She needed plan B. She opened her journal and began writing furiously. Something brilliant would come to her. It always did.

Tuesday · December 5 · 4:52 p.m.

Shit, shit, shit. This old broad is trying to ambush me, force me out, and I'm not having it. I am in control, and she hates me for it. She's always hated me, but so what? I don't need anyone's fucking approval to exist in this world. I'm an island, dammit. Hate me or love me, I'm still here in this life and in this body. Poor pitiful-ass Dahlia is just about gone, anyway. What's left of her is hanging on by a thread, and she doesn't have the strength to hold on much longer. I can feel her melting away little by little. It's almost sad, really, that it had to come to this. Bottom line, dammit: I am stronger now than I have ever been, so Baby and that quack doctor can eat me. I can't believe she stole my keys and took my shit. Who knew she had it in her? She has balls after all. It's funny how some old people decide to become useful before they die.

Where the fuck is Milky and that kid, anyway? If I could just have a few minutes with him alone, I know that he'd love me, and in time, he'd want me more than he ever wanted her. I deserve this life. I deserve to be loved, and more important, I deserve to be free. He'd make Baby go away if I asked him to—send her back where she came from. I need to find him and show him how good we could be together. Convince him that I was the one he should have chosen in the first place—screw his brains out until he gives in. He's a man. He'll succumb. They all do; it's in their blood.

In the meantime, I'll go to this stupid-ass session with the shrink and play crazy. Ha-ha. Of course, I know it'll be a complete waste of my time, but she and four-eyes will figure that out eventually. Both of them are going to analyze me to death until I find Michael, my husband. My husband—yeah, I like the sound of that. My husband, my husband, my husband. How in the hell am I going to sit through all this psychobabble bullshit without losing precious brain cells? Jesus, I'm going to throw up in his office—blow chunks right on his rug. That'll end the session in record time. I know. I'll make them think that there's a chance to get Dahlia back. Yeah, baby, that's it! It's time for me to call the shots here. Now who's outsmarting whom? They don't know who they're messing with. They don't know what I've been through to get here, and dammit, they don't know me. I am a survivor here, now, and always.

Shit. I need a mojito bad, and I wish to God Pocahontas would stop banging on the door.

CHAPTER 42

"Breathe, girl, breathe," Mercy told herself. How could her life be unstable, so much more complex in the span of a few short hours? Nothing would ever be the same again. She came to that realization when it was over, when he'd left her. Change scared her more than most, and she could admit that to herself now without fear of being exposed. Lucius would know soon enough that she'd betrayed him. He'd sense the gospel of it and smell it in the air. He was creepy that way, just like his aunt.

She slipped underneath the water in the bathtub and contemplated staying there submerged until warm liquid inched up her nose and flooded her lungs. She could drown quickly and take the easy way out. In the end, who would miss her? Her parents were dead, and she was too vain to have any girlfriends who gave a damn about her. It would probably be days before Lucius even realized that she was gone, and that would be just as well. It was, after all, what she deserved, and no one knew that better than she. Still, in spite of an impending violent depression, her nipples hardened and her insides throbbed with the memory of him. Him who loved her, him who touched her, him who said he could forgive her anything. She came up for air and discovered her hands nestled between her legs rubbing, prodding, and searching for that feeling that had finally set her free.

Mercy was forty-one years old and had just experienced her first orgasm, with a man who wasn't her husband. She was scared and confused at the same time and wondered how she was going to get through the rest of the night without screaming his name. She couldn't say it at all, couldn't wrap her mouth around the syllables, for if she did, Lucius would know with certainty that her soul had flown open as easily as her legs. What was she going to do? How was she going to exist in a house that was growing tired of holding multiple confidences in its walls? In the beginning, the house had been loyal to her, guarding her secrets, protecting her sins. But now she feared she had given it one sin too many, and it, like everyone else, would turn on her in due time.

Maybe if she avoided him, stayed as far away from him as possible, erased the memory of his tongue dancing with her clitoris, she could survive here. Mercy reached for a towel and shook her head in resignation. Who was she fooling? She knew her survival depended on whether the matriarch returned. The mere thought of being in Aunt Baby's presence caused her face to spasm in protest. She accepted that her twitching would most likely give her away the moment Aunt Baby glided through the door. The woman would see right through her. She always had, and this would be no different. She leaned against the wall for support and sank toward the cold linoleum. There was nothing she could do, no place she could go, and no one who could understand. Truth was stalking her. She could feel its breath lifting the hairs on the back of her neck. She knew that she should turn around and confront her enemy and finally rid herself of the lies that confined her, but running was all she knew how to do.

CHAPTER 43

Dante Culpepper replayed the day's events in his head repeatedly. His world had changed drastically in the span of a few hours, and the day wasn't even over yet. With his mind stuck in constant rewind and his heart beating faster than normal, Dante struggled with simple duties and strained to shift his focus to other matters for fear of going insane. But much to his dismay, no matter what he did, he couldn't stop thinking about their time together, and he couldn't figure out how he was going to get through the rest of the day without her. Concentration eluded him, and common sense was long gone.

He was a nervous ball of conflicting emotions, and he vacillated between what he yearned to do and what had to be done. Anger, regret, and a multitude of other feelings assaulted his state of mind, and he was immediately ashamed. His brain hissed that he'd made a horrendous mistake, but his heart pleaded with him to run up the stairs and find her, comfort her, and sink inside her all over again. Instead, he'd waited outside the preparation room clenching and unclenching his fists, wondering how he was going to face his brother. He'd felt the music reverberating on the other side of the sterile white doors and knew instinctively that Lucius wanted to be left alone. He'd stepped forward, paused, and reached for the door several times. He didn't know what was going to come out of his mouth once he was in there, but he did know that if he didn't face Lucius at that moment, he'd never be able to. Somehow, someway he had to salvage what was left of his honor. He had to try to redeem himself.

The exchange had been normal and strange at the same time. Lucius had focused on his work, and Dante had waited for the right moment to confess what he had done. The moment had never come, and Dante was relieved. Perhaps nothing needed to be said. Perhaps he and Mercy could exist in the same house and behave as if they'd never been wrapped around each other. Or perhaps he, too, was finally succumbing to crazy. He was going straight to hell for this. He just knew it.

Now he stood in Percival Tweed's house prepared to interrogate the old albino and a man he didn't know. He thought some fresh air would help clear his mind. There had to be some kind of resolution between him and Mercy before his mother returned, or a plan of sorts, because Aunt Baby would know, plain and simple. She would take one look at both of them and smell betrayal. In time, maybe his mother would forgive his transgression and his brother would learn to trust him again. He inhaled deeply. He didn't want to think about what Aunt Baby would do to Mercy. His mama said once that she'd put aside her Choctaw ways and sell her soul to the devil to wreak devastation on anyone who hurt somebody she loved. After all this family had done for him, he couldn't be the one who destroyed it, and he had to make sure no one else did either.

He walked the grounds until his heart rate returned to normal and ended up standing on Percival Tweed's doorstep. The stranger whom he'd seen earlier was listening intently to what the albino had to say. Dante heard his name and knew that his problems were just beginning.

Milky jumped when he heard the voice behind him. He immediately stood and offered an introduction, but the man speaking didn't seem to notice. He continued to address Mr. Tweed, and it was obvious they knew each other.

"Please continue."

"I think I'm done talking now. I'm plum tuckered anyhow, I'll tell you that."

"It doesn't seem like it to me. It looks like you're bent on stirring up some trouble here, Percival."

"No," Percival Tweed responded calmly, "you've done enough of that for everybody."

"I don't know what you mean."

"Boy, you know exactly what I mean."

"Excuse me," Milky interrupted, "can somebody tell me what's going on here?"

"Sir, I don't know who you are or how you became involved with Mr. Tweed, but this is really a family matter."

"Then that's a good thing. Michael, looks like you got here just in time for a family get-together," Percival said. "I guess it's up to me to make the acquaintances here." Percival Tweed walked toward the two men and leveled his eyes on Dante. "Michael Chang, this is Dante Culpepper, Lucius's only brother and your wife's uncle."

"I see. I think under the circumstances I need to go back to the hotel. I'm tired and I've heard enough for one day." Michael sighed. "I need to call Isabel, anyway."

"We'll speak again," Percival added, and watched Michael walk toward his car. And then he looked at Dante for a long time. Neither of them spoke or moved. Each assessed the other methodically and without hesitation. Dante opened his mouth first, but Percival silenced him with a look.

"Sit down," Percival commanded.

"Mr. Tweed, I don't have time for—"

"I said, sit down." Percival spoke sternly and retrieved a letter from his desk drawer. "I have something for you."

CHAPTER 44

Buried alive. That's how she felt—entombed under layers and layers of emotional concrete. She was on the outside looking down at herself pounding on triple-pane glass while watching her mouth move. She was a life-sized dummy, a real live ventriloquist act, but who was pulling the strings? Who had their hand thrust up her spine bending her every which way, manipulating her mind? She screamed a thousand soundless screams and no one heard her, no one who mattered. "Help me," she'd sobbed from wherever she was, and after a time, there was only one reply. "Go away," the voice hissed. "There's nothing left for you here."

She'd heard that voice lately, weaving in and out of her brain, but it was usually a whisper, a faint murmur that she'd thought she'd heard. Now it was deafening, and it brought with it a cacophony of vibrating noise. In the space she clung to, the voice taunted her and dared her to lose her mind. She tried to remember when her relationship with the voice had morphed into something twisted and acrimonious. It hadn't always been this way. The voice used to help her, soothe her, and tell her she was precious and worthy. The voice had always promised to protect her and keep her far away from the people and places that frightened her the most. But now the voice had abandoned her, and she struggled to make sense of it all. "Why?" she asked, and trembled at the immediate reply.

"Because," the voice yelled, "I don't love you anymore."

Dahlia could feel herself shrinking and was humbled by the experience.

"Leave me alone," Dahlia whispered, suddenly very confused. "Just please, leave me alone."

There were doors where she was, and some doors were thicker than others. The thickness represented pain and suffering. She didn't know how she knew that, but she did. And these doors beckoned to her to open them, lured her by name, and enticed her with freedom. Still, she retreated from the emotion that tempted her, dangled agony in front of her face as if she were supposed to embrace it and hold on for dear life. "No. No!" she shouted, and slipped further from a reality that she could see but not touch—feel but not grasp. As she hoped, the first door seemed to be moving away just out of her reach, and as it moved in distance, she experienced a welcome sense of alleviation. Breathing even became easier and required less effort. The doors led to somewhere she was in no hurry to go, and contentment and fear seemed a better option. Here wasn't really so bad. Here was comfortable, here was safe, and here was where she'd stay.

Although she'd told herself this nonsense before, her conviction to abandon herself never lasted. No matter how long she stayed in that dark place that protected her from what was authentic, she knew the floating doors would eventually return and she would have another opportunity to make a decision. Stay or leave. Sink or swim. She'd visited this place so many times that it had begun to feel like home—a welcome illusion. Even in the deep recesses of her mind, where she felt anchored but held on to nothing, truth resided strong and alive, pulsating inside of her. There was a way out, but it was she who had to take it—she who had to fight for her life. Her life waited on the other side of those doors, and the only way out was to reach up and open them all.

CHAPTER 45

Dr. Kelly flipped through his notes. He'd read them repeatedly, and each time, he marveled at the complexities of the human psyche. In all his years of practice, he had never encountered a patient quite like Dahlia. He had, of course, reviewed other cases of dissociative identity disorder—or multiple personality disorder, as clinicians like to refer to it—but he hadn't experienced one up close until now. Dissociative disorders were once considered a rare and mysterious psychiatric curiosity. And some practitioners in the field of psychiatry refused to believe such an affliction existed at all, even after the release of *The Three Faces of Eve* and the much-better-known *Sybil*. Now, after years of scientific scrutiny, dissociative disorders were understood to be fairly common effects of severe trauma in early childhood.

Dr. Kelly still didn't know enough about Dahlia's life to ascertain exactly what had occurred, but something had traumatized her—something or someone terrifying enough to shatter her very foundation and splinter her mind into unrecognizable pieces. He was committed to helping her rediscover herself and put the fragments of her life back together. All he needed was time and cooperation.

He'd canceled all his previous appointments. He'd done that a lot this month, and he informed his lovely wife that he would be otherwise occupied with a patient emergency. She wasn't thrilled but she understood, and he adored her for it. He glanced at his watch, anxious to begin. Dahlia or Phoebe was due to arrive momentarily. He took a deep breath and prayed that his $100,000 Harvard education, years of experience, and two failed marriages had prepared him for this session. Everything he had learned and all he had become led him to this exact moment. If he wasn't ready now—if he couldn't help cure her—he wasn't worth the paper his degrees were printed on, and worse yet, Dahlia would be lost forever, and he couldn't let that happen. And it's not like he hadn't had to commit patients before, because he had, but this one, this one had to be saved from herself.

He was strangely drawn to her, and it pained him to acknowledge his emotional attachment, but he could now admit why he felt obligated to cure Dahlia Chang. He'd had a daughter once, Gweny, from his first marriage years ago. She'd wrestled with mental illness as a teenager and eventually died from an overdose of meds when she was only seventeen years old. He'd blamed himself for years for not recognizing the signs sooner, for not being a better father, a better therapist. He lost his Gweny, his marriage, and his own sanity for a while. If it hadn't been for Lionel Durbin, he'd have been running around Trafalgar Square like a loon in his knickers. If Gweny were still alive, she'd be the same age as Dahlia right now. Maybe she would have married a nice bloke and followed in his footsteps. Maybe he would have been a grandfather by now. Maybe. He knew it was unhealthy to dwell on the past and become personally involved in an ongoing case, but Dahlia needed him. When he looked into her eyes, he saw Gweny—strong, sassy, terrified Gweny. He saw a scared little girl reaching out to him, begging him to help her. And he would help her this time, by God, or die trying.

Aunt Baby dialed home on her cell phone. Dante had gifted her with the shiny silver contraption last Christmas, and she could count on one hand the number of times she had ever used it. People at home always knew where to find her, she'd said then, so why the hell did she need a cell phone, anyway? She still couldn't believe that she could call somebody from the middle of nowhere without wires and a jack. Good Lord, what were they going to think of next? She'd been so busy fussing with Loony Tunes sitting next to her that she'd forgotten to call home and tell her family that she'd arrived safe and sound smack dab in the middle of the twilight zone. Funny, though, no one had called her. God only knew what was happening in that house without her. She shook her head and stared out the window. For all she knew, the world was coming to an end. If she smoked, she'd be on her second pack by now. She sat next to her grandniece in the Yellow Cab and felt no connection to her at all. To some, she thought, her feelings would seem preposterous, but Dahlia was gone for now, and the woman eyeballing her was a stranger.

Aunt Baby was relieved when the cab stopped. She needed to get somewhere and rest her bones, but more important, she needed to decide what to do next. This Dr. Kelly couldn't keep Phoebe, and Aunt Baby couldn't leave her. She'd promised Dahlia, and she'd die first before she disappointed that girl again. So there was only one thing left to do. She was going back home to Dallas just like that, and she was taking crazy-in-the-head with her. As gifted as she was, she couldn't heal this child by herself, and she refused to rely on an outsider who didn't know a thing about her family. Since that day, no one in the Culpepper family had ever spoken about what had happened, not the day after, not in more than twenty years. It was time for a few people to open their mouths. It was time for her to open hers. And whether they were all going to hell or not, it was time for the truth. Baby Marseli dabbed her forehead with her mother's baby ivory lace handkerchief and immediately felt better. Leaving Pasadena was the sensible thing to do for everyone. She would threaten Phoebe if she had to, drug her and tie her atop an Amtrak train, and they would survive this and live to heal another day. Perhaps on some level Dahlia would sense their destination and realize once and for all that there was no shame in going home again.

CHAPTER 46

Milky hung up the phone and questioned himself again for being here instead of with his precious daughter. Isabel was fine with his mother, but she wanted him to come home. She missed Mommy, she'd said. Well, that made two of them. And where was Mommy? she'd asked. He'd lied to his daughter like he always did, and he hated Dahlia for that. It had been two days since he'd spoken to his wife. No one was picking up at home, and as usual, she wasn't answering her cell phone. She was gone yet again, and for the first time, he began to fall apart. Suddenly he was plagued with destructive scenarios and failed outcomes. What if this trip was a colossal waste of time? What if Isabel was emotionally scarred because both her parents were gone? What if his marriage was over once and for all?

Dammit, his life didn't used to be this complicated. His life used to make sense, much like his award-winning culinary creations. Right now he should be in his restaurant putting the finishing touches on foie gras; instead, he was in Texas, of all places, yearning for his family and pondering the nutritional value of grits. Yeah, he was losing it for sure and would most likely be certifiable by noon if he didn't pull it together fast. What good could he do Isabel or Dahlia if he didn't get a grip and remember why he was there in the first place? "Get up, Michael," he yelled. "Get up!"

He sat on the edge of the king-sized bed in the famed Adolfus Hotel and attempted to make sense out of everything he'd learned yesterday about the Culpepper family. Although he was only interested in information that related directly to Dahlia, he was fascinated by it all. He sensed that he had to understand where she came from to truly know her. He wished he'd had a tape recorder because he had no idea how he was going to absorb all of this new information. Names, dates, and people he had never heard his wife mention were now swimming around in his head with worry, fear, and sixteen different recipes for smothered chicken. And as much as he had acquired from Percival Tweed, he knew that there was plenty left unsaid. There was more to know about this family, much more. Today he'd go back there, take notes, and ask more poignant questions. Today he'd meet his father-in-law, Lucius, whether it was the right time or not. Determined and back on track, Milky headed toward the shower. There was no time to waste; the albino was waiting.

Rest evaded Percival Tweed for the first time in a long while. He wasn't accustomed to being so affected by life's twists and turns. He had always been a spectator, not an active participant in the drama that surrounded the Culpeppers. Of course, deep down, he knew that wasn't necessarily accurate, but he'd convinced himself that it was. Besides, he'd only interfered when it was absolutely necessary. He'd only stepped in when Baby Marseli was involved. And the truth be told, if he had to do everything all over again, he wouldn't change a thing.

He had been up and down all night deliberating on whether he was doing the right thing by running his mouth about other folks' business and, more important, by giving Dante the letter.

He hadn't read the letter, but he could only imagine what secrets were revealed after all these years. "Prettybaby, forgive me," he whispered. Jesus, Mary, and Joseph, what had he done? And why had he agreed to give the boy the letter in the first place? After all, he wasn't a real blood member of this family, even if he'd been a part of it for as long as he could remember.

At 3:00 a.m. or sometime thereabouts, Percival decided that sleeping wasn't necessarily that important anyhow but helping Baby Marseli any way he could was. She had always been his priority, and after forty years, that wasn't about to change. They were never ones for talking, but they communicated effectively just the same. He thought of her and all she did for him, and his heart melted. From the moment she gazed into his eyes, he knew that she saw clear through to his soul. No other woman had ever looked at him that way again, but Baby Marseli still had that same look in her eyes every time she saw his face. Good God, he loved her for that. He loved everything about her.

Normally people like him were supposed to shy away from the sun for obvious reasons, but afflictions that affected other albinos never bothered Percival. He wore his wide-brimmed hat and glasses when he ventured out in the sun, but only because he wanted to. He tired of folk staring at him all the time. The glasses and the hat usually kept the finger-pointers at bay.

When he first started working at the Culpeppers' he discovered a porcelain container filled with an odd-smelling white substance on his front porch. The note attached explained how to use it, and he'd been rubbing that homemade lotion all over his body ever since. As a result, he never had a problem with the sun—or anything else, for that matter. He never had to ask where the concoction came from either. He just knew. And even now, years later, Baby Marseli kept him knee-deep in that cream. She made sure that he never needed anything at all.

After ruminating over two biscuits and a frosty glass of buttermilk, Percival Tweed decided to confess whatever came into his throat first to Michael and Dante, and he didn't intend to leave anything out either. No sense in doing anything halfway, that wasn't his style. He had to go the distance for Baby Marseli. He had to make it easy for her to come on home, back to Dallas—back to him. She was returning any day now with trouble attached to her hip. He didn't need any confirmation; everything inside told him so. He leaned back and waited for Michael or Dante. He figured one of them was due any minute now, and Percival was ready, ready to release it all, or so he thought.

CHAPTER 47

The more things change, the more they stay the same. Just when Lucius thought he had a handle on life, Dante's dead mama shows up in his mortuary. No note, no warning, no nothing to prepare him for the revolving drama that was obviously his life. It seemed to Lucius that no matter what he did, turmoil always seemed to find him. He was mentally exhausted and pained for his brother. He didn't know if he was doing the right thing by not telling him, but he knew that he couldn't let Dante embalm his own mother. There was something unnatural about that—embalming your own blood—something that changed you forever and rocked your soul from its foundation.

Lucius had a permanent soulache, and he accepted that. The ache carved into his soul was inevitable after what had happened, after what he had had to do, but Dante deserved better. He had been through enough already. He'd come into this world covered in pain, and Lucius resolved that his little brother wouldn't leave the same way. Lucius was wrapped in enough anguish for the both of them. He adjusted the volume on his stereo and attended to the final details. She had to be right; she had to be perfect, and he would make it so for his brother's sake. He covered her lower extremities and sewed her eyelids shut. Oddly enough, he experienced an intense feeling of longing for his own mother, but the moment passed, and he compartmentalized his own needs, just like he had always done. And in that instant of swallowing his emotions raw, Leezel Diezman became family and not just a stranger who spent time on his long steel table.

Finally, after she was fully prepped, he decided to rest, but not in his own bed upstairs. Rather, he reposed on the black leather couch that decorated his expansive office. He knew he should have crawled in bed with his wife and whispered soft velvet apologies. He knew he should have offered some kind of explanation for his erratic behavior, but he couldn't engage her—not now. God knows he couldn't. With "Naima," another 'Trane masterpiece, playing softly in the backgroud, Lucius Jeremiah Culpepper eased into a restless slumber and dreamed of his life before the tornado, before the children, before his parents left him for good.

CHAPTER 48

Mercy flinched when she heard the knock on the door. It was her husband, and she had no desire to see him. She didn't know why he didn't just come in and berate her some more. Well, if he were waiting for her to acknowledge him, he'd be standing on the other side of the door all night. Either life was a maze of incomprehensible connections or the Almighty had a wicked sense of humor. Either way her life had fallen apart since she'd fallen in love with her husband's brother. She'd never have believed she could think such ungodly thoughts or fiend for someone other than Lucius. But recently, ungodly thoughts emanated from every vital part of her anatomy and propelled her to do ungodly things.

He knocked again. She couldn't answer. She waited. Nothing. Why didn't he just come in? Why wouldn't he simply get it over with? Earlier, before Dante, she would have flown to the door grinning like a lovesick teenager eager for attention, but now she just wanted him to go away—disappear and leave her to her guilt-ridden fantasies in peace. She placed her head between her knees and rocked to a rhythm that had become pleasurable and familiar. Time would not slow for her, and she couldn't make her husband wait forever. After a few minutes, the persistent rapping ceased, and she slid under the covers, grateful that Lucius had chosen not to intrude. She admired the hand-etched crown molding on the ceiling, fidgeted with the folds of her cherry red nightgown, and wondered if Dante was thinking of her.

Dante locked himself in his room and tried not to imagine the worst. After last night's terse exchange with Percival Tweed, his fears were confirmed. The old man knew what he had done. The knowing had been in his eyes and all that he didn't say. His instinct was to run away—vanish in the wee hours of the morning on one of his extended vacations. That was his modus operandi when he felt out of sorts and overwhelmed or when being in the house began to cause him acute discomfort. But he couldn't leave that way. He refused to be a coward any longer. There was a monsoon brewing around him, and this time, he was keenly aware of the injuries it would bring with it. It didn't catch him off guard like the last one. He had created the disturbance now beginning to contaminate the very air around him, and he resolved to step forward and do something. This time, he wouldn't stand on the sidelines with his mouth open while his family fell apart.

Calamities, he had learned over the years, attracted other calamities and clumped together, much like a cancer intent on metastasizing. And before anyone realized what was happening, they morphed into something palpable, taking on a life of their own. When disaster befell the Culpepper family, the effect of that particular disruption never seemed to leave the house. Instead, the aftermath or the residuals wandered around and waited patiently for something else equally wicked to keep them company. There was enough latent misfortune traveling through the house to begin with without him adding another ruination for the original mass to absorb and grow stronger.

Dante breathed the newly transformed air and thought of his mother. He had bedded his brother's wife, but he was still somebody's son. He should have called Aunt Baby by now and made sure she'd arrived all right. He should have done a lot of things, but unlike most people, he had a different kind of mother. He didn't remember when he first realized how unique she was, but he was certain it had been very early. He'd heard enough stories to know what she had done for him, how she had saved his life and rid him of unimaginable scars, both emotional and physical. He knew that he'd probably be dead and in the ground if it weren't for her. Aunt Baby was connected to many people, but their bond was extraordinary, and from what he'd been told, it always had been. No, he couldn't ring her—not now, not yet, not with his feelings for Mercy so close to the surface, so close to being exposed. Baby would sense his emotional distress right through the phone and strip him naked—that was the nature of their relationship. He had to end it with Mercy first—stuff his feelings for her way down in the core of his heart where they belonged. Severing all ties with her was the only way, and then, when things appeared to have returned to normal, he would leave the business for good and sign everything over to his brother. It was the least that he could do.

Decision made, he retreated further inside himself and conjured up every facial expression, every exchange, every curve and nuance to magnify Mercy Blue. He adored her more than she would ever know, and although he'd deluded himself for a minuscule space in time, a part of him had always known that he was destined to love her from a distance. Dante focused with an intense certainty. He needed a strong image to sustain him on his journey without her, an indelible print of their time together. He dozed off reminiscing about the taste of her, and when he awoke, he remembered that the albino had given him something. At the time, so many things were crowding his mind that he'd folded the letter and shoved it in his inside jacket pocket and had forgotten about it until now. The old man wouldn't tell him what it was, and he had to admit that a part of him didn't want to know, so he'd distanced himself from it and had almost thrown it away.

He examined the outside; his name was written in a flowery scrawl he didn't recognize. It was probably a note from some decedent's family member thanking him for a job well done. He commenced reading unaware that his perception of himself was about to change forever. His lungs swelled; his heart began to beat to a familiar rhythm, and for a moment he was unable to breathe.

CHAPTER 49

"Well, is he here or not? I don't have all damn day."

"Calm down," Aunt Baby hissed. "The man knew we were coming. Lord have mercy." Aunt Baby looked at her watch: 9:00 a.m. Just how long would it take to crack Phoebe's head open and pull her niece on out of there? The door opened, and she determined to find out.

"I'm glad you were able to make it. Hello. We spoke on the phone. I'm Dr. Trevor Kelly. And you must be Phoebe."

"Well, you always were a genius, Trevor," Phoebe answered first.

"Please excuse her, Dr. Kelly. I can offer no explanation for her manners. I'm Marseli Culpepper, Dahlia's grandaunt." Phoebe rolled her eyes at no one in particular. "Now, before you begin doing whatever it is you've got to do, I need to ask you a few questions."

"Ms. Culpepper, as per our conversation on the phone earlier, I'm afraid that I can't discuss Dahlia's . . . er . . . ah . . . Phoebe's case with you without her . . . or their . . . permission. I am bound by doctor-patient confidentiality. Do you understand what I'm saying to you?"

"Son, do I look like I have a learning disability? Do I look crazy in the head to you?"

"No, ma'am. I just wanted to inform you that—"

"I don't care, Trevor," Phoebe interrupted. "She can listen to whatever you have to say. She'll probably drug it out of me later anyway. Can we get this show on the road already? Christmas is coming."

"Phoebe, are you saying that you don't mind if I discuss your condition with your aunt? And you don't mind her sitting in session with us? Is this correct?"

"I see you're still thick in the head and getting thicker by the minute. You know, you should really consider getting your ears checked. That wax buildup is a bitch. Look, I said fine already, and I told you before that she's not my aunt. She's not anything to me but a pain in the ass, much like you."

"Well, all right, then, both of you may come on in and chat for a while. Ms. Culpepper, may I speak to you outside for a moment?"

"I thought you'd never ask."

While Phoebe waited inside his office, Dr. Kelly addressed Aunt Baby. He had to be allowed to run the session his way without her interference, but he was also aware that she most likely had information that would help him reach Dahlia significantly sooner. Diplomacy was key here. For Dahlia's sake, he had to approach this matter delicately, as Dahlia's aunt appeared to be a formidable woman. He opened his mouth to speak. "Ms. Culpepper, I'd appreciate—"

"I know, son, but let me tell you how this is going to work. I'll give you today with her and maybe tomorrow if you look like you know what you're doing, and then I'm taking her home whether you're successful or not."

"Ms. Culpepper, I don't think you understand the severity of

Dahlia's condition here. Dissociative identity disorder is not something that can be cured or fixed overnight. The course of treatment is long-term, intensive, and often quite painful, as it generally involves remembering and reclaiming the dissociated traumatic experience. I've explained all this to say that she needs consistent treatment and medical attention to heal. The memory must be faced, experienced, metabolized, and integrated into Dahlia's view of herself. As I've said, this will be excruciatingly painful for her. I need more time."

"No, Dr. Kelly, I understand everything. It's you who's working completely blind here, but I'm willing to give you a chance to help make this right. I see how much you care, how much you want to rescue her."

"I'd appreciate your cooperation here. I know she had to have been faced with an overwhelmingly traumatic situation from which there was no physical escape. I'm betting you know what happened to her."

"Of course I do, Dr. Kelly."

"Well, whatever information you can give me about what occurred in Dahlia's past would really—"

"No. You're the doctor. Let's see what you can get from her. If Dahlia wants you to know, she'll come out some kind of way and tell you."

"What if she can't, Ms. Culpepper? What if she's not strong enough?" Dr. Kelly persisted.

"She's strong enough," Aunt Baby countered. "She just doesn't know it yet. She's a Culpepper. She can get through anything, even this."

"Look, I know you mean well, but it will take a lot more than your beliefs to cure your niece. What you're proposing won't work. It just doesn't work this way. With all due respect, this is my area of expertise. Let me do my job and help Dahlia."

"Life is my area of expertise, son, and I've seen more in my time than you could ever imagine. So, you do your thing, and

I'll do mine. In the meantime, I'll sit on in there with y'all and watch. If you need something from me, I'll help when I can. Like I said, the most you've got right now is today and tomorrow."

"Why?" Dr. Kelly questioned. "You just said that you were taking her home. Can't she come back the day after tomorrow?"

"Home," Aunt Baby answered softly, "is where she came from and not where she lives now. Home is where this all began, and home is where it will end, around family, around people who love her."

"Where exactly are you referring to?"

"She never told you? Dahlia never told you where she was from?"

"We were working up to that in previous sessions," Dr. Kelly responded defensively.

"Oh, I see." Aunt Baby smiled. "Well, let's see what happens in there, and then we can talk more afterward."

Dr. Kelly opened his office door, made sure Aunt Baby was comfortable in his chair, and stared into the angry eyes of a woman he was determined to know.

FREE

Percival Tweed wasn't accustomed to second-guessing himself, but ever since he had given Dante the letter, he'd been consumed with worry. He'd been in possession of that letter for fourteen days, and each day it rested in his desk drawer, he'd tried to burn it, but he couldn't destroy what didn't belong to him. It just wouldn't have been right, plus he'd promised her, and Percival Tweed was a man of his word. About a couple of weeks ago, she'd sent for him out of the blue after a forty-year hiatus. A man had called and asked him to come to Parkland Hospital as soon as possible. He went that afternoon—left ten minutes after the call—but nothing could have prepared him for their reunion. Leezel was waiting, clinging to a life that wanted her to let go. She reached for him, and he held her close for a long time.

She handed him the letter with a shaking hand, and they both knew whom it was for. "Are you sure you want to do this?" he'd asked, pained for her and yet afraid for Baby Marseli. "Please," she'd whispered, "do what you think is best." "Leezel," he'd responded. She placed her hand on his face. "He has to know," she said. "I want him to understand that I didn't want to leave him." She wanted to say more. She tried to say more, but she became too exhausted to continue and lapsed into a coma from the effort. Doctors filled the room, and he was immediately ushered away, left alone again with his thoughts and now hers on paper. So much would be different now. So much would change. He ran his hand along the champagne-colored envelope and prayed to God to give him the strength to do the right thing. Now it was done, and the only thing he could do was wait. Sweet Jesus, what was next? Everything seemed to be moving so fast, and heaven help him, he didn't have to open his front door to know that Dahlia's husband was on the other side waiting—eager and anxious for answers. He opened the door, handed Michael a cup of coffee, and motioned toward the kitchen. He sensed the boy would be most comfortable there. "Knew you'd find your way back out here," he said, and sat down.

"I'm here for my wife. I want to help her in any way I can. She's not well," Michael offered, and sipped his coffee.

"I know. She hasn't been right for a long time now."

"Why is that, Mr. Tweed? Why hasn't she been well?"

"I think it's best her father tells you that. I'll tell you everything that led up to that." Percival looked away, troubled.

"Mr. Tweed, I hope I didn't cause you any problems last night. Dante, is it? Well, he didn't seem too happy to see me."

"Dante, don't mind him. He's got other things on his mind, and you aren't one of them." Percival paused. "He's as good a place to start as any. You said earlier that you wanted to know about him. I'll tell you on one condition."

"Okay," Michael answered quickly.

Percival decided once and for all what was going to be said and what would remain inside him. And after some intensive reflection, he figured he'd know what to let go of when the time came.

"What I tell you here today about Dante Culpepper can't ever leave this here house. Do you hear me?"

"Yes already, and after you tell me this, then will you take me to see Lucius?"

"I think I can do that. We should be right on time." Percival rose and paced the kitchen. He swore once to Leezel a long time ago that he would never speak of her to anyone, but he didn't think she'd mind now, seeing as how she'd gone to glory and was lying up yonder. So it was, he would begin with her story and reveal a secret that he'd kept safe for more than forty years. "Well, it was 1964. Folks were fighting, the world was going crazy, and, let's see, it was four years before Dr. King would be assassinated. Seems like now that none of that compared to what was happening right here in Dallas. Cities were burning, and a baby boy was left up yonder on the doorstep. Michael, I'm telling you, it was the beginning of peculiar times, and you know, I remember it like it was yesterday. I remember it all."

CHAPTER 51

Leezel Diezman could have sworn on a stack of Bibles shipped straight from Jerusalem that she'd been struck by lightning. Lightning had shot through her eyeballs, traveled down her spine, and settled in her bones, nearly causing an internal combustion of sorts. How in the world could she return to her ordinary life now? She knew the explanation for what she experienced back there was deeply inadequate, but she couldn't think of any other way to describe her feelings for the tall, cocoa brown boy she'd met at the Balamikki Jazz Room.

Unbeknownst to her father, she'd been sneaking down there on Friday nights when he thought she remained behind at the bakery with the others, kneading dough like a loser. Now she couldn't focus on anything or anyone else but him and the way he stared at her. Oh, yes, he wanted her; she knew it, and she was willing to give him everything she had, including the clothes off her back. Maybe next week she'd get a chance to touch him, and perhaps he'd want to reciprocate. She'd allow him, of course, to explore her completely. That was without question. She would dance like she was one of them, sip the tan liquid in the short, fat glasses, and wait for him to notice her. She was in love with the tall cocoa brown boy, and when her father found out, he would kill her for it. She was seventeen, miserable, and stuck in a place and a time that didn't understand her. She'd emigrated from Düsseldorf with her father and brothers a decade prior, and had been wild as a coyote ever since.

Leezel Adeline Diezman had two lives: one of them had been decided for her before she'd been born, and the other she'd chosen herself. Her father, Wilhelm, always believed that females were only worthy of being spoken to if they were attached to a man. She knew he was full of shit at a very early age and questioned him incessantly, often catching him in a myriad of contradictions. She suspected he didn't like her much, and that was okay because she wasn't especially fond of him either, but he was her father nevertheless, and girls were supposed to honor their fathers. However, it didn't take her long to realize that every time she honored her father, she dishonored herself. So something drastic had to be done at once or her existence would begin to resemble everyone else's around her. Leezel refused to end up like the other fräuleins in her community, married to some dreadful man whom she didn't love, baking his schnitzel and scrubbing his floors. She was unfit for such drudgery, and nothing her father said would make her accept his choices for her.

After Leezel's mother died, Wilhelm moved to America with all of them in tow and opened a German café in North Dallas. In spite of her father's sour disposition, it thrived in no time at all, and she grew up not really wanting for anything except a life of her own. Her brothers, two of whom were dumb as sticks, were able to make decisions—come and go as they pleased—but she had to do what she was told: clean the house, prepare the borscht, pour her father's lager. And still, while she temporarily became the dutiful daughter whom he demanded, he plied her with useless commentary. She was too smart for a girl. She had too much mouth for a girl. God had surely cursed him.

She'd wanted to go to college like two of her brothers, but her father had said no. He would not waste his hard-earned money that way. She was already too smart for her own good, too clever for anyone suitable to ever want her. So, when her father informed her that he'd chosen the man she would marry, Leezel decided she had nothing to lose and delighted in discovering every aspect of herself. She opened her own bank account and stopped eating German food. She hated German food. It was mediocre, much like her family, and lacked spontaneity. She wore frosted pink lipstick every day and bobbed her long, blond hair. Of course, her father punished her, beat her, and threatened to send her back to the land of her birth, but she knew he didn't mean it. He was getting old, and she was the best baker in the café, better than he had ever been, better than her mother. Her breads boasted a bold, distinctive quality unlike any other. Customers could always tell the difference between the breads she baked and breads baked by her father or her brothers. People craved her creations and returned for more, always inquiring as to her whereabouts. So in spite of his foul temperament and idle threats, her father needed her, and she needed a way out. Heaven help her, she would cut herself a new path any way she could. She would turn her back on her father, her brothers, and her way of life before she married one Otto Potoshnik—a man who resembled a potato and reeked of day-old sauerkraut. There was a whole wide world waiting for her, and she ran toward it with open arms.

The Balamikki Jazz Room was located on the corner of State and Hugo streets near downtown Dallas. It was owned by a cream-colored Creole man named Kersey with two wives, and everybody who was anybody in the jazz world had graced its stage at one time or another. The club boasted an eclectic mix of people, young and old, black and white, the law-abiding and the dangerous. It was the kind of place where a person could relax for a spell and forget about the combustion of the outside world. Oftentimes folks who sat together at the Balamikki would never have spoken to one another anywhere else. Cultures collided, and here that was a good thing. The owner had a penchant for the company of young girls, so he allowed them in most times as long as they behaved and didn't start a ruckus.

Percival Tweed spent time there now and again when he desired a respite from the monotony of his life. He wasn't upset about his choices, nor did he want to make a change. He was content with where he was, and had no intention of leaving as long as Baby Marseli remained. There were so many times that he wanted to ask old man Culpepper for her hand in marriage, but he figured the old man would be offended, refuse, or worse, send him away. Being away from Baby Marseli wasn't an option, so he swallowed his courage repeatedly and loved her still in the privacy of his own heart. She was unusually sad right now, and he had to find a way to carry her burden. When she frowned, he ached, and when she smiled, he rejoiced. And so it was and would continue to be until the day he dug his own grave. He fantasized about her for hours while he listened to the likes of Nancy Wilson sing "Guess Who I Saw Today" with Cannonball Adderley on alto sax, his baby brother Nat on cornet, and Roy McCurdy on drums. His ears were in heaven, and oftentimes his heart was in hell. The Balamikki was jumping, but no one ever bothered him, so he was able to drink his poison in peace and focus on ten thousand ways to make Baby happy.

He noticed the white girl right away sitting at a table by herself pining for someone she had no business even thinking about. She was that German girl from North Dallas, and he'd heard tell that her father was one of them Third Reichers. Lord, she was either extremely brave or decidedly insane. Either way, she wasn't any of his business, or so he thought. He had a feeling, though, that he should watch her closely—pay attention to whatever situation she found herself mixed up in. So, not one to ignore his gut feelings, he visited the Balamikki Jazz Room three times more a month than he should have, listened to Ahmad Jamal tickle the ivories, and waited for fate to deal him a new hand.

CHAPTER 52

My dearest Dante,

I have always wondered what I would say to you if and when I could ever muster the courage to say anything at all. I am struggling as I write this letter because I know that there are not and never will be any words to convey my emotions about what happened. If you are reading this, then I am gone from this life and am finally free from my feelings of guilt and self-hatred. You see, I was never the same after I let you go, and I suppose that is no surprise. How could either one of us be what we once were? I think that would be impossible. Real pain changes you, my love, changes every cell in your body until you become someone else. I know that who you would have been before that night is completely different than who you are now.

I want you to know that I thought about you every day, and I think of you still even during my last hours on this earth. I need you to understand that I wanted you, that I loved you, and that I would have done anything to spare you the pain you suffered because of me. Please try not to think badly of me. I did the only thing I knew to do to save your life and to salvage my own.

The night you came into this world seems like a lifetime ago, but I can still smell you when I close my eyes, and I can still feel you in my arms warm and secure. You had my mouth and your father's nose, and you were a thing of beauty, so small, so precious, and all mine if only for a short time. Trust me, a mother never forgets these things about her child. You were born on May 16, 1964. And a few days later there was a horrible accident, a fire, and you were injured beyond comprehension. My love, I was so scared that you were going to die, and I believe you would have perished if it weren't for Percival and the woman you know as your mother, Marseli Culpepper. Percival Tweed was my angel, and he helped me at a time when I had lost everything: my family, my house, and almost my life.

I was so young then, Dante, young and naïve, and I actually thought that I could control the world around me, but nothing that night was under my control except for my decision to give you away. There is no justification for my cowardice, but I was hurt, terrified, and lost in a moment that has continued to haunt me. Percival swore to me that Baby could heal you and that no one would care that you were half-white at all—half German, in fact, not that it matters at this point. "Black folk are used to raising other people's children," he said, and I believed him. He promised that you would be loved and cherished in spite of me, and so I handed you to him along with a part of my soul.

Marseli Culpepper is a good woman, a gifted healer, and I know that she has been and will continue to be a wonderful mother to you. She is everything Percival said she was and more. My life has been incomplete without you in it, and baking bread for you on Wednesdays all these years was the only way that I could be close to you. I hope that you enjoyed what I had to offer, and I hope that you tasted the love I created for you. I did not want to intrude on your life, but I want you to know that I've seen who you are. I've watched you from a distance, sat

*next to you on a plane, and touched your hand once in a
restaurant in New Orleans. You are a fine man, a man that
any mother would be proud of, and I am honored that you
came through me even though the journey was a torturous one.
I know there has been sorrow in your family, but believe,
Dante, that your heartache will pass and your life will move
forward full of joy and countless blessings. When you think of
me and you begin to wonder, close your eyes and feel my
embrace. Know that I am never too far away. I wish you well,
my son, and I leave you with my heart, my love, and my
promise that I will watch over you always.*

Your mother,
Leezel Adeline Diezman

Dante sat on the edge of a chair facing the door for hours. He
read the letter over and over again searching for a truth that
maybe he'd missed the first few times. He was numb and yet sa-
tiated simultaneously. He knew that she had left out vital information, and obviously she'd had her reasons, but he didn't care.
It didn't matter anymore who his father was or why he was left
on the Culpepper doorstep. His mother loved him, and that
made all the difference. He was suddenly filled with an intense
emotion that he couldn't quite describe, and there was only one
person, one woman, he wanted to share his feelings with. Despite the tug-of-war going on in his heart, he opened his door
and went to find her.

CHAPTER 53

There is a moment in every woman's life when she knows the path she is on is no longer acceptable or the space that she occupies has become too small. Mercy was filled with the prospect of lateral movement, and change was beginning to feel less terrifying. She pulled her knees to her chest and glanced at her husband's side of the bed. It was after midnight and he wasn't there—not that she'd expected him to be. It was finally clear that Lucius would rather be anywhere else but with her. It had taken her exactly twenty-four years, four months, and six days to figure that out. And now that she had a sense of clarity about the direction of her life, there were things that needed to be said, and 1:53 a.m. was as good a time as any. She slipped into her robe, walked down the stairs, and was about to call out for Lucius when Dante spun her around from behind.

"I've been waiting for you," he said, "hoping that you could feel me nearby craving you. I almost came upstairs to your room, but I didn't want to take any chances."

"Slow down," she whispered. "He's not there. I was just going to find him. Dante, we—"

"Shhhh," Dante interrupted. "Not now. Find him later."

Mercy could hear the music wafting through the house, and she knew wherever Lucius was, she wouldn't be able to reach him. She had fooled herself into thinking that she could make a difference in his life but had only succeeded in corrupting her own. She hesitated, but only for a moment, and looked behind her for a husband who wasn't there. When she turned to face Dante to tell him that they shouldn't and that they had already gone too far, she became lost in his eyes. He needed her. She could feel it, and for the life of her, she couldn't remember the last time she had been needed.

Caught up. Swept away. Lost inside a place that he didn't recognize, Dante allowed his emotions to dictate his actions. Every sentiment within him threatened to explode and fill any available space with his myriad conflicting conclusions. What to believe, what to do, what to say, how to be floated in and out of his mind until he was nearly dizzy with indecision. All aspects of his life from the moment he read the letter spun out of control, and for once, he didn't want to stop the roller coaster. He chose to ride it, afraid and excited simultaneously, with both hands in the air. The outcome didn't deter him, and neither did the consequences. He ceased thinking about who he was and who he was becoming and concentrated on making sure that there was nothing else trapped inside him—nothing else that needed to escape. He pulled Mercy into a closet at the end of the hall, pressed her against the wall, and pretended for a moment that all was right with the world. "Take your robe off," he whispered. "Let me feel you."

CHAPTER 54

"Well? Are we going to sit here until I die of boredom?"

"Just give me one moment, please. Do you mind if I record this session?"

"I don't give a damn what you do as long as you do it quickly."

Dr. Kelly adjusted his glasses and glanced from Phoebe to Aunt Baby. He wished the older woman could have been more helpful. It certainly would have made his job easier if she'd shared what she knew about his patient. No matter. He was determined to find out what had happened to Dahlia and, more specifically, what had created the dissociations she was presently experiencing. Ultimately he had to ensure that she came back to him for help. He didn't believe that removing her from her home right now was the best course of action, but he wasn't about to challenge that aunt of hers. He had to show her that he could be of service here. He had to make them both trust him. He addressed his client first. "I don't think we've been properly introduced. I'm Dr. Trevor Kelly."

"It appears you've misplaced some brain cells since the last time we spoke. You know who I am."

"Yes, but I'm a believer in fresh starts, so humor me. What's your name?"

"Phoebe."

"Do you have a last name, Phoebe?"

"Graham. My last name is Graham, okay? Write it down."

"How old are you?"

"Younger than your patient."

"Which patient are you referring to?"

"Jesus, Mary, and Joseph. We're going to be here the whole fucking day if you insist on asking such asinine questions."

"Phoebe, I need to make sure I have all the facts. I'm being thorough, that's all."

"Fine. Whatever. I'm going on twenty-six. Yeah, that sounds about right."

"Where are you from?"

"Dallas."

"Really?"

"Yes, really. What, you don't hear my southern accent?" she responded with a twang.

"Do you still have family in Texas?" Dr. Kelly pressed. He noticed that she rolled her eyes at Aunt Baby before she answered.

"No, I don't have any family there. My family is here."

"Who's here?"

"My husband and my stepdaughter."

"The hell you say," Aunt Baby interrupted.

"I see. What about your parents?"

"I don't have parents. She had parents—inadequate, dysfunctional parents."

"What about them was inadequate and dysfunctional?"

"Well, let's see, the mother was a total whack job, and the father spent more time playing with dead people than he did with his own family."

"Right, then. How did that make you feel?"

"Personally, I didn't give a rat's ass about those people, but she hated them."

"Who, Dahlia?"

"No, Hillary Clinton. Of course Dahlia. That's why we're here, right, to talk about Dahlia?" Silence. "Ah, come on. What's with this beating around the bush shit? Baby, do you hear this? The good doctor here wants to know about your Dahlia. Would you like to do the honors, or shall I?"

"Looks to me like your mouth is working just fine," Aunt Baby acknowledged.

Dr. Kelly continued. "Phoebe, it sounds like you're very angry. Are you angry?"

"Yeah, you could say that."

"Yes, but would *you* say it?"

"I thought I just did."

"Why are you so angry? And are you angry at anyone in particular?" Dr. Kelly continued.

"I'm angry at her"—Phoebe pointed at Aunt Baby—"for not being able to mind her own damn business and for never being where she's supposed to be. As a matter of fact, your whole family sucks, do you hear me? Not one of you is worth a damn dime. None of you did what you were supposed to do. None of you gave a damn about Dahlia! I am the one who protected her, and now you're both trying to destroy me."

"That's not true," Dr. Kelly replied urgently.

"No, it's not," Aunt Baby added.

"You see, Phoebe, no one here wants to harm you in any way. We only want to understand you, understand how you arrived here at this moment."

"Please, do I have stupid written across my forehead? I'm not falling for any of this bullshit. You can both kiss the crack of my ass."

"Enough!" Aunt Baby interrupted, standing. "Just stop it right now."

"Or what? And since you're up, you might as well take the floor. Why don't you tell him about her family—your family, Aunt Baby? Tell him how fucked-up everyone is in that house. Why so quiet, old lady? You don't have anything to say now?" Phoebe rose from her seat and began to walk toward Aunt Baby, her voice getting louder and louder.

"Phoebe, please calm down," Dr. Kelly pleaded.

"Did you know, Dr. Kelly, that Dahlia's father, Lucius, married a woman half his age after his crazy-assed wife, Reva, wigged out and went psycho on everybody? And that the new wife of his, Mercy, is a liar—a no-good, worthless, prevaricating, sway-back slut? And, oh, by the way, Baby, did your son finally grow some balls and get a piece of that?"

"What nonsense are you saying?" Aunt Baby asked calmly.

"Ladies, please, everyone just calm down," Dr. Kelly attempted to interject.

"Dante has always wanted to screw her brains out. Oh, I'm sorry, you didn't know that? I thought you knew everything, Baby. As a matter of fact, she's probably on her back right now with her thighs high to the sky comparing him to his big brother."

Aunt Baby slapped her hard, but Phoebe kept erupting like the hit didn't faze her at all. Dr. Kelly rose and stood between them.

"I think we should all sit down right now and discuss what just happened here. Everyone please sit down."

"How is Percival anyway? Is the old freak still around after all these years digging graves before people actually die? And what about you, Baby? Still talking to your dead mother—and grinding up shit that doesn't do a damn thing for anybody? Hmmm, and you people call me crazy. Crazy is where you come from, Baby. Crazy is in your blood."

CHAPTER 55

His mama had named him Verdell, but folks at the joint called him Popeye and not because he had abnormally large calf muscles. He was aptly named because his eyes were so enormous that they looked like they were going to pop out of his head at any moment and cause a commotion. Leezel wouldn't have cared what anyone called him; she longed simply to call him hers. He was unlike any Negro man she had ever seen—fair-skinned almost like foreigner skin and eyes so green that she felt weak in the knees whenever he glanced her way. His hair fell in soft curls around his face, and she thought he resembled some kind of mocha-colored movie star, if there were such a thing. His big ole eyes didn't dissuade her from wanting him, and from what she could tell, they didn't scare any other women away either. She noticed the way the black girls scrutinized her, and she was keenly aware of how they looked at him, but they didn't love him like she did. They couldn't give him what she could.

All she needed was space and opportunity to ensure that Verdell understood just how far she was willing to go to get what she desired. She didn't give a damn about the consequences, and she couldn't care less about what she was supposed to do or whom she was scheduled to wed. She'd found the man of her dreams, and that was the only thing that mattered. Leezel took a deep breath and squeezed his hand on the way out of the club. She had nothing to lose and only pleasure to gain. She prayed that he would follow her, but he didn't. He did, though, send a fellow after her with a few kind words and a phone number. She eagerly accepted both and headed home to dream about their life together. She had her proverbial foot in the door, and by next week, he'd be calling her name and eating her hot buttered rolls.

Wilhelm was waiting for her with a pint of lager and a wide leather strap as she climbed through the window of her second-story bedroom. He ordered her to tell him where she had been and whom she had been with, but she refused. He said that her brother Boris had followed her across town where those animals lived and saw her socializing with them like her blood wasn't pure. He called her a whore and demanded once more that she confess whom she was going there to see. She declined, and he struck her again and again until she blacked out.

The next day, she stood bruised and battered with her father and her brothers next to Otto Potoshnik and vowed before God and man to be his wife and bear him many healthy sons. She lasted all of six days before she used the phone number tucked securely in the lining of her brassiere.

CHAPTER 56

He had listened to 'Trane, Miles, Bird, and even Ella to no avail. He could stall to every jazz genius in his expansive collection, but in the end, the music would cease and he'd still have to walk up the stairs and face his wife. Procrastinating any further would only make matters worse and prolong the inescapable. It was morning, and nothing had visibly changed. He was a mortician with a wife and a life he never should have had.

He didn't know why this exchange with Mercy felt distinctly different. They'd had arguments before and always managed to navigate their way back to the status quo, but he sensed that the status quo had changed. He felt the energy twirling around the house, reverberating off the walls, dancing to a rhythm he was loath to remember. He strode out of his office and took the stairs two at a time. There were things that needed to be said, and he'd promised the Almighty that he would stay in the present and bear witness to his life truthfully and without reservation. It was time he told her the truth. It was time he opened his heart and confronted one of his biggest mistakes.

When he arrived, she was waiting for him, fully clothed and strangely calm. He'd expected her to yell until her throat closed and demand as always what she knew he was incapable of giving her. He'd anticipated a scene and had prepared for the worst but found that he had to adjust to a new reality, a different Mercy, a Mercy whom he did not know. He tensed. He didn't like surprises ever. They caught you off guard and left you questioning your own truth. It was best to know what was coming around the corner. He would have had a chance that way—to survive, to be a better man—if he had known what to expect. Lucius had recently surmised that there had to be more to life than merely surviving the unwanted surprises that caught him off guard and enduring the bombshells that he should have seen coming a mile away. The space between them was heavy—laden with a lifetime of unfulfilled needs and countless disappointments. He fought back tears and acknowledged his failings.

"I never loved you," he whispered.

"I know," she said. "I know."

CHAPTER 57

They met often, and always at his small house in South Dallas. They figured no one would ever find her there in the colored section of town, sprawled across his bed. Her father didn't speak to her much anymore except to make some snide remarks about her penchant for dark meat. Leaving was easy: her husband, Otto, was clueless to her clandestine wanderings. He didn't know anything about her and didn't care, either. He only concerned himself with their newly gifted shares in her family's business, impressing her father, and of course sauerkraut. They had been married for four months and still had not consummated their ramshackle union. Otto asked her out of habit to oblige him every few days or so, and she always politely declined, preferring to knead dough or wash the walls instead.

Meanwhile, she and Verdell made love every chance an opportunity presented itself. She didn't believe in wasting precious time, and neither did he. She baked him various German delights, and he introduced her to delicious pleasures like collard greens and hot-water cornbread, red velvet cake, and buttermilk biscuits. She ate heartily, loved intensely, and promised him the world. He pleased her and pledged never to let her go. She thought she had her life all figured out. The pregnancy changed everything.

Unlike some women who step out on their spouses and become pregnant, Leezel Diezman knew without a doubt that the baby inside her belonged to her lover. As she had never had intercourse with her own husband, passing the child off as his was out of the question. She confided in Verdell that she was in the family way, and like a gentleman, he offered to marry her right and proper. In another lifetime, that solution would have worked if she weren't a white girl in Texas and already married. She found herself in quite a conundrum. Her options were limited, and time was not going to accommodate her needs.

As much as the thought revolted her, Leezel decided to return Otto's unwanted advances, convince him that he had the world's most powerful sperm, and pray that the baby resembled her and only her. It was possible. She was pale even for a white girl, and Verdell was so fair. She formulated a plan and immediately felt better about her chances for success. When the time came and she had saved enough money to open her own bakery, she and the baby would leave Otto, and no one would be the wiser. She'd start her own business and run her own life in her way on her terms. So on Monday nights between eight fifteen and eight twenty-two, she opened her legs and gritted her teeth. Self-worth clashed with pride, and pride evaporated with logic. A lie was born, and God help her, wrapping her mind around it was easier than she'd anticipated. By the end of Leezel Diezman's first trimester, she'd convinced her oddly shaped husband that he didn't repulse her at all, and Otto, in turn, told a surprised Wilhelm Diezman that he was going to be a grandfather.

Percival noticed that the white girl didn't frequent the Bala-mikki as much as she used to, and neither did the redbone. Something was amiss with those two, and he'd already sensed the outcome, smelled it like rain. The gal Leezel was a different kind of woman, and Verdell would be lucky if he didn't get shot messing around with them immigrant white folk. He'd heard that the gal's daddy was a mean ole son of a bitch, and that husband of hers was as dumb as a bucket of rocks. Hell, a man had to be an idiot not to know his wife was slipping and sliding through town with another fella grinning all the damn time. He sipped his rum and coke and listened to an animated Thelonious Monk grunt and groan through a lively tune called "Straight, No Chaser." He tapped his foot to the rhythm and thought of Baby Marseli, what he'd heard and what he'd seen earlier that day. He'd been standing outside the kitchen sneaking purple tulips onto the back porch for Baby when he overheard her speaking to her mother, Oceola Moon. Now he knew along with everyone else in the house that she conversed with her dead mama from time to time, but it was the first time he'd witnessed the one-sided dialogue with his own eyes.

"Mama, I had that dream again last night, the one where I was reaching for that child. Um-hmmm. I know it was only a dream, but it was so real. I woke up again wanting, wishing for something I know I'm not supposed to have. Yes, I accept who I am and what I was meant for in this lifetime, but that doesn't mean I don't ever think about what could have been, wonder what it would be like to have a child of my own. My time's passing, I know that. But don't worry about me. I'll do what I always do, say my prayers and be thankful. I am grateful, mama. I'm grateful for everything you ever taught me."

It was as if Baby could see her own mother the way she spoke, answered, and spoke again. He knew he shouldn't have remained and intruded on her privacy, but he was compelled to stay there crouched underneath the windowsill until she was done and her mama's spirit was gone. Witnessing Baby Marseli have a conversation like that with thin air scared him a little at first, until he reminded himself that all of Dallas thought him peculiar as well, and he felt perfectly normal—most of the time, anyway. He'd left then in deep thought wishing that he could do more, praying to the good Lord for a miracle. Baby Marseli had been helping people all of her life, treating folks when no one else would. She was an angel walking, and all he could do was bring her pretty flowers in a jar.

Percival ordered another rum and coke. He had a tall order to fill. Somewhere out there, there was a child without a mama or a mama who didn't want her child. He braced himself for the work ahead, because the joy of his heart required much more than purple tulips to make her happy.

CHAPTER 58

"Ms. Culpepper, as you can see, Dahlia needs serious psychological help, and I can't help her if you take her to Dallas."

"Well, Dr. Kelly, you're just going to have to help her when she returns. Her life is here; her husband and child are here. Trust me, she'll be back."

"Perhaps I should have a session with her alone. I think it would be beneficial."

"I know you do; however, I'm going to do what I should have done a long time ago. Wrap it up, Dr. Kelly, we've got someplace to go."

Aunt Baby felt a surge of confidence. She'd watched Dr. Kelly work for more than two hours and realized her own power. She didn't have any fancy Harvard degree, but she knew what had to be done here. His way was to keep Dahlia here talking for hours about nonsense until she experienced some kind of breakthrough. That was the word he'd used. Well, what if she didn't respond to him at all? What if she kept talking for days, weeks, and years? Phoebe was strong now and only seemed to be getting stronger by the minute. Aunt Baby resolved to help her niece the only way she knew how. She walked out of the office and dug around in her purse for her cell phone. Dahlia's cure was three states away, and Baby couldn't waste any more time getting her where she was supposed to be. She dialed home, and when Dante answered, she knew immediately that something was wrong. "Brother, can you hear me?" She held the phone close to her ear and waited for a response.

"Mom, I've been waiting for your call. How is Dahlia? Is everything all right?"

"What's going on down there, Dante?"

"Nothing that you need to be worried about. Did you see the baby, Isabel? I bet she's a big girl now."

"Boy, don't you lie to me, you hear? I've got enough trouble on my hands without you telling tales."

"Well, I think you should know that Dahlia's husband is down here."

"Michael's there at the house with Lucius?"

"Not at the moment. He's most likely with Percival; at least, he was last night."

"Lord have mercy. Percival is talking to Michael? I knew something was going on what with the way my big toe has been hurting."

"Mom, Percival invited him to his house. Michael is probably there right now getting a lesson on Culpepper family history."

"Has he spoken to Lucius yet? Has Lucius told him anything?"

"Not that I'm aware of, and anyway I don't think it's Lucius that we need to be worried about these days."

"Dante."

"Yeah?"

"Is that all?"

"Yeah, Mom, that's all."

"There's nothing else you'd like to tell me?"

"No."

"I see. Well, then I need you to do a favor for me, son."

"Anything. What is it?"

"Call the airline and get me two plane tickets."

"Are you sure? I mean, how in the world did you talk Dahlia into coming back here?"

"You just be at the airport to pick us up and let me worry about Dahlia."

"Okay. Give me a few minutes and I'll call you back with the flight information."

"Dante."

"Yes, mom?"

"Hurry, son. We need to come home, and we need to come home fast."

Baby closed her phone and narrowed her eyes. Something was brewing back home, and Dante was keeping it from her. *Well,* she thought, *it's about time for this mess to come to an end.* She was worn out, and the real work hadn't even begun yet. She wasn't surprised that Michael had found his way to Dallas. She'd always figured he'd show up sooner or later demanding answers to questions Dahlia would never have tolerated. So it was for the best that he was there, and she hoped Lucius would speak to him like family, open up about everything. Baby thought of Percival and immediately smiled. Instinctively she knew he was laying the groundwork for her, doing what he could to make her task easier. He had always looked out for her, and she loved him for that. She would need his help when she got home. She would need everybody's help to do what must be done.

Phoebe inspected her nails and called Dr. Kelly an incompetent English asshole for the third time. This entire mind-probing shit was getting on her nerves. The fool actually asked her if he could speak to Dahlia. He'd even asked her in a couple of different ways, as if she were retarded or something. Jesus, she didn't know what part of "hell, no" he didn't understand. He, too, obviously thought she had "dumb fuck" scrawled across her forehead. The man was exasperating, and she wanted to pop him in the neck one good time and watch him choke to death, but she figured that would get her locked up in the county somewhere. Baby would stick it to her good, too, probably call the police herself. She knew the old woman would do anything to get Dahlia back, but Dahlia was gone to a place that neither of them could reach. Why couldn't they both see that and accept her? Some people needed to be hit in the head with a brick.

She had to get out of here. She was tired, and her head was beginning to hurt. Answering stupid questions and eyeballing Baby had given her a migraine. She had to find Michael before these two turned her into an alcoholic. He would help her and tell everybody to leave her the hell alone. She stood and reached for her jacket. Phoebe had had enough of people telling her what to do. She turned to face Baby, who'd returned. "I'm through here, and I'm not coming back. This was a waste of my time."

"I agree," Baby answered.

"Really," Phoebe responded sarcastically. "That makes me feel so much better."

Dr. Kelly interrupted. "Ms. Culpepper, Dahlia . . . er . . . Phoebe—" Both women silenced him with one glance.

"Phoebe," Baby called, oblivious to Dr. Kelly's attempts to control their conversation.

"What?"

"You feel good, do you? Feel like you're in control?"

"Hell, yeah."

"You feel strong, right—like you can handle anything, go anywhere, and face anyone?" Baby stared so intently into Phoebe's eyes that Phoebe was the first to turn away.

"This is bullshit," she spat. "I'm going to look for Michael. I'm going to find my husband."

"You mean Dahlia's husband, don't you?" Baby continued gently. "I think you should come on back home to Dallas with me tonight."

"And why would I ever do that? Why on earth would I go anywhere with you?"

"Because home is where you began, and home is where Michael is waiting for you right now."

CHAPTER 59

It was raining where Dahlia was—stinging rain, the kind that you sought refuge from, the kind that drove you to higher ground. She was folded in a corner unprotected from the elements with nowhere to run except through the first door that stood tall and thick waiting for her. Suddenly, being in the rain wasn't as comforting as it used to be. This time, the deluge began as a trickle, a summer misting of sorts, and eventually transformed into a downpour. Water collected around her ankles and slowly inched its way toward her knees. Soon she would drown, without incident and without fanfare. She blinked salty tears, and the water was at her waist. Panic embraced her, and she willed herself to stop shaking. Still it rained harder, and it was cold, so very cold. She found it difficult to breathe, but she managed to move forward a little at a time, even though the water threatened her survival.

She stepped toward the door, and the onslaught lessened. Relief and fear collided inside her soul, and she was temporarily paralyzed with indecision. Her momentary lack of movement brought the water to her chest, and she wondered how long it would take for her to die. Die, death, gone. The concept floated around and filled the space she occupied. She allowed the possibility to envelop her senses completely and without hesitation. One word traveled through her, and she clung to it, wrapped her heart around it like a life preserver. "No," she said, when the water beckoned her home. "No."

She waded closer to the door and was amazed at how quickly the water receded. She wished there were someone, anyone, to hold her hand, but she was alone in a space that didn't allow visitors. She reached the massive door and nearly swam back to the corner. She was terrified, and being washed away in a flood almost seemed preferable to exploring what was on the other side of the rain. Her head throbbed and she was exhausted from the journey, but she closed her eyes, grasped the doorknob, and turned.

"Hello, baby doll," the woman said on the other side. "I've been waiting for you."

Dahlia looked around and wondered where she was. Strange, she was eleven again, and she felt whole and alive, innocent and restless. The nice lady motioned her forward and reached for her hand.

"Baby doll, do you remember who I am?"

Dahlia shook her head "no" but felt pangs of familiarity.

"Here, sweetness, let me help you."

And then, like magic, memories from her life that she'd believed were long gone danced all around her. Images reflected off the walls, pranced over the pink canopy looming in front of her, and shimmied across the floor.

"Yes, I remember you now," Dahlia whispered, with a wide smile. "What happened to you, Mama? Where did you go?"

CHAPTER 60

Leezel swelled, Otto beamed, and her father was uncharacteristically silent. Spending time with Verdell had proved to be difficult, but she was able to steal a moment away now and again throughout her pregnancy. Everything seemed normal at home, and her plan appeared to be working thus far; however, something troubled her. It wasn't any one thing that she could put her finger on exactly; it was more like a feeling that she couldn't quite articulate. At first, she thought maybe she was overreacting due to an abundance of female hormones, but that wasn't her style, so she waddled from day to day and hoped that the feeling of doom that was growing inside of her with the baby would vanish along with her leg cramps.

Percival Tweed was nobody's fool. There were rumors circulating all over Deep Bellum about a blond-haired German girl keeping company with a pop-eyed yellow hammer. Percival decided to pay a visit to the German café one day in North Dallas in the white section of town. Under normal circumstances, a black man would have been stopped three or four times just for standing on the sidewalk over there, but Percival didn't concern himself with other people's stupidity. He had a feeling he simply couldn't shake, so he walked in the door and asked to speak to Miss Leezel. Customers stopped what they were doing and gawked at the odd-looking black man with the wide-brimmed hat who'd strolled into a white café like it was the most normal thing in the world.

"Yes, may I help you?" Leezel inquired, aware that her father was watching.

"I come here to inquire about that bread you're baking." Silence. The girl's father began to walk toward them from the other end of the bakery.

"You want to buy some of my bread?" she asked, confused.

"Ifn you ever decide to be charitable, Miss Leezel, I know a place where you can deliver that bread safe and sound. I know someone who would appreciate all of it, love it like she made it herself."

Three men surrounded him, and the father growled, "Get on outta here, boy. We don't serve your kind here."

Percival ignored the pink-faced man and continued to address Leezel. "Ifn you need to find me to donate that bread, and ifn you need my help, my name is Percival—"

Unable to control himself any longer, Wilhelm jumped in front of Percival and in so doing knocked the hat from Percival's head. "*Gehen Sie von heir aus der neger!* Now git on away from here. She doesn't need your help, freak, and she's not baking you or anybody like you any goddamn bread."

"Pappa, please, don't say such things," Leezel pleaded. "All he wants is some bread."

Percival Tweed retrieved his hat from the floor and turned to face Wilhelm Diezman. He removed his black sunglasses, something that he never did, and answered him directly, flashing unsettling yellow eyes. "I'm not a freak," he said quietly. "And you ought not to use the Lord's name in such a disrespectful way, Mr. Diezman. He won't like it. He won't like it at all."

"Is that right?" Wilhelm hissed.

"Well, something tells me you'll be able to ask him yourself soon enough." Percival nodded in Leezel's direction. "Tweed, Miss Leezel," he continued, as he walked calmly out of the bakery. "Percival Tweed."

Percival's mama, Caldonia Tweed—God rest her soul—had always told him to look for the pieces in people that weren't necessarily obvious. "Ifn you pay attention," she'd said, "soon enough you'll see what's missing." Something was definitely missing in Leezel Diezman's crusty old daddy. Even in the worst of men, he'd seen a part of them that was redeemable—a love for their family, a love for their God. But this man was different in a way that prompted Percival to say a few prayers to Jehovah on Leezel's behalf. Wilhelm Diezman lacked all that was decent and honorable in a man. He was evil, and evil wasn't ready to retire anytime soon.

CHAPTER 61

"Lucius, there is something that I need to tell you, something that I should have told you a long time ago."

"No, me first. Let me say what I have to say, or I'll never say it. I took advantage of you, Mercy. I used you to take away my pain. I used you to help me forget what happened, forget Reva, Dahlia, the kids."

"It hasn't worked, has it, Lucius?"

"No, it hasn't, even after all these years. I genuinely believed I was doing the right thing at the time. No, that's bullshit. I—"

"Stop it."

"Mercy, I'm sorry."

"I said, stop it. Stop apologizing to me," Mercy screamed.

"What?" Lucius interjected, confused. "Isn't this what you've wanted—for me to talk to you—for me to be honest about my feelings?"

Mercy began to laugh at the irony of it all. Now, after all this time, after she had compounded her sin and betrayed him once more with his brother, he was actually apologizing to her.

"What is it? What is so damned funny?" Lucius demanded.

"Trust me, Lucius, if I don't laugh, I'll fall apart again, and we both know how much you hate that. You didn't use me, Lucius. You didn't do anything to me that I didn't deserve."

"Don't be ridiculous, Mercy. I was thirty-one years old and you were barely eighteen when we married. I was a grown man with grown-up problems and responsibilities, and you were a child—seven years older than my own daughter, for God's sake. You didn't know what you were getting into. You didn't sign up for this, for me." Lucius waved his arms around and stared out the window. He didn't want to have this conversation. He couldn't face her anymore.

"Did you know, Lucius, that I've had a crush on you since I was twelve years old? I had a crush on a grown man, a married man with a family. It's funny, I know. I was a little girl then—a foolish little girl. I should have gotten over you, been attracted to boys my own age, gone to college, and made something of myself, but I didn't; I couldn't. It was you, Lucius. My life has always been about you until now."

"What are you saying?"

"I'm saying that I came to you. I came to this house of my own free will. I asked my parents to help me get a job here, and I knew exactly what I was getting into—or at least, I thought I did. I've made some mistakes, terrible mistakes."

"No, Mercy, the mistakes have been mine. I had no right to expect so much of you. I had no right to ask you to save me."

"You're not hearing me. That's the problem with you, Lucius. You don't know how to listen. You can't feel anybody's pain except your own. I have to tell you something about that day."

Lucius finally turned to face her. "Leave it alone, Mercy. That day didn't have a damn thing to do with you."

"No, Lucius, you're wrong. That day had everything to do with me."

"Why are you bringing this up now? What is the point of bringing this up now? You were so young then. You probably don't even remember it anymore. For me, it's different. It's always been different. I remember it, dream it, relive it whether I choose to or not. Living without remembering for me is impossible. Why can't you understand that?"

The telling of repressed revelations seemed to be happening in slow motion. She saw her husband's mouth moving, but the words no longer made any sense. He didn't know what he was saying. He couldn't fathom what she had done. Strange, this wasn't how she thought it would be when she told him, but so much had transpired, and she couldn't adopt any more lies. She wanted to be free from her life, from her deceptions, and from this house. He would hate her and so would Dante, but their collective hatred was a price she was now willing to pay for her life back—for her freedom. She swallowed hard. "Lucius," she said softly, "that day, Dahlia—"

"I don't want to do this!" he shouted, and began to walk away. She reached for him, he stumbled into her arms, and Dante burst through the door.

"Lucius," he declared, wide-eyed and out of breath, "Dahlia's on her way home."

CHAPTER 62

Leezel grabbed her abdomen and begged the nurse, Mrs. Stroud, at Baylor Hospital to give her something—anything—to help alleviate the throbbing pain. The baby was coming, and she writhed in agony while it struggled to escape her womb. She called out for Verdell and wished he were with her instead of her dim-witted husband and father. Her prayer for a swift delivery was answered, and she was in labor for a mere three hours.

"You're a very lucky girl," the nurse said.

Leezel pushed and breathed and pushed. "It's a boy, Mrs. Potoshnik!" the doctor exclaimed and smiled. And suddenly his smile was replaced by an expression she couldn't quite identify.

"What?" she asked, fearful for her son. "What's the matter with my baby?" No one answered, and then she knew. By the looks on their faces, she knew. The now stoic-faced nurse handed her the whimpering child, and Leezel wept at the sight of her perfect, light-brown, green-eyed, full-lipped baby boy.

Three days later, no one uttered a word on the ride home, and her father refused to look at her or the baby. She wasn't surprised and prepared herself for the worst. She imagined that he wanted to kill her. Otto, of course, followed Wilhelm's lead and ignored her attempts at casual conversation. There wasn't really anything of substance that she could say without acknowledging that she'd just delivered a black baby who obviously didn't belong to her husband. Maybe no one would ever speak of it. Maybe she and the child would both survive the night to see tomorrow, and maybe she expected too much.

Later, when they believed she was sleeping, she heard them whispering about her, plotting in low tones to do God knows what. She was in pain, frightened, and she didn't know what to do or whom to call. At her urging, Verdell had left town for a while for his own good, so she was alone with a child to protect in a house with men who thought her an abomination. They saw her as something worse than a whore for what she had done. "No one must ever know of this disgrace. *Keinem muss diesen Kind sehen,*" she heard her father tell Otto in German. "No one must ever see dis child." She braced herself. It was only a matter of time before he came for the baby. Leezel nursed her precious boy and picked up the phone. There was someone who would help her—someone who could save her son. If only she knew how to find him. If only she remembered his name.

Percival awoke to a ringing phone in a cold sweat. Creole Kersey from the Balamikki was on the line, mad as a wet hen for being disturbed by some crazy white girl over nonsense. "What the hell you doing getting caught up in Popeye's mess, man? That white girl's going to get you both killed," he'd hollered into the phone. "Even you have to watch yourself on this one, Percival. Man, that daddy of hers don't like no bloods. Heard tell he was one of them Nazis back in the day." Percival dressed quickly. He didn't know what was happening, but he knew that he had to get to her fast. She had tracked him down in the middle of the night, and that meant that she was in a heap of trouble over that baby. He hurried—drove like the wind and prayed that he would get there in time. Sweet Jesus, let him get there in time.

"Oh, my good God" was all that he could say when he arrived

at the Diezman place. A man was screaming, sparks were flying, and the back of the house was already filled with smoke. He ran around the back calling out for Leezel, hoping that she wasn't there—praying that she had phoned Creole Kersey from somewhere else, anywhere else. He stepped over a man's charred body still twitching in the doorway and discovered Leezel in a room shrieking, desperately trying to smother a flaming pillow with her bare hands. Only it wasn't a pillow; it was that precious little baby on fire, and neither of them could stop screaming.

CHAPTER 63

Leezel Diezman. Leezel Diezman. Dante rolled the name back
and forth in his head and tried to remember where he had heard
it. It was 3:00 a.m., and sleeping at this point was not a realistic
option. He'd been in the closet with Mercy for more than an
hour giving her everything he had again and again, and even the
thought of her legs wrapped around him wasn't enough to calm
him down. He was exhausted from their passionate encounter,
and yet he knew when he'd had her straddled against the wall
that his night was just beginning.

It was only a matter of time before he found his way to the
prep area. It was silent and peaceful, and he worked best that
way. The jazz greats had retired for the night, and so had his
brother. He was grateful for the solitude. Seeing her was something he needed to do alone. On some level, though, from the
moment he'd read her words, he felt her presence close to him—
only he didn't realize how close. He searched for the paperwork
and finally found it in Lucius's desk, which was unusual. It wasn't
where it belonged, but then neither was he. Everything seemed
to be out of place. It wasn't necessary to read the particulars, but
he did, anyway—absorbed their contents deep into his marrow.

His mother was in this room in drawer number four waiting patiently to say good-bye.

He clicked on the soft overhead lights and touched cool steel. "I can do this," he told himself. "I have to do this." He took a deep breath, pulled open the drawer, and looked at a face that mirrored his own.

"I don't hate you anymore," he said calmly. "I don't understand everything that happened that night, and by the grace of God, I don't remember, but I know you loved me. I can feel it now." He paused and looked around. "I've had a good life here, Leezel, and you chose the best mother for me. I want to thank you for that." He reached underneath the sheet and caressed her hands. They were hands that bore a lifetime of scars. They were hands that had held him once. "I wish I could have known you," he continued. "I wish that I could remember the time you sat next to me on that plane, but I don't. Jesus, I don't. I wish that I could tell you how much I loved your bread and how much I looked forward to it every week. Thank you for thinking of me. And God knows I wish more than anything that I could hold you now and tell you that I forgive you." Dante felt himself breaking from the inside out and leaned to kiss her on the cheek. It was then that he noticed her feet, and his breakdown became complete. "Oh, mother," he cried softly. "What happened to you?"

CHAPTER 64

Aunt Baby settled into a window seat in first class. She hated planes and couldn't believe that she was actually belted in a 747 about to fly home with the other one. She rang for the stewardess, because Lord, she needed a drink desperately. The doctor had been none too happy about seeing them go, but she'd promised him that Dahlia would return soon, ready to begin repairing her life. It was all coming together now, and she was glad—relieved, in fact, that the worst of it was still to come. Their lives were moving forward again, and that was what was most important. Stagnation and denial had cost them so much, but after today, their family would no longer be immobilized by the events of one tragic day. They could move on, forgive, and learn to love one another again. That was the best she could hope for. That was what she lived for.

She watched Phoebe nod off in the seat next to her and wondered what Percival was doing. Did he think of her as much as she thought of him? Did he wonder what she was doing, and did he sense that her heart was breaking? Did he know that she loved him and that she always had? No. Most likely his mind was somewhere else far away sharing her family's saga, remembering once again what they had all tried a lifetime to forget. Phoebe seemed ready, though, to waltz down memory lane, or at least she claimed she was completely in control up until the time they both boarded the plane. She'd been complaining of a migraine ever since they left Dr. Kelly's office, and that was a good sign. Headaches meant change, and headaches meant that baby doll was fighting the good fight. Her Dahlia was strong, and Baby sensed that she was trying to climb out of whatever hell she had put herself in. Even though Dr. Kelly told her it was a mistake to bring Dahlia home, Baby was sure it was the only real option. Her mama had always told her that, to cure an illness, you had to get to the root cause of the problem. If she attacked the root cause and healed it, then it stood to reason that Dahlia had a chance to reclaim her life. Exhausted and slightly tipsy from Puerto Rican rum, Baby began to doze off. She took one last glace at Phoebe and worried that she would try to run but relaxed immediately. They were on a plane coasting at an altitude of thirty thousand feet. Where in the hell was the heifer going to go?

Round and round and round they went, holding hands and giggling until their bellies hurt. And then the laughter was replaced with pain. It seemed as if every inch of Dahlia's body was convulsing, and she cried out for help. "Mama, Mama, make it go away. Make it stop hurting."

"I can't, my precious. The only person who can make it stop hurting is you."

"I don't understand."

"Stand up straight, baby doll, like your Aunt Baby taught you, and walk with me."

Dahlia shook her head "no" but allowed her mother to guide

her. Her mama led her toward another door, and she froze. She was tired already; she wanted to rest, and she wanted the ache in her head to disappear.

"If you come with me, you'll feel better, I promise."

"Okay. Mama?"

"Hmmm."

"Do you love me?"

"Yes, darling, but not enough—not like I should have."

"Why not?"

"Well, because I was sick way down in the inside where you can't see it."

"Mama?"

"Shhhhh, baby doll. We're almost there."

"Where are we going?"

"To your brother's room, my love. He's been waiting for you for a long time."

CHAPTER 65

"My God. So what happened in that house?" Michael questioned incredulously.

"I don't rightly know till this day. We didn't speak of it then, and we only spoke once more after that night. Leezel Diezman handed me that burned-up baby, and you know, I don't think she ever really intended to give that child up, but it was for the best, considering what happened. He was so tiny, and he didn't look like a baby anymore after what they had done to him. She begged me to help her save him and to keep quiet about what I'd seen. I wrapped the poor child up as best as I could and left him on the doorstep of the one woman—the only woman—who could give him a chance at a normal life."

"Aunt Baby."

"Yes."

"Does anyone in the family know that it was you who left him on the porch?"

"You do, and someone else will soon enough. If you ask me, that's already two people too many."

"Mr. Tweed, this was a fascinating story, but I don't understand what any of it has to do with my wife."

"Well, it doesn't have anything to do with her directly, but I figure now you're prepared."

"Prepared for what?"

"Everything else you need to know."

"I just want to know about my wife, her life, and her parents."

"I can't tell you nothing about that, son, but I know someone who can. Come on, now. We 'bout done here."

Michael stood and followed Percival out the door.

"Where are we going?" he asked.

"Up yonder to the house. It's time you met the rest of Dahlia's family."

Lucius paced and contemplated what he was going to say to his firstborn. They hadn't laid eyes on each other in more than fifteen years. And as much as he missed her, he was terrified of facing her after all this time. Dahlia, his beautiful Dahlia—losing her had nearly killed him. Mercy and Dante were trying to tell him something, but he didn't hear them, and soon they were no longer in his field of vision. The whole house was weeping around him, and in moments, he was standing over his wife, Reva, or what was left of her. Abruptly, someone grabbed him, and he was once again forced into the present. He looked at Mercy and addressed Dante.

"My baby is coming home," he said.

"I know. I don't know how Mama did it," Dante answered.

"It doesn't matter. This time, I'm not letting her leave until I make things right." Mercy began to cry. Both men turned to her in surprise. "What's the matter, Mercy girl?" Dante asked softly.

"Oh God" was all she could say.

Lucius left Mercy and Dante when he heard the doorbell. He raced toward the sound, struggling desperately to maintain his composure. It couldn't be Dahlia and Aunt Baby already. He opened the door with Dante not too far behind.

"Morning, Lucius," Percival said. "This here is somebody I think you ought to meet."

"Percival, this isn't the best time. My daughter's coming home today. Dahlia is finally coming home."

"Mr. Culpepper," Milky interrupted, "you've spoken to Dahlia?"

"No, he hasn't," Dante interjected. "I spoke to my mother, Aunt Baby. She's been in Pasadena with your wife all this time. They're on a plane right now. They should be landing in a couple of hours."

"You two know each other?" Lucius asked, confused.

"Yes, we've met briefly," Milky answered, staring at Dante. He quickly refocused and offered his hand. "I'm Michael Chang, sir, Dahlia's husband."

"Michael has been spending quality time with Percival Tweed since he's been here," Dante added, avoiding Percival's eyes. Lucius glanced at Percival. "Did you tell him everything?" Lucius asked quietly.

"No," Percival answered. "Not my story to tell. I'm going on home now. I've done my part here."

"What in the hell is going on?" Michael yelled. "What in God's name have you people done to my wife?"

"Come in, Michael," Lucius said, and placed his hand on Michael's shoulder. "We should talk."

CHAPTER 66

Dahlia held on to her mother's hand and stared at the little boy playing with his trains. She didn't know him, and her first instinct was to bury her head in her mother's skirt like a child. She looked down at herself again. She was some kind of strange child-adult construct. She resembled a child but was starting to feel more like a grown-up with every passing moment. It was frightening and liberating at the same time.

The boy appeared to be about seven or eight, and seemed quite content to remain where he was. He didn't notice them initially lingering on the outside looking in, but then he saw her and smiled. A tiny smile at first—you know, the way kids do sometimes when they're up to something mischievous. She grinned back and walked toward him. He looked familiar and smelled like home.

"Come play with me, baby doll. You never play with me anymore," he whined.

"That's funny, I don't remember playing with you at all. What's your name?" She looked to her mother for help. "I think he knows me."

"Of course he does, baby doll. That's your brother, Jazz," Reva announced.

"Who are you talking to, crazy girl?" Jazz asked with a laugh.

"Oh, baby doll, he can't see me."

Dahlia picked up a train and started pushing it around the track.

"Choo-choo," Jazz began in a singsong voice. "Choo-choo-choo-choo-choo."

A room was opening in her mind—a room that had been sealed for most of her life. "Keep out," the voice said harshly. "There's nothing for you here." Ignoring the enemy within seemed to be less difficult. She railed against herself, straining to recall what had been lost. New memories sprang forth—so many that she became dizzy. The harder she pushed, the more they came, one right after the other. One minute she was in her purple pajamas helping a man decorate a tree. The next she was sitting at a table drinking hot chocolate and showing a little girl how to tie her shoes. And then children were calling her name and squealing in delight. She picked them up and twirled them around. She wasn't a stranger; she was somebody's sister, and she was adored. Dahlia looked at the boy through new eyes and realized that he was exactly the way she remembered. "You're right, Jazz," she said, as she reached for him. "I never play with you anymore."

He wrapped his little arms around her, and they laughed and played for a long time. And then he was gone, and she grasped achingly for the space where he had been. The feeling of pure loss was so powerful that she almost blacked out from the intensity of the moment. "Where did he go?" she asked Reva, who was now sitting crossed-legged in front of her.

"Home, where he belongs."

"I had a home once."

"Yes, you did," Reva answered. "And you still do. You just

have to find your way back there. You see, you're lost now, and that's all right. We all get lost sometimes."

"Have you ever been lost, Mama?"

"Oh, yes. And once I became so lost that I couldn't find my way back home."

"What did you do?"

"I came here and waited for you."

"What in the hell for?" the voice interrupted.

"Did you hear that?" Dahlia asked.

"No," Reva answered, and vanished before her eyes.

"Over here, crazy," the voice continued, but it wasn't just a voice anymore. The sound was emanating from the mouth of a woman standing in the doorway.

"Who are you?" Dahlia asked.

"What, you haven't figured that out yet? Christ, you're slow."

Dahlia narrowed her eyes. "I remember you. You used to be my friend, but you're not my friend anymore."

"Aaaah, that's not true, and to prove it, I'm going to give you a little piece of advice." The woman began to walk toward her, and Dahlia cowered.

"What is it? What do you want from me?"

"Look, doll, stay out of business that doesn't concern you. You can't go home anymore, and you know you can't listen to your mama. She was crazy then, and she's still crazy now. You can't trust a word she says."

"And what about you?" Dahlia asked, willing herself to stand and face the stranger who knew her.

"Me? Well, you've always been able to trust me."

"You're the voice."

"Um-hmmmm."

"I don't even know your name."

"Yes, you do," taunted the woman. "Say it."

Dahlia hesitated and then spoke softly. "Phoebe," she mumbled.

"Come on, girlfriend. Say it with conviction. Say it like you mean it."

"Phoebe," Dahlia said louder. "You're Phoebe."

"Yes," Phoebe answered with a smirk. "My, my, my, I think she's got it."

CHAPTER 67

Percival walked the long way home. He couldn't remember the last time he'd been so fatigued. He'd said more in the last few hours than he had in several years. And yet he was far from being finished. There was more to be said, and he welcomed the release. Since he was doing all this communicating, he figured he might as well free everything else he'd been holding in for a spell.

He reached his house and left the front door ajar; Dante wouldn't be far behind with a thousand questions. When he looked at Dante now, it was hard for him to imagine the baby that he used to be. His survival was a miracle, and Percival thanked God every day that he'd gotten to Leezel when he did. By now, he guessed Dante had read the letter and figured out that his mama was lying up yonder only a few feet away. And as if that wasn't enough, the fool boy had gone and parked his car in somebody else's garage—his brother's garage, no less. Sweet Jesus on the cross, what a mess. Percival shook his head. These kids today just didn't have any respect for what was right and proper. He spoke aloud: "Dante Culpepper, what in the world were you thinking?"

"I've been asking myself that same question," Dante replied from the doorway. "Percival, I need to speak with you if you have a minute."

"I reckon you do, son." Percival motioned for Dante to sit down. "I reckon you do."

Dante removed the letter from his pocket. "She wrote that there was a fire. She said—"

"Look, son, I don't rightly know what's in that letter there. Your mama asked me to give it to you after she passed, and that's what I did. If it had been up to me, I wouldn't be discussing this now, but I figure you got a right to know where you come from. You know what she wanted you to know, and that's good enough for me."

"Can you tell me about her?"

Percival sighed and told Dante what he claimed he remembered about that night. He didn't tell him everything, though. He didn't see what good it would do for the boy to know that his grandfather had tried to burn him alive. Some secrets should never see the light of day, and Percival decided right then and there that what really happened that night would go to the grave with Leezel, where it belonged.

"I know this is plenty for you to handle right now, finding out about your mama and all, but I believe there are other matters you should be attending to and other folk you should be thinking about."

Dante opened his mouth to speak, but Percival held up his hand. "I know what you want from me, and I aim to give it to you, but you're going to have to clean this mess up you done got yourself into—and the sooner, the better. You and I both know that your mama will find out about you and Mercy by the end of the day, and I don't want Baby being hurt by any of this foolishness."

Dante looked Percival in the eyes at the mention of Mercy's

name. "I didn't mean for any of this to happen, and I can't begin to explain my feelings for her. It wasn't a casual thing for me. I—"

"Son, stop. You don't owe me any explanation. I know what it's like to love a woman your whole life, see her every day, and not be able to touch her—watch her in pain from a distance praying to the good Lord that you could hold her in your arms just once and make everything all right."

Dante stood and walked toward Percival. "Is there something I should know here?"

"I guess there is," Percival answered. "I love your mama, the woman who raised you, like I love my life, and I have been in love with her from the moment I laid eyes on her. If she'll have me, I swear I'll die trying to make her happy."

Neither man spoke for a while. The space between them vibrated with relief and opportunity, and each revealed more than he had anticipated. There was an invisible bond that connected them in a way that Dante would never understand. For most of his life, he had been suspicious of the albino but comforted by his presence at the same time. It was an unusual feeling that he was never quite able to identify. He thought that perhaps his reaction to Percival had something to do with the way Percival loved his mother, but now he knew without a doubt that it was something else; something inside him recognized the connection. They'd had more in common than he could ever have believed. He still wasn't sure how to process his own feelings about Leezel and Percival's involvement but he wanted to move forward from it once and for all, and he wanted his mother to be happy. She deserved that and more. After all, she would need someone to look after her when he left the business. Dante peered over into yellow eyes, eyes that had always seemed frighteningly familiar, and offered a gift. "Percival, I was wondering if you could do something else for me."

Percival met his gaze.

"I should stay around here and make sure that Lucius doesn't need any help. Could you pick up my mom and Dahlia from the airport?"

Percival smiled through tired eyes. "Yeah, son, I can manage that."

CHAPTER 68

Lucius sat across from his son-in-law and tried not to bombard him with a thousand questions. There was so much he wanted to know about Dahlia and Isabel, but he sensed that this wasn't the right moment for him to fish for information. This particular time and space belonged to him to do what he should have been doing all along. He didn't know where to begin, and hoped to God that he could honor the truth without losing himself in the process. He looked around his office and allowed a lifetime of pain to work its way out of his soul. "I was in here the day it happened, the day I got the call. It was right before Christmas, and Dahlia was eleven then."

"What happened, Mr. Culpepper?" Michael asked softly.

"Has Dahlia ever spoken about that day to you? Has she ever spoken about her mother, Reva?"

"No, she doesn't talk about this place or you or her family. She told me once that she was very young when her mother died. She also said that she had no memory of her at all."

Lucius closed his eyes. He wished he could erase Reva as easily, and Lord knows he'd tried, but she was everywhere. Sometimes he could even swear that he smelled her perfume curling around corners and lingering in the hallways. He longed to be rid of her, and he wished to God that he could stop hating her. Reva. The name alone tormented him. He strained to remember a time when he loved her. He must have loved her once—he was certain of it—but all he could remember was the day she died and took what was left of his life with her. Moments from that day often floated in front of him, sometimes like stills from a twisted dream, and he'd tried on numerous occasions to convince himself that they were someone else's recollections. But they haunted him just like Reva, and now they flooded his senses whole and intact, sewn together for him to see all over again.

"I remember I felt funny that morning, and I didn't know why. Nothing was visibly different, but I knew something was wrong. I could feel it. I don't know any other way to explain it to you. Dahlia's mother was sick and had been sick for quite some time. She had the kind of sickness that people don't like to talk about around here. Back then, there weren't any fancy names for what she had like there are now. We all thought that she was just a little touched in the head, but I know now that Reva was mentally ill. There, I've finally said it out loud. I swear I didn't realize that she was capable of hurting anyone—not like that, not my babies. My brother, Dante, had just come back from a trip, and I was happy he was home again. It was a busy day, and I was preoccupied with work. Six bodies needed to be laid to rest, and supplies had to be reordered. Aunt Baby was off somewhere, so I told Dahlia that it was her responsibility to watch her mother and her brother and sister."

"Wait a minute," Michael interrupted. "Are you telling me that Dahlia isn't an only child?"

"She wasn't then, but she is now." Lucius looked away as guilt enveloped him, creating a pain in his chest that was almost unbearable.

"Are you all right?" Michael inquired.

Lucius waved his hand and wiped the perspiration now trickling from his forehead. "What happened was my fault, and I blamed it on my eleven-year-old child. I should have been there. I should have been the one taking care of Reva, but I wasn't. I was preparing to bury my own children; I just didn't know it at the time."

Lucius remembered gripping the receiver in his right hand frozen in disbelief. "Mr. Culpepper, there's been an accident," the voice said on the other end of the line. And then Dante's voice: "Lucius, Reva's gone, and she took the children with her!" Everything happened so fast, and in the blink of an eye, his life as he knew it was over. One minute, he was a husband and the father of three, and the next, someone was telling him that everyone he loved was dead.

CHAPTER 69

Phoebe shifted uncomfortably in her first-class seat. Why the hell was she on an airplane anyway drinking cheap red wine? She couldn't believe she'd agreed to such bullshit, and for what? She should have refused Aunt Baby and waited for Michael at home. He would have returned eventually to get the kid, but no, she had to chase his ass down in Dallas of all places, like a suspicious housewife on a rampage. How pathetic. She rolled her eyes in disgust; she detested Texas—fucking hillbillies, all of them— and she couldn't stand the sight of any of those Culpepper bastards either. Michael better be there, or else she was going to show them what crazy really was, give them all something else to remember. She was through playing head games with people. It was time to move on with her life and finally be rid of excess emotional baggage, but then again, there was a battle brewing with an old friend, and she planned on being an active participant.

It had been years since she'd been back on Haven Street, but that didn't matter. She was sure nothing had changed for the better. People were still dying, the albino was probably digging his way to China by now, and Lucius was most likely shoving cotton up somebody's ass. No one there had a clue about her or what she was willing to do to protect herself. Crazy didn't scare her. She was born of madness, and felt quite at home in chaos. And now that she thought about it, there was one person she looked forward to seeing again, one person who thought she'd gotten away with murder. She smiled at Aunt Baby and pulled her seat back into the upright position for their descent into Dallas/Forth Worth International Airport. Phoebe reached in her purse and refreshed her lipstick. She had a man to claim and a long-overdue appointment with a bitch in a red dress.

Dahlia awoke in a room covered from floor to ceiling with mirrors. As much as it troubled her, she was forced to look at herself from every angle. Soon her reflections morphed into different versions of Dahlias she'd once been. The experience was overwhelming, and she strove to remain conscious and focused. She tried closing her eyes periodically but realized that ignoring what was in front of her face was only a temporary solution. When she was finally able to gaze at the multiple reflections without fear, she stared into the eyes of a grown woman. Her head began to ache again, so she sat down and wondered how her mother had ended up in a place like this.

"I didn't feel too well," her mother said, as she walked in out of nowhere.

"I was just thinking about you."

"I know," Reva answered. "Every time you think of me, I can feel it no matter where I am."

"I can't feel you."

"If you really wanted to, you could. Remembering me hasn't been a very pleasant experience for you, and I'm sorry for that, but I'm afraid it can't be helped under the circumstances. I was sick, honey, and my sickness had nothing to do with you."

"I don't feel well most of the time either. Maybe I belong here."

"No! Don't ever let me hear you say that again," Reva said sternly. "This is no place for you. You are stronger than I ever was, and you can go home whenever you choose. The power is yours."

"I'm scared."

Reva smiled and opened her arms. "You can do this, baby doll; you're almost there. Hold on." Dahlia laid her head on her mother's lap, and for a moment, it felt like home.

She was alone again, standing in front of another door. She heard a child crying on the other side, and she instinctively called out to her. The name that passed her lips was a name she'd screamed in a thousand nightmares. "Livia," she said, and turned the knob once again, "I'm coming." The scenery changed, and she found herself once more in unfamiliar territory. She stood outside a very large house that was surrounded by trees and flowers. She inhaled, and the scent of jasmine made her smile. She looked around and tried to remember where she was. Somehow she knew she'd been here before. She'd spent time here in her dreams, and had run from here in her nightmares. The child's cry intensified, and Dahlia experienced feelings of sadness and severe agitation. Olivia needed her, but her feet refused to move. She was paralyzed from the waist down and listened helplessly while the child continued to wail for help that she was unable to give. The ground quivered beneath her, and she strained to break free. "Help!" Dahlia cried out to a figure now standing in the doorway waving. "Help me, please!" she pleaded. "I'm sinking."

"I know. Isn't it wonderful?"

"Please help me!" Dahlia pleaded.

"No. Not anymore."

Dahlia concentrated on the sound of Olivia's voice and tried again to move her legs, which were now starting to buckle underneath her. She jumped blindly, struggling with all her might, and took one laborious step at a time until she reached the entryway. "Move, Phoebe," she said to the figure blocking her path. "Move the hell out of my way. I'm coming for you, and I'm going to get my life back." She breathed deeply, suddenly sure of herself and unafraid, ready to do whatever was necessary to get through the door. Phoebe vanished, and Dahlia rushed into the house to find Olivia. She had to comfort her baby sister, feel her heartbeat one last time before it was too late.

CHAPTER 70

Percival Tweed took meticulous care in dressing. He was picking up Baby Marseli, and there was no time for mistakes. This had been the longest day of his life, and he knew it was just beginning for Michael. He adjusted his tie and looked at himself in the mirror—something he never did. He, too, had tried to forget that day, but like a few other days in his life, it hung around to keep him company. The worst of it was the pain that it had caused Baby Marseli, pain that he couldn't take away from her, pain that he felt somewhat responsible for.

He saw her the morning of the accident. She was on her way to help somebody on the other side of town, and he didn't think it was a good idea, seeing as how the tornado was coming and all, plus he didn't have a good feeling about her leaving in the first place. They exchanged pleasantries, and as always, he kept his opinions to himself. "Good morning, Percival," she said. Lord, even then, she looked like an angel walking. He tipped his hat and asked her if she needed a ride. "Well, how many people are going in the ground today?" she inquired.

"Well, I done dug six graves, but I had to dig three more—one regular, two small," he answered.

"Lord, I hope it's nobody we know. No parent should ever have to bury their child," she'd said, and Percival nodded in agreement. He never knew who was going to die on any given day. He just sensed how many graves to dig. He couldn't rightly explain it. That was just the way he had always been, and God help him, it never occurred to him that he'd dug those three extra graves for Baby Marseli's kin or that he should have told her to stay home. That day, after Reva did what she did to those poor children, he wished Baby had never seen those graves, and he wished they hadn't spoken at all, because she was wracked with guilt for leaving, and he hated himself for letting her go.

Percival drove in silence. He'd been talking all day and couldn't think of one word to say to Prettybaby. He'd asked God for help sorting this mess out before he left home, and prayed until his knees were stiff for the Culpepper family. He hoped that everything would work out for the only real family he had ever known. He hoped that Dahlia would finally be able to forgive her father for what he did, but mostly he hoped that Prettybaby would take one look at him and know right away how much he loved her, and then, God willing, he wouldn't have to say anything at all.

The plane hit the tarmac, and Aunt Baby called on every ancestor she could recall. This had to work, and if it didn't, she'd go ahead and lose her mind right along with Dahlia. There were moments when she thought she saw glimpses of her niece when she looked at Phoebe, moments when she wanted to reach over and pull her close, but Phoebe was still there eyeballing her, nagging the flight attendant for another vodka tonic. Baby wanted to strangle her and put her out of her misery. But she knew that Dahlia was fighting, and Baby willed her precious niece to hold on just a little while longer. They'd be home soon enough, and Baby was determined to get Dahlia back, pull her out with her bare hands if she had to. Baby rubbed her right arm, which had fallen asleep during the flight, and briefly thought about her own life. She should have traveled more and seen the world. She should have taken more time for herself, and most important, she should have loved the only man who smiled at her every day for no reason at all.

Baby scanned the area for Dante and started to get nervous. What if he was late? What if Phoebe ran? And what if nothing she did brought Dahlia back to them? Ugly memories interrupted her present worries, and she tried her best to keep them at bay, but they were resurfacing one after the other, begging for her undivided attention. She shook her head "no," but she still saw what was left of those babies laid out on Lucius's steel table covered in blood. She began to second-guess herself. Maybe Lucius had been right all along. Some stories should never be told. Baby didn't realize she was crying until she felt the moisture creeping down her face. She closed her eyes, and when she opened them, Percival Tweed was standing in front of her smiling as usual.

"What are you doing here?" she whispered, suddenly self-conscious.

"I'm here for you, Prettybaby. I've always been here for you." He caressed her face with such tenderness that she began to tremble.

"Get a room," Phoebe said, rubbing her temple, but neither seemed to hear her. Baby kissed Percival's hand, and she knew then that he knew there was nothing more to say. The healer recognized her soul mate, and in that moment, she knew everything would be as right as rain. They drove toward home in silence with an irritated Phoebe in the backseat, and Baby spoke for the first time since they'd left the airport.

"Percival, I think it best that we make an unscheduled stop on the way. It's time now."

Percival saw the pain in Baby's eyes, and he didn't have to ask her any questions to know exactly where she wanted him to go. He placed his large white hand on top of hers and changed course. He headed downtown to Elm and Corinth, to the place where Dahlia had originally lost her mother, her family, and her mind.

CHAPTER 71

"Mercy, I think we should talk. We can't keep pretending that nothing ever happened between us."

Mercy ignored Dante's pleas and tried desperately to control the spastic muscles wreaking havoc with her face. From the moment she learned Aunt Baby and Dahlia were coming home, her entire body had transformed into a virtual war zone. She had been tic-free while Aunt Baby was away, and now she was a twitching mess. By the time they arrived, she would most likely explode into a thousand pieces. She prayed for an aneurysm to strike her dead the way it had struck her mama, because dying right here, right now would be easier than facing Dahlia Culpepper. She felt Dante grip her shoulders.

"Talk to me, dammit," he said urgently, but he couldn't comprehend what was working its way out of her stomach and into her throat. She began to hyperventilate, as the lie was now throbbing on her tongue, making it difficult for her to breathe. She saw the concern on his face and wept all over again.

"Mercy, I do love you," he said, in an attempt to calm her down.

"You won't after today," she choked, and ran toward the attic.

Her suitcases were stored there, and she was certain that she would need them before the day was over.

Mercy Blue was a sophomore in high school when she began working for the Culpeppers. Her friends didn't understand her bizarre fascination with mortuary arts, but she didn't care. She was beyond them and couldn't be bothered with childish distractions. She'd learn how to embalm dead people herself if it meant that she could be close to Lucius Culpepper. Everyone in Dallas knew about the Culpeppers. People in her neighborhood talked about them in the market, at the beauty parlor, or anywhere there were grown-folk conversations. At first, she didn't think much of all the chatter, but women consistently described Lucius Culpepper with the same unbridled passion. "Lawd take mercy on my heathen soul," her cousin Marie Ann used to say. "I'll kill my husband today and drive his body over there myself if I thought I could get next to Lucius Culpepper." And of course, that would be followed with "I heard that. Cuz, you know, they don't grow 'em like that anymore." Or "The Lord ought not to make a man that fine. It just ain't right." And "Girl, the Lord didn't have nothing to do with that. That's the work of the devil himself trying to tempt us all out of our drawers." And on and on it went until Mercy had to see what all the fuss was about.

It wasn't long before she got her wish. Somebody her mama knew died, and she found herself staring into the eyes of the most beautiful man she had ever seen. She decided right then in the middle of Kenny Harper's service, God rest his soul, that she was going to marry that man. And it didn't matter to her that he was already married with three children. He was her destiny, and that's all there was to it. Obsession had become her way of life. After considerable coaxing, her mama, Lucille, was able to get her a job at the mortuary after school when she was fifteen, and she learned how to apply makeup to the nonliving from an old woman named Miss Flossy. Of course, she spent as much time there as she could and waited for the right moments to get his attention and win his heart. That crazy wife of his pretty much stayed in her room, but those children were always around raising hell and keeping him away from her. Mercy didn't like kids, and she could tell that kids didn't really like her all that much either.

On that day, the day of the tornado, she was frustrated and annoyed that the object of her affection hadn't given her the time of day. All she needed was a few hours of uninterrupted time to convince him that she could be everything that he needed—the wife that a man like him deserved. He wasn't happy with Reva Culpepper, and everybody knew it. It was a wonder that none of those children was as funny-acting as she was. Mercy was in the foyer trying to figure out a way to ask Lucius to take her to lunch when Dahlia came flying down the stairs talking loud again about her nutcase mama.

"Mercy," she'd said, all excited and out of breath, "my mama is taking me and Jazz and Livia out for ice cream. We're going to Swensons!"

Mercy remembered looking at the girl like she'd lost her natural mind. Everyone at the funeral parlor knew damn well that Reva Culpepper wasn't supposed to leave the house by herself ever, let alone drive anywhere with those children.

"Are you sure you ought to be doing that?" Mercy had asked her. And then she heard Reva calling, and Dahlia ran happily toward the sound of her mother's voice.

"Tell my daddy that we went for a ride with Mama, okay, Mercy?" Mercy had nodded while Dahlia continued.

"She feels good today, and we'll be back in a little while," Dahlia had called back over her shoulder, and then they were gone. Mercy knew that there was something wrong with an unstable woman driving her children to get ice cream in the middle of a tornado watch, but the only thing she could think about was seducing Lucius Culpepper. With his wife and children gone, he would finally notice her. Maybe, just maybe, Miss Sophea wouldn't wreak any havoc anyway. She remembered how happy she felt then and how she prided herself on her ingenuity. Dante had passed her shortly thereafter in the hallway.

"Hey, Mercy girl," he said, with a goofy grin, "have you seen the kids anywhere?"

"No," she replied with a straight face. "Maybe they're upstairs playing." She walked away, nearly skipping with anticipation, and went to find the man of her dreams. At that moment, in that split second of deception, she sold her soul to the devil and changed the course of everyone's lives around her forever. Dahlia was in a coma for weeks after the accident, and no one knew what Mercy had done. She held her breath then, hoping that the little girl had forgotten about their conversation earlier that day before the tragedy. She'd heard that that happened sometimes in cases like these when a person suffered severe head trauma. She had been lucky for years because the girl had never mentioned a thing. When Dahlia left for college right after high school, Mercy was relieved. But she always believed that she was on borrowed time with Lucius Culpepper after that, and that one day her luck would come to an end.

On the third floor, in the middle of the attic, Mercy Blue gathered her Louis Vuitton luggage and buried her head in her hands. Aunt Baby was coming for her, and this time, she knew Dahlia would remember everything.

It had come to this—sneaking away like a spineless coward. A part of her had always known that she'd most likely leave the Culpepper house the same way she came in. Her entrance was unexpected and duplicitous, and so would be her departure. Perhaps, in time, when she was stronger, she could come back here and make things right with the people she'd hurt. She hoped that Dahlia and Lucius could finally make peace with each other, and she prayed that Dante would forgive her.

She had no idea where she was going, but the unknown intrigued her. She no longer liked who she was, and she intended to change that. Maybe she'd go back to school. Maybe she'd move to New York. And maybe in time she could look at herself again and not feel shame and regret. Whatever she did, she'd start over and cut a new path for herself. If she worked real hard, she'd find out where she belonged. Mercy packed what she needed and left her wedding ring on Lucius's nightstand. She wasn't afraid anymore of living a life without him. She had some money saved for a few rainy days. Lucille had made sure of that—always taught her to keep a little something for herself.

Mercy Blue stood in the doorway and managed to smile. She knew two things for sure: (1) she never wanted to step foot in a funeral parlor again, and (2) she loathed anything red. She was so damn tired of the color red. She straightened her olive green skirt and closed the door for the last time.

CHAPTER 72

"Oh, my God," Michael whispered. "Oh, my God. How could she not tell me this?"

"Don't blame Dahlia, Michael. I don't think she even remembers what happened. It was as if Jazz and Livia didn't exist at all. We all did what we could to make it easier for her—well, except for me. I forbade anyone in this house to speak about the accident or ever mention Reva's name again. They were difficult times, and I dealt with them the best way I knew how. Unfortunately, what I did afterward didn't make things any easier for Dahlia or for anyone."

"There's more?" Michael asked, incredulous.

"Yeah, son. There's more."

One week after the funerals, Lucius threw himself into his work. Aunt Baby and Dante tried to convince him to take a few days off and go away somewhere, but he wouldn't hear of such a thing. His baby doll was still in a coma; how could he possibly go anywhere? He worked tirelessly day and night until he fell down where he stood from exhaustion. He couldn't stop moving. He couldn't slow down for even a moment or his mind would go back to the corner of Corinth and Elm and he'd die all over again. He barely spoke to anyone and lost weight from refusing to eat. His appetite disappeared along with his smile, so the rest of him didn't matter.

He traveled back and forth to Parkland Hospital for three months, praying constantly that his baby doll wouldn't die. If she left him, too, there would be nothing else for him to live for, no reason for him to ever open his eyes again. It was a miracle, the doctors said, that she was alive at all. No one had heard of anyone surviving such a horrific collision. "Someone up there was looking out for her," they'd repeated to him every damn day, like that made him feel any better at all. Aunt Baby slept in the hospital night after night on an old cot next to Dahlia's bed and spent hours talking to her about everything and nothing. "You know, she can hear you, Lucius," Aunt Baby told him all the time. But he couldn't talk to her. He couldn't confess that he was angry with her for disobeying him, and he couldn't admit to his oldest child that he hated himself for not knowing what he should have known.

He and Aunt Baby were with her the day she came out of her coma. Dahlia opened her eyes and looked right at him. "Say something to her," Baby pleaded, when she saw his hesitation. Lucius held her hand, and she responded by squeezing his finger. He struggled to say the right words, but remnants of his own twisted guilt flew out of his mouth instead. "Why didn't you come get me?" he yelled. *"You were supposed to come get me!"* Baby pushed him out of the room then and slapped him hard. "She's lost enough already!" she hollered at him, in front of God and everybody. "My God, Lucius, she's just a child." He burned with anger and plunged his fists into the walls, screaming hysterically outside his daughter's room. Lucius wailed for the family that had been stolen from him, and he cursed the wife he couldn't punish for making him trust her. He screamed again and again for the first time since he'd had to identify a mangled Reva and embalm his own children. So complete was his breakdown that he didn't grasp the gravity of his actions until it was too late. He receded inside himself, oblivious to the poison he'd just injected into the brain of the one he loved the most.

Now, at the core of her soul, Dahlia believed that she was the cause of her mother's madness and that it was her fault that everyone in the car was dead. Her father blamed her, and this was more than her heart could bear and much more than her mind could hold. She would live, but she couldn't face him the way she was. At eleven years old, she protected herself the only way she knew how. Her mind splintered into a million pieces, and when they came together again, Phoebe was born.

CHAPTER 73

"What the hell are we doing here?" Phoebe yelled. She was nervous, and her damn head was hurting again. It was that bitch hoping to get the jump on her. She could feel Dahlia trying to return, breathing down the back of her neck. Phoebe climbed on top of the railroad tracks and waved her hands in the air. "What are you trying to pull, Baby? Is this shit supposed to frighten me?"

"No," Baby answered. "I just wanted to know if you remembered what happened here."

"Hell, I don't know. I wasn't here for the fireworks, but I heard it was quite a show. I mean, it was on the evening news and everything, made y'all famous," she added sarcastically. "Jesus, Percival, can we leave now? I'm tired." Phoebe looked around and paused. She wanted to keep walking but found that she was unable to move her feet.

"I don't need you anymore," Dahlia screamed loud and clear, disorienting Phoebe, interrupting her thoughts.

"Fuck!" Phoebe said, and sat down instead, unconsciously absorbing the moment. "The girl wants a fight." She rubbed her temple in disgust and tried to hold on to a life that didn't belong to her. "Not now," she yelled. "Not yet!" She dug her fingernails into the palm of her hand and blinked back tears. She couldn't breathe, and her head felt like it was about to explode.

Aunt Baby watched closely, with Percival not too far behind. She didn't know if she had done the right thing by bringing her here, but it was a risk she took willingly. She waited with clasped hands for a sign from Dahlia. If she was still in there, coming here would either pull her out or seal her in. But the Culpepper women were strong of mind and courageous of heart. Dahlia was descended from a long line of formidable women, women who walked on water, women who could fly. Each one before her had survived some special kind of hell and thrived, so Baby Marseli knew at the core of all that she was that baby doll could survive even this.

It was quiet where she was, peaceful and serene—almost eerily so. It was a kind of calm that she didn't recognize at all, and that frightened her. No one spoke to her, no one came through doors that weren't there, and there were no signs to guide the way. There was, though, a familiar feeling welling inside her that she could easily identify. Love. It coursed through her, and she welcomed the intensity of it, allowed it to fill her up and spill out into the space she occupied. A different reality began to ease its way next to her, and she threw her head back and tasted the possibilities. There were people waiting for her to love them. Somewhere there was a little girl who needed her mother and a husband who longed for his wife. Dahlia stood by herself with the knowledge that she was nearly there, nearly ready to open the last door. What existed beyond the door would be the absolute worst of it, and she knew that as surely as she knew that Phoebe wouldn't go down without a fight.

Dahlia placed her hand on the door and heard turbulence knocking from the other side. She snatched her hand away and wondered how long it would take her to see whatever it was that she'd spent a lifetime hiding from. She thought of Isabel and balled her fists like a child. She was somebody's mother, and mothers were supposed to protect their children, keep them from harm's way. She would fight for Izzy. She would fight for Milky, and finally she was ready to fight for herself. Her life was precious, and she wasn't about to sign it over to anyone.

She leaned against the door and pushed. "Give it up," the voice said. "It's over." Dahlia pushed harder, ignoring the voice that told her she was going to die, until the door gave way. For a split second, she saw her entire life flash before her eyes, and then, without warning, Sophea took her and ripped her right out of the doorway. She was flying and then falling down, down, into outstretched arms. Reva held her close and caressed the side of her face. Her mother began to cry, and Dahlia rushed to wipe her tears. Reva shook her head and backed away slowly. "It's time now, baby doll," she said. "Come take a ride with me. I can't leave you. God help me, I can't leave you."

Dahlia followed her to a burgundy Mercedes and watched as the younger version of herself slid into the car with Jazz and Livia. She tried to speak to them—tell them that a powerful storm was brewing—but they couldn't hear her, and after Dahlia climbed in the backseat, neither could Reva. She was a reluctant spectator, a voyeur of her own life. She was suddenly overcome with trepidation, and she wanted to flee, but she couldn't leave them, and this time, she refused to leave herself. Sophea raised hell outside, and Dahlia could only watch from the passenger-side window. It had begun to rain, and she tensed with worry. Reva spoke, and Dahlia felt the bile rise up in the back of her throat. She'd heard these words before.

"Baby doll, tell your brother to be quiet while I'm driving. Livy, listen to your sister. Everybody come on now and settle down. We've got to get away from here."

"Aren't you afraid of Miss Sophea, Mama?" Jazz asked. Reva

rolled her eyes. "Boy, please. Do you think a little old tornado is going to scare me away? Umm-umm, the scary things are in the inside. You remember that, you hear?"

"But, Mama—" Jazz continued, until Livy pinched him. "Ouch! Mama, Livy hit me!"

Dahlia remembered that she didn't want anything to interfere with her double dip of lemon custard, so she'd snapped at her brother and sister.

"Jazz, hush up now or Mama gonna take us back home and we won't get anything. Livy, give Jazz back his train. Mama, are you going to get some ice cream, too?"

But Reva had stopped talking, and Dahlia didn't want to upset her any further by running her mouth, so she tried to enjoy the ride until she realized that they were a long way from home and had already driven past Swensons. Reva's driving became erratic, and the car seemed to be going faster, but no one noticed except her.

"Mama. Mama, where are we going? I thought we were getting ice cream." And still no answer. Jazz looked at her and shrugged his shoulders. Livia began to cry. Dahlia rocked back and forth in the car. Oh, Jesus, this wasn't just a nightmare.

"Mommy," Jazz called in a singsong voice. "Mommy."

Reva stopped the car near the tracks on the corner of Corinth and Elm and eventually turned to face them. "Hey, baby doll," she said with a smile, "how about I take y'all to see a real live choo-choo train?"

"Yeah!" Jazz squealed. He was so excited, but Dahlia knew that something wasn't right. She didn't feel well. Her stomach was in knots, and her mother wouldn't talk to her anymore. She wanted her father, and she wanted to go home. Jazz was the first one to see the train, Livy cried softly, and Reva rolled the windows down. "The air from the tornado needs to flow through," she said, to no one in particular. Wind whipped through the car, and Dahlia yelled for Livy to hold on to something. "Mama, roll up the windows," Dahlia shouted, "or Sophea's going to get us."

"No, this is cool," Jazz screamed at the top of his lungs, as one of his toy trains flew out the rear window. Reva started the car, and it didn't take long for Dahlia to realize where she was going.

"Mama, what are you doing?" Dahlia yelled. "Mama, noooo!"

Time paused and continued and paused again while Dahlia watched the destruction of her family in slow motion. She'd reached back and tried in vain to grab her baby sister's arm, and then Livy was gone in seconds, snatched through the windshield like a rag doll. She never saw what happened to Jazz. She only heard him calling for her, crying for his daddy. The tornado was all around them, pushing and pulling—hissing sweet nothings in her ears. It didn't hate her, it chided. It was only doing what it was supposed to do. She could hear the siren blaring in the background, and she thought about her family. Did her father miss them? And did he know they were gone? She wondered if she'd feel pain when she died, and if there was lemon custard ice cream in heaven. She wondered if she'd ever see Livy and Jazz again, and if God was going to punish her mother. She hoped that he would. She thought about Aunt Baby and hoped Oceola Moon was waiting for them on the other side.

Dahlia braced herself for impact and covered her face with her hands. She couldn't stand to see any more, and for the life of her, she couldn't recall what hit them first—Sophea or the Amtrak train. She screamed for them all, and then it was over.

CHAPTER 74

Lucius couldn't sit still anymore. He paced back and forth in his office, aware that Michael's eyes were trained on him. He had already said so much, and he didn't think there was anything more to add, but there was a question in Michael's eyes, and Lucius wasn't prepared to answer it.

"Mr. Culpepper, why? How?" Michael was interrupted by an intrusion that Lucius welcomed.

"Come in," Lucius said, and looked at his brother. "I thought you were going to the airport."

"I decided to stay here. Percival is picking them up."

"Percival?" Lucius said, with a raised eyebrow.

Dante looked at his watch. "Their plane landed over an hour and a half ago. They should be here by now."

"What could be taking them so long?" Michael asked, concerned. Dante and Lucius looked at each other. "It's been a long time since she's been back here, Michael," Lucius answered. "Be patient."

"Lucius," Dante said softly.

"We're done here. Dante can answer any other questions you have. I'm sorry. I have to get some air."

"Mr. Culpepper," Michael called after him, but Lucius was gone. He'd had enough, and he didn't want the boy to see him bawl like a baby. He had to be strong now. His baby doll was on her way home.

Dante sat down in Lucius's chair and addressed Michael. "I'm sorry if I was rude to you yesterday. There's been a lot going on here, but that's no excuse for my behavior."

"I understand. Apologies aren't necessary," Michael offered.

"You have no idea how hard this is for him," Dante said.

"And you have no idea how hard this has been for my wife and my daughter. I'm starting to understand Dahlia better now. I can see why she is the way she is."

"Our family was devastated by what happened, and it still is. The day Reva drove those babies in front of that train, we all died in one way or another. I can't imagine how hard it's been for Dahlia, but I know how impossible it was for my brother."

"How could he have blamed Dahlia for what happened? What kind of father would do such a thing? Do you—does anybody here have any idea what this has done to her?" Michael countered. "God, how can we come back from this?"

"Michael, I'm not excusing what Lucius did, but he barely survived. Something inside him snapped that day just like Dahlia; he's never been the same since. None of us have. His whole life since then has been a train wreck. The day of the accident, I went looking for Dahlia and the other kids. I tried to keep my eye on things while Lucius worked because I knew how focused he got. I usually checked on them every couple of hours or so, but that day, I couldn't find them anywhere. By the time I realized where they were, Reva was halfway down the street with those kids. I ran after them, but she wouldn't slow down, and I couldn't catch her. I tried to get a car to stop and help me follow her, but I couldn't find anybody, so I ran back here. Trees were toppled over, people were screaming, and a house four doors down had been ripped right off its foundation. It was chaos, pure chaos. And by the time I got to Lucius, Reva had—Jesus.

"Anyway, Lucius and I drove like maniacs, and I couldn't look. Sophea had calmed down by then, but you could tell she'd been there. She left her mark all over Dallas that day. The police wouldn't allow him anywhere near the wreckage. It took nine of us to hold him back. And then the arrangements had to be made, and he refused to allow anyone to touch Jazz, and my God, Livia was in pieces." Dante began to weep, but he continued. "She was found two miles away from the scene of the accident. We begged him to send the kids to another mortuary, but he wouldn't hear of it. They were his babies, he said, and no one else could take care of them like he could. He sent Reva's remains away, though, to a mortuary on the other side of town. He didn't care who put her back together, and he didn't want to see her again even in death. And at first, he wouldn't even allow her to be interred here with the rest of the family.

"Three days after the accident, while his daughter was still in a coma, Lucius embalmed Jazz and Livia by himself, and Aunt Baby couldn't convince him otherwise. Morticians aren't supposed to prepare their own families, for obvious reasons, like doctors aren't supposed to write their own script. We all thought he had lost his mind, but there was nothing any of us could do. He locked himself in the prep room over there, and we heard "Someday My Prince Will Come" by Miles Davis over and over again for the next forty-eight hours. Till this day, he won't listen to that record anymore. I can't imagine doing what he did. I couldn't have done that—prepared my own family—and walked around the next day or the day after that like nothing ever happened. I think when he blamed Dahlia in the hospital, he was still in some kind of shock. That was over twenty years ago, and he hasn't spoken about it until now. None of us have."

"How did he go on after all that? I don't know how you begin to survive something like that," Michael said.

"What's more important here is whether or not he'll survive the rest of the night."

CHAPTER 75

Phoebe finally slept, and Dahlia opened her eyes to a life she'd fought hard to get back. It was vivid and alive with possibilities. She felt distinctly different in a way she couldn't quite articulate and wouldn't be able to for some time. Her head was free of noise, and the newfound silence felt wrong and awkward. It was foreign to her because it wasn't what she was accustomed to, but clarity was a beautiful, yet sobering sensation. And she eagerly integrated it with the rest of her fledgling emotions. She began to experience various states of mind almost simultaneously: fear, love, pain, sorrow, and anger. She was caught in an all-encompassing whirlwind, and she fought hard to stay grounded. She would not lose control. She was an unfinished masterpiece, an intricate riddle yet to be solved, and still a woman in need of many things to make her whole again.

Her experience was reminiscent of the time she awakened from her coma years earlier. She was surprised that she was able to make that connection. So much was beginning to make sense to her now. Just like she remembered being in a coma, she remembered that her little sister, Livia, liked chocolate, and she remembered that she missed her father after all. And she did have a mother once who combed her hair and read her stories, made her homemade fudge, and held her in the middle of the night when she was scared. Yes, her mother had hurt her once on a December afternoon, but her mother had also loved her the only way she knew how. Reva wanted to end her pain, and Dahlia accepted that all her mother had tried to do was take her babies with her. That was the way she chose to remember Reva, and the decision sat well with her soul. Dahlia recalled a lifetime in a span of eight short minutes, and the knowledge so overwhelmed her that she collapsed under the weight—weight that she'd been carrying for twenty-five years. She placed her face on smooth steel tracks and sobbed for Jazz and Livy. The pain, both emotional and physical, was so intense, so debilitating, that she became paralyzed where she lay. She would never know what went through Reva's mind that day, and she couldn't comprehend why she was the only one who lived. She began to lose herself in grief and regret until strong, pale hands lifted her and held her close.

Lucius saw the car coming up the winding driveway and took several deep breaths. He would end his own life right now if it would make his daughter's any less painful. He was prepared to do whatever she needed him to do to make things right between them, even if it meant cutting his own heart out. Dante squeezed his brother's shoulder and offered words of encouragement. "You can do this," he whispered. "We're all here for you." Dante walked to his mother and wondered what had happened to Mercy. He hadn't seen her since they last spoke, and he noticed that her Mercedes was gone.

Michael ran to meet the car. He wanted to be the first person his wife saw. He wanted to tell her how much he loved her, and he wanted her to know that he couldn't begin to understand what she was going through but he'd stand with her until it was over. He had devoted his life to her, and he'd be damned if he'd give up on her now. For Isabel and for his family, he'd stay until Dahlia was well enough to leave.

Dahlia walked out of the car and into Milky's arms. The house and everything around it was exactly the way it was in her dreams. Nothing had changed, and yet everything had changed. She glanced at Aunt Baby and inhaled the moment. She had lived here once a lifetime ago. She remembered she used to chase her brother around the backyard and play hide-and-seek in the attic with the round window. She remembered how much she loved gumbo and fried green tomatoes. She remembered growing lemon verbena with Aunt Baby and learning to braid her long hair. She saw a man standing tall on the front porch and remembered that, once upon a time, she had a father who adored her and a family who refused to let her die. She remembered the smell of the magnolia trees in spring and her Uncle Brother's famous grilled cheese sandwiches. And finally she remembered above all else that she was loved and that she still had plenty of love to give.

Exhausted, she released Milky's hand and walked up the stairs alone to meet her father. "Daddy," she said, with tears in her eyes, "I'm home."

"How many times do we have to talk about this? How many different ways can I tell you that my mom played chicken with an Amtrak train and lost?"

"As many times as it takes for you to be cured," Dr. Kelly asserted.

"I feel fine. I feel better than I have in a long time. I can talk about it now. I know what happened wasn't my fault."

"That's good. How is your father, by the way?"

"He's okay, I think. He left the mortuary business, you know, and he's taking up saxophone lessons. Right now, he's somewhere in Paris wrapping up some unfinished family business."

"Really? What about his wife—Mercy, is it? Did you ever have that chat with her?"

"No. She's gone, and I think it's for the best. I'm still working on forgiving her for what she did. If she was still around, I'd tell her that," Dahlia answered, and looked out the window.

"Have you had any headaches lately?"

"Little ones, but not like I used to. I know what you said, Dr. Kelly, but I think Phoebe is gone for now. I don't feel her the way I used to."

"Very well, then. Are you sleeping?"

"Sometimes. I still have nightmares every now and then, but they don't paralyze me anymore, and my husband is so supportive of my illness."

"And how is Michael—and Isabel?"

"They're both fine. Actually, I need to get home."

"Do you have a pressing engagement this evening?" Dr. Kelly asked, closing his notebook.

"As a matter of fact, we're taking my Aunt Baby and Uncle Percival to dinner at Milky's restaurant."

"Splendid, then. Lovely woman, your Aunt Baby. Are they visiting for long?"

"They stopped by on their way to Italy."

"Well. I shall see you next week, then, same time?"

"Wouldn't miss it," Dahlia said with a smile, and opened the door to leave. "Dr. Kelly," she called.

"Yes, Dahlia."

"Thank you for everything. Thanks from the both of us."

CHASING SOPHEA

Gabrielle Pina

A Reader's Guide

A Conversation with Gabrielle Pina

Q: Where are you from, and how did you come to know so much about life in Tornado Alley and the outskirts of Dallas, Texas?

A: I'm from Dallas, Texas, and I survived a tornado with my grandmother and my uncle when I was a little girl. My grandmother used to tell me stories about tornadoes, and I guess they stuck with me.

Q: What else about your upbringing in Dallas did you find seeping its way into this novel?

A: Aunt Baby reminded me of my grandmother a little bit. She always had a concoction for everything. She always had a cure for an ailment or something to make everything right with your soul.

Q: What motivated you to combine so many different sources of spiritual strength?

A: Often when you are truly in crisis, you need to pull from everything the creator has to offer. One solution to a problem doesn't fix everything. Truth is sometimes found in places you least expect it, and you have to be of open mind and open heart to absorb its effects fully.

Q: Why did you choose a funeral home as the Culpepper family business?

A: I've always been creeped out by funeral homes, and researching them was one way for me to deal with my own uneasiness. Also, the thought of someone growing up in a funeral home intrigued me.

Q: Why did you choose to write about the experience of someone with dissociative identity disorder (DID)?

A: I've always been fascinated with DID and other mental disorders. More specifically, what causes the brain to rewire itself and then correct itself in the blink of an eye? DID is such a multifaceted disorder and one that isn't necessarily common in the African American community. I wanted to explore what happens when an otherwise strong woman is tempted by and surrenders to madness.

Q: Who is the first person to recognize Phoebe?

A: Aunt Baby recognizes Phoebe soon after the accident. However, Baby doesn't know what to do, how to classify the illness, or how to begin to fix it. And her failure shames her. In the end, she commits to heal Dahlia, and she is just as determined to redeem herself.

Q: What about Dahlia allows her to survive the Sophea experience, unlike her mother and siblings?

A: Dahlia survives the Sophea experience because she is supposed to. Her experience and her life are meant to be a testament for the people around her.

Q: There is such intense color imagery in *Chasing Sophea*— Mercy Blue and her red dresses, Reva's being a "brown blur," even Michael (Milky) had to be given a colorful name. Can you explain the significance of these colors?

A: Mercy's fascination with red dresses represents her feeling that everything in her life is out of control—her livelihood, her emotions, and her relationship with Lucius. She needs to feel like there is one thing in her existence that she can control. Buying and wearing red dresses is that anchor for her. She is attempting to communicate nonverbally to those around her. "Look at me. I'm special. I'm worthy. I'm alive."

Colors in the novel represent the multitude of shades in our lives—vividness, evolvement, and ultimately change. Also, the colors represent layers of burgeoning insanity, not just in Dahlia's life but in everyone else's as well.

Q: Please explain Lucius's compulsive attraction to unstable and insecure women.

A: A universal law is that you attract who you are. This truth, much like rain, is unavoidable. From the time he was a child, Lucius yearned to be loved but was abandoned by the first woman in his life. He never really recovered from his mother's departure, and as a result, he is emotionally stunted, unstable, and insecure. In choosing women, unconsciously on many different levels, he is choosing himself. Emotional stagnation begets nothing but spiritual retardation and vice versa.

Q: Which character was the easiest for you to write? Which was the most difficult?

A: Aunt Baby was the easiest for me to write because I saw her immediately. Dahlia was the most difficult. There is so much more I could have written about her, but then the novel would have been six hundred pages.

Q: In the last sentence, you write, "Thanks for everything. Thanks from the both of us." Who else?

A: Why, Phoebe, of course. I wanted Dahlia to understand that DID cannot be miraculously fixed. Before Dahlia can even begin to heal, she needs to acknowledge her alter and realize that the healing process could take years.

Q: Were there other journal entries that you wrote for Phoebe aside from those included in the novel?

A: Yes, there were several other journal entries. And no, I can't share them. They're sealed for Phoebe's protection.

READING GROUP QUESTIONS AND
TOPICS FOR DISCUSSION

1. In her interview, Gabrielle Pina says that we choose ourselves in our mates. How does this play out in other relationships in the book? Do you think this is a true statement?

2. Lucius is a very complex character: seemingly deep and thoughtful, yet neglectful toward almost every living person. What role do his aloofness and relative calm play in the storms of Dahlia's life? How do these traits manifest themselves in his other relationships?

3. Do you think most husbands would react to their wives' psychological illnesses the way Milky does? How would you react if you suspected that someone close to you had a mental illness?

4. Aunt Baby and Percival remain calm even in the toughest and craziest of situations. How does their patience influence their decision making and their love for each other? How does it impact their abilities to help others?

5. Some of the most important characters in *Chasing Sophea* have names that imply multifaceted relationships (Uncle Brother, Aunt

Baby). What does Gabrielle Pina suggest about the changing/mutable roles of family members, especially in times of crisis?

6. Forbidden lust and temptations recur throughout this tale. Who succumbs to temptation, and what does it reveal about their personalities?

7. Aunt Baby is a great mother to Dante, even though she didn't give birth to him. Lucius is distressed at the way his mother abandoned him. Dahlia certainly suffered at the hands of her mother, and Isabel seems to have as well. What does Gabrielle Pina suggest about mothering and how motherly love impacts families?

8. Revelations and reckoning are dominant themes in this novel: everyone brings a different element of truth to light. In talking to Dahlia, Baby reassures her that the world will keep spinning even when they discuss the truth. What truths move this story forward? Are there any you wish had been explored further?

9. Discuss the various methods for healing described in this book. Which are the most effective? Why?

10. The Culpeppers have always been set apart from the rest of the world: by Jim Crow laws as well as by the nature of their profession. How does their social and geographic isolation help or harm them?

11. What was it that Dahlia needed to learn from Reva, Livia, and Jazz in order to heal?

ABOUT THE AUTHOR

GABRIELLE PINA received her MA from the University of Southern California Master of Professional Writing Program. She is a lecturer at the University of Southern California and a member of the adjunct faculty at Pasadena City College. She lives in Southern California with her husband, Ron, and her children, Julian, Maia, and Langston.